HOUSE OF DANGER

"Well, there you are," he said. "That's the place that you're bound for."

"Why do you wave me on, Chip?"

"Because that's where your trail lies, ain't it?" he answered. He was irritated.

"Are you going to stay behind?" I asked, more and more alarmed.

"What should I wanta go in there for?" he asked me, as sharply and as unreasonably as before. "They'd only sink a knife into me between the shoulder blades, so's I wouldn't know the face of him that stuck me. No, no, Joe, old son. That's your job . . . the entering of the house."

I felt the color draining out of my face. My skin felt puckered with cold fear.

"What sort of people are they, then, in yonder?" I asked. "Is that a murder den?"

He started to shake his head, and then, fixing his eyes steadily and coldly upon mine, he nodded several times, slowly. "Yeah," he said, "there's been murders done in there. . . ."

MAX BRAND
THE OATH OF OFFICE

LEISURE BOOKS   NEW YORK CITY

A LEISURE BOOK®

November 2000

Published by special arragement with Golden West Literary Agency.

Dorchester Publishing Co., Inc.

276 Fifth Avenue

New York, NY 10001

"The Fall and Rise of Newbold" first appeared under the title "Chip and the Cactus Man" by Max Brand in Street & Smith's *Western Story Magazine* (1/10/31). Copyright © 1931 by Street & Smith Publications, Inc. Copyright © renewed 1958 by Dorothy Faust. Copyright © 1998 by Jane Faust Easton and Adriana Faust Bianchi for restored material. Acknowledgment is made to Condé Nast Publications, Inc., for their co-operation.

"The Ivory Portrait" first appeared under the title "Chip Champions a Lady" by Max Brand in Street & Smith's *Western Story Magazine* (1/24/31). Copyright © 1931 by Street & Smith Publications, Inc. Copyright © renewed 1958 by Dorothy Faust. Copyright © 1998 by Jane Faust Easton and Adriana Faust Bianchi for restored material. Acknowledgment is made to Condé Nast Publications, Inc., for their co-operation.

"The Oath of Office" first appeared under the title "Chip Traps a Sheriff" by Max Brand in Street & Smith's *Western Story Magazine* (1/31/31). Copyright © 1931 by Street & Smith Publications, Inc. Copyright © renewed 1958 by Dorothy Faust. Copyright © 1998 by Jane Faust Easton and Adriana Faust Bianchi for restored material. Acknowledgment is made to Condé Nast Publications, Inc., for their co-operation.

The name Max Brand™ is a registered trademark with the U.S. Patent and Trademark office and cannot be used for any purpose without express written permission.

ISBN 0-8439-4796-9

The name "Leisure Books" and the stylized "L" with design are trademarks of Dorchester Publishing Co., Inc.

Printed in the United States of America.

THE OATH OF OFFICE

TABLE OF CONTENTS

The Fall and Rise of Newbold

This story first appeared in 1931 under the title "Chip and the Cactus Man" in Street & Smith's *Western Story Magazine* in the issue dated January 10. In it Frederick Faust, writing under his most well known pen-name, Max Brand, introduced his youthful character, known only as Chip, who appeared in a trio of stories, collected together, here, for the first time. Unlike other on-going characters created by Faust, such as Reata or Silvertip, Chip is not the hero of the stories. The concern is rather with his influence on others. Consequently, Faust's original titles for these stories have been restored since they more aptly describe them.

Chapter One

"Where the Trouble Started"

If he had had a quarter of an inch of rain a year, Newbold could have raised cattle in Hades. For that matter, we all felt that his range was a little worse than Hades—it averaged only a shade more than a quarter of an inch of rain most of the year. What saved him, of course, was the western half of the range, where the westerlies piled up clouds at certain times of the year and gave that smaller section of his land a good drenching. When the grass petered all out to the east and south, we had to get the cows started through the teeth of the passes and work them over to the green section. They were a humped-backed lot, all gaunted up with thirst and the grass famine, before we got them to the western range, however. After they hit the green feed, they went at it so hard that a lot of them were sick at once, and a good number always died.

No wonder! Nobody but Newbold could have ranged cattle at all on the remainder of that mangy range. We used to say that he gave his cows a college course in gleaning, and that a Newbold yearling would gallop half a mile for a blade of grass and run three days for a drink. There wasn't much exaggeration in the second remark, either.

Somebody with a mean nature, plus a sense of humor, gave Newbold his start by making him a donation of his first ledge of the range. That was when he was sixteen. That land raised nothing but coyotes and a few foxes, and even the foxes were out of luck in the district. A bear will dine on anything, from roots to grubs and wasps' nests, but self-respecting grizzlies simply broke down and cried when they had a look at Newbold's gift of land.

But Newbold didn't cry. He was raised with the silver spoon, at that. Old Man Newbold had made a fortune in lumber, another in cows, another in gold dust, and still another in land. But he used it all on high living and faro. He used to work up a new faro system every year or so, and then he would go on a big campaign, but the faro always won. Take it by and large, faro always will. It beats the white men, and it beats the crooks.

So the old man died and left one son and heir, and that boy, who had been raised soft and high, was chucked out into the world with nothing much but hope to fill his poke. Then, as I was saying, an old friend of his father's gave the kid a wedge of desert that was already overcrowded by a fox, a coyote, and half a dozen rabbits, all sinews and fur.

But Newbold took the gift with thanks. He started with about a cow and a half and a burro, by way of livestock. When big outfits were driving back and forth across the range and lost young cows and yearlings going across the boy's sun-blasted land, he picked up those dying cattle for half the price of their hides, and then, as we all said, nursed them with pain and promises until they could walk.

I think that cows were afraid to die on Newbold's hands; they had an idea that the earthly paradise was anywhere off his range, and they kept fighting and fixing their sad eyes on the future until they graduated and got to the butcher at last.

Yes, Newbold progressed so rapidly that, when he was eighteen, he fixed his eyes on more of that range. He took a trip clear to Chicago and walked in on the fellow who happened to own the rest of hell-on-earth. When this man heard that Newbold wanted to buy, he looked him over and saw that he was all brown steel, like a well-oiled engine. He offered to rent him the range for about a dollar a year, but finally he sold it for something around a dollar an acre, which was sheer robbery, except for the green western valleys, which I have spoken of before.

So Newbold went back West again and got him some more batches of cows that had used up their first chance in life down to last half drop. From year to year he walked his skeletons back and forth across his range, and lost a lot of them, but made a heap of money on the rest.

He took that range when he was sixteen. He expanded it when he was eighteen. And for fifteen years he raked in dollars off the rocks and blow-sands. In a good, fat country, I don't think he would have done so well. He was one of those geniuses who knows best how to make something out of nothing. He was a cactus among men.

At thirty-three, he looked forty-five. He was the hardest heart, the hardest driver, and the meanest boss in the world. He fed worse and paid less than any other outfit. But still he always managed to keep a crew together. In the first place, he was straight; in the second place, he treated himself worse than he treated his men; in the third place, he backed up his boys as though they were his blood brothers when they had a falling-out with sheepherders or any other poachers; and in the fourth place, and, most important of all, any 'puncher who could say that he had lasted out a whole year with Newbold was sure to get a job wherever he cared to roll down his blankets and pick out a string.

The fourth reason was the one that brought me to his place. That, and because I had heard of him since I was a youngster, first as "the boy cattle king," and secondly as "that hardcase, Newbold."

He was a hardcase, all right. His only relaxation was a fight, and even in that line he didn't get much relaxation after a time. He became too well-known. Now and then somebody who wanted to make a reputation went up to the ranch and looked for trouble, but that man either turned up his toes on the spot, or had to be shipped out for a long list of repairs.

It got so that Newbold would ride sixty miles to wrangle with a neighbor or to take up a remark that somebody else had said somebody else had heard about him. But even these long rides finally began to bring him in very short returns, and all that Newbold could do was to fight the weather, and the prices, and the railroads—three things that even Newbold couldn't beat. Even so, he just about got a draw, as a rule.

I think it was because he was running out of trouble, except enough to kill five ordinary men, that he finally thought of raising hay in the western valleys of the range. It was one of those paper schemes. You sit down with a map and draw a lot of lines. You fence in a lot of the best ground, and then you buy mowing machines and rakes, and you cut the crop and cure it for hay, and you make a road through the passes, and when the eastern range is as bare as grandfather's red head, then you have a lot of first-rate feed to stuff into the cows and pull them through until the next quarter-inch rain comes along and washes more mud and a little water into the tanks.

That was the scheme of our boss. A good, big scheme. And a scheme that might do wonders. The trouble was, in the first place, that fence building, and road making, and mowing machines, and two-horse rakes, cost money. However, Newbold stuck in on the scheme, and he did it in the true Newbold way. You would think that he would just sit down and write off an order to a big manufacturer of agricultural implements, and pretty soon we would go down to the railroad station and debark a trainload of everything covered with shining new blue, and red, and green paint.

But Newbold didn't do that. He was ten miles too mean for that. First he got a one-legged machinist and a seventy-year-old blacksmith, both of them willing to work for board and tobacco. Then he put up a bowlegged shed, and he went away from the ranch on a three-week trip.

All through the West, now and again, a big farmer or rancher dies and his family splits up, and the first thing that is done is to sell off all the implements. As soon as the paint is rubbed off a gang plow or a mowing machine, it's old. As soon as it's old, it's not wanted. It may have been worked six months or sixteen years. That doesn't matter. It's simply old. I've seen a hundred-and-twenty-five-dollar mowing machine sell for five dollars, and a forty-dollar subsoil plow sell for one dollar, and a seventy-five-dollar running gear for a wagon auction off for seventy-five cents, and a five-hundred-pound heap of iron junk—chains, hammerheads, plowshares—knocked down for a dollar and a quarter. Even junk dealers are not interested when it comes to bidding in on farm wreckage.

Newbold was not proud, in that way. He went out and collected. He attended half a dozen sales, and, first of all, up came a forge and a lot of blacksmith's tools, and that sort of thing. And then we got an order to break mustangs to collar and harness, and we went down to the station and began to haul junk forty miles overland to the ranch. It was a long job, and a mean one, and those mustangs could kick off their harnesses faster than school kids can shed their clothes on the rim of a swimming pool.

But there was the whole mass and heap of stuff, at last. And first of all, he set to work at the forge under the tutelage of the blacksmith of seventy years, and the more intelligent of us—I was not one—were put under the one-legged machinist. He and the blacksmith, do you see, were to supply the brains, and we 'punchers were the hand power! It was a mean scheme, but, then, Newbold was always mean. It was a cheap scheme, but Newbold was always cheap.

We worked for weeks straightening the knock knees of wagons that had developed flat feet and rheumatism a generation before. We patched harness with second-hand rivets, rawhide, and baling wire. We took out the mysterious insides of mowing machines, and operated, and put them back again, praying all together. We unrolled miles of knotted, tangled, spliced, and rotten second-hand barbed wire. A roll of barbed wire can play as many tricks as an outlaw mustang, and buck as high, and hit as hard, and bite as deep. Besides, it never gets tired.

But, to make it short, finally we fenced, and plowed, and sowed, and cut, and raked, and windrowed, that land and the hay crop from it. Then the boss saw that we could never haul that hay in the loose clear across the passes over the so-called road that he had made. He had to get a machine and bale it. And that was where the trouble started.

Chapter Two

"Men and the Machine"

We got a fourth-hand device called a hay press. The name of it was Little Giant. But it was misnamed. It wasn't little. It was a full-grown giant, when it came to making trouble. It had to be a giant, because it succeeded where everything else had failed.

Newbold had not really minded the stretch of trouble that he called a cow range. He liked it. The harder the fight, the more he was pleased; the longer it lasted, the better grew his second wind. Climate or no climate, rain or no rain, prices or no prices, he raised cows, he made men herd them, and he coined money.

That's why I say that the hay press was a real giant, because, single-handedly, it licked Newbold. It put him on his back. He was a new man when it got through with him.

I never quite understood the workings of that machine. When he got it, it looked like a cross between a traveling crane and a moving van. It was these things, and something more. It had all the habits of everything, and none of the virtues. It broke the heart of the machinist, and it nearly killed the poor old blacksmith. I shall never forget how he used to sit with his head in

16

one hand and a broken piece of iron fixture in the other, too tired to swear and too worried to sleep.

I remember right well that day we finally hauled the hay press through the worst of the pass, having pried and prayed it over jutting rocks, through tight squeezes, mile after mile. We had chucked stones under the wheels in time to keep it from lurching forward down a slope and crushing the mustangs that hauled it. We had thrown a log under it in time to keep the obstinate fool of a thing from running backward into a ravine. I remember the day for these reasons, and because that was when a pinto beast, working in the swing, clipped me on the point of the hip with a well-aimed kick just as I was jumping out of range. But most of all, I remember it because that evening a man rode into our camp and sat down to eat with the boys.

He was Dug Waters, whom most people in those days called White Water, for a lot of obvious reasons. Mostly because, here and there, he had made as much noise and done as much damage as a river at the flood. He was a tall, gentle-looking man with a good deal of Adam's apple and an embarrassed smile. He had a way of crowding into corners and seeming to beg everyone not to notice him. But the boss noticed him, you can bet.

That fellow Newbold always had a good look at any stranger who sat down to eat his meat at our camp. As I said before, it was the worst chuck that ever was put before cowpunchers, and heaven knows that cowpunchers never got much of the cream, no matter where they hung their bridles and tried to call home. But Newbold would watch a penny in the shape of a piece of sourdough as closely as a jeweler could watch a fine diamond.

At the table was where we liked him least. He hauled up to where Waters was sitting and asked him his name and business, and, when he found out that it was White Water himself, the boss almost choked. He told Waters to start for the skyline as soon as possible, and that the shortest road would probably be the smoothest. He said that he had never turned an honest man from his door, but that he would walk ten miles and swim a river to take the hide of a skunk.

Our boss was a known man, but so was Waters, for that matter. The moment we heard his name and saw how quiet he

17

was, we knew that he was really a dangerous fighter. I've never seen it fail. A fellow of many words never has so many bullets in his magazine. The quiet fellows who seem to think their way from word to word are the ones who wreck a saloon when the time comes, and shoot the tar out of a whole sheriff's posse when they're pursued.

White Water was exactly that sort of a fellow, to judge by the look of him and to listen to his reputation, but he didn't pull a gun on Newbold. Yet I've never seen a more cold poison than there was in the eye that he turned on the boss.

Finally he said: "Newbold, I'm a sick man. I'm bound on a long journey, and I haven't eaten a morsel for two days. I'll tell you one thing more. I'm not begging on my own account altogether. I'd see you hanged before I'd do that. But I'm asking you to let me sit here and eat a square meal. I haven't a penny to pay you, but I'll give you the bridle off my gelding yonder. I can ride him just as well with a halter."

We all watched the boss pretty carefully at this. I think that almost any other man in the world would have thrown up his hands when he heard and saw the straightness with which White Water was speaking. But Newbold was all chilled steel. He was the stuff that they put in the nose of armor-piercing shells.

"Your bridle and you be danged together," he said. "Get out of this camp before I throw you out! You're a thug, and a thief, and a gunman, and I hate your breed. If you're sick, you're not as sick as I'd like to make you. I'd like to see you and your whole breed drop and the buzzards start on you before your eyes were dark. Now, start along before I use my hands on you!"

I thought that it would be guns, then, and a mighty neat fight, because it made no difference to the boss. Perhaps he preferred fists, but he was just as much at home with knives, or guns, or clubs even for that matter. It was a sight to see him there with the red light shaking from the fire over his long, lean, loose-coupled body.

But Dug Waters only looked up at him for a moment as though he were seeing a game bird, away off in the sky. Then he surprised us a good deal by saying: "You don't have to throw me out. I'll go."

With that he got up and left us, and the amazing part of it

was that not one of us, in speaking of the thing afterward, thought that Waters was yellow. We all agreed that he must have had something on his mind. Pete Bramble said that he saw Waters stagger as he raised his foot to the stirrup to go off. And every one of us agreed that he had told the truth and was a sick man. He had the white look of a fellow with very little blood in his body—little good blood, at least.

Pete Bramble, after the boss had rolled into his blankets, looked around him at the silent circle of us and said: "That's gonna bring us bad luck. That's going too far. When a man's sick . . ." He stopped and puffed at his pipe.

The cook was standing there in his shirt sleeves, the fire shining on his greasy, red arms. "When a man's sick?" he echoed. "No, when he's hungry! Aye, or even a dog, when it's gaunted all up!"

I think he was the worst cook in the world, but I loved him for saying that. We all did. For two or three days hardly a man cursed him for the way he made the coffee or burned the beans.

The next day we got the hay press down to its first location and set her up. It's a hard thing to describe a hay press. In the first place, it's a job I don't like. The less I have to think about hay presses, the better pleased I am. In the second place, I never understood them, and I never wanted to. But I can say that this thing that turned big hay into small, so to speak, was a long box set upon one end, with a beater in it that worked up and down on long irons. The power that worked it came from four squeaking mustangs that scratched their way around and around on a circle, hitched to a beam. Halfway around the circle they were lugging to pull the beater up; the other half they were lugging to jam the feed down. It was run, run, run for them except when the bale was made, and then the power driver yelled—"Bale!"— and dropped an anchor board that held the power beam in place until the bale was tied with wire.

The first thing that we did was to start out a fleet of four Jackson bucks. For the benefit of 'punchers who never saw a Jackson buck, I'd say that it's a thing with a lot of iron-shod and pointed wooden spears that stick out in front. Two horses work behind this line of spears with a wooden, open bulwark in front of them, and behind them sits the driver on a seat that has a single plow wheel under it.

It was my job, at first, to drive one of those Jackson bucks. I admired the contraption a good deal, right at first, but I used up my admiration plenty before the day was an hour old. The trick was to start out with the teeth of the machine hoisted, and, while running empty like that, the clumsy brute was sure to start sliding on a downslope where there was no downslope to see, or zigzagging over bumps where there were no bumps to find. I ask any cowpuncher to imagine what a pair of bronchos only half broke to the saddle and a quarter broke to harness would do with that sort of a stall of wheels weaving around them.

They kicked, and bucked, and threw themselves backward, and then they started to run away. But the cards were stacked against those bronc's. They were tied in front, and they were tied behind, and they were framed in on both sides, and, when they tried to bolt, I just lowered the spears into the ground, and, after they had plowed an acre or so, they admitted that they were beat.

So was I. I was kind of chafed a little, to tell the truth. I thought that riding for years in a saddle had given me an outside lining as tough as leather, but I was all wrong. That iron seat on top of that jolting, jouncing, jarring plow wheel found all sorts of new and tender places that I didn't know were on the map.

Finally, the bronc's were convinced that it was no good, so I started their work, which was to pick up as many shocks of hay as the buck would hold without spilling and shove them up to the back end of the hay press. The bronc's would ram the load home well enough, but, when it came to backing up, they couldn't understand. They simply balked. Pete Bramble lighted matches and burned off their chin whiskers before it dawned on them that there were two ways of going, and one of them was back.

But still, it was a hard job. Between pulling my arms out of joint to back my ornery team of nags, trying to steer that danged side-wheeling invention, and being bumped like a hiccuping rubber ball until my heart and stomach changed places and my liver and lungs got scrambled together, I was ready to quit by noon.

So I went up to the boss to tell him my idea, and there I had my first sight of the kid. I have to take a new breath before I start talking about him.

Chapter Three

"Red Hair"

This kid was about fifteen, I should say, very big for his age, and with a pair of smooth shoulders—the sort you see in a well-made mule. He looked young, but you could see that the bull was only beginning to appear in his neck, and the mastiff in his jaw, and the mischief in his eye. His face was covered with bright-red freckles.

"They're the sparks and the coals of fire that come out of the top of his head," said Pete Bramble one day.

For his hair was just the color of fire—red fire. This pug-nosed boy was sitting on a rock, chewing a straw, and looking like a simpleton, which is a talent that no grown man can divide with a fifteen-year-old brat. He had on about half a hat, with his red hair burning up through the holes in the roof. He had on a shirt that was minus a collar and one sleeve. His trousers were a sawed-off pair that once had fitted a man, and a big man at that. His feet were bare, and so were his calves with white marks on them where the thorns had scratched. Take him all in all, he looked like a young mountain lion with the fur peeled off and the hide tanned.

The Oath of Office

I looked at this young limb for a while, and then I sashayed up to the boss. He gave me the nearest relation to a smile that could be found in his house—about a fifth cousin, say.

"How is things, Joe?" he asked.

"Kind of monotonous," I said.

"Monotonous?" he says.

"Well, chief," I said, "I come up and hunted for your shindig because I heard that there was some action to be found around your place."

"Why, Joe," he said, "I've always aimed to keep the boys amused and with enough to do so they won't have to be rocked to sleep at night. I used to keep minstrels and such to soothe them down, but then I decided that I'd have to look up more for them to do. Matter of fact, I haven't had no complaint like yours since I can remember."

"That's a funny thing," I said, "and I'll bet you ain't been keeping your ear peeled close to the ground. Well, it hasn't been so bad, mostly. Breaking in ten, twelve trained outlaws that you call range ponies every year was one pleasin' feature that we all looked forward to, especially me."

"I always guessed that you did, Joe," said the boss. "You look so plumb graceful in the air."

"There was other good features, too," I said. "Like drinking tank water when the wriggles have to be strained out of it and vinegar mixed in . . . and eating beans twenty-one times a week . . . and exercising our jaws like lawyers on beef that we never could convince. And the ship's biscuit was entertainin', too, because it was a lot of fun to rap a chunk of it on the edge of the table and see the weevils come out and take notice who was callin' at the front door of their old home."

"Why, Joe," he said, "it seems that I've been running a regular vaudeville show to keep you boys amused. I didn't know that I was laying myself out to do that."

"A regular college, too," I said. "Couple of years up here would make a man pretty handy with some of the dead languages, because it's a cinch that your cows don't understand no living tongue. There's some medical trainin', too, because anybody that can nurse your yearlings through one of these winters ought to be able to set up a first-rate practice giving the rich

23

and the old and the feeble another ten years of life."

"That's an angle I never thought of," he said. "I guess that I ought to start to charge admission, and here I've been all the time paying out regular wages."

"It's been a terrible mistake," I said. "The boys all been wanting to speak about it, but you know . . . some fellows, they break right down when they find that they can't give away a lot of their dough. We all thought that you must be one of that kind."

"I see how it is," he said, a lot more patient than I ever expected him to be. "My mistake is being too big-hearted and generous all the time."

"I hate to tell you," I said. "I hate to complain, but that's the truth. Look at the way you put up a roof all patterned with holes, like an open-work shirt, so's we could see the stars while we were lying in the bunks. A plain cowpuncher, he don't expect that much care and thought and trouble on the part of his boss, though I must admit that it was handy to know when it was raining, and we could always tell when the cows was likely to freeze to death by the way we felt in the bunkhouse."

"I see it all, now," he said. "I've just been too kind!"

"Boss," I said, "I'm a humble man, and I don't like to complain, but the hard truth has gotta come out. We're a rough lot, and a thick-skinned lot, and we have to be treated that way. Still, for the sake of education, and all that, I've stuck along on the job, but today is too much. There ain't enough to do on that Jackson Creek to keep me awake."

"Joe," he stated, "you fair make my heart bleed. Sitting there on that soft iron seat has sort of culled you."

"Yes," I said, feeling my way along, "about half a yard of hide has been culled right off me. And a fellow like me that has been used to riding Thoroughbreds out of Thunder and sired by Lightning, you can't expect him to have his hands full with nothing but a pair of those pets that I've been driving all morning."

"They've been too well taught," he said. "I can see that."

"Yes, chief," I said, "the fact is that it ain't barely possible to keep them from reciting their lessons all day long. They've been marking up a hundred per cent on me all the time!"

"It's hard to bear."

24

"Yes," I agreed. "I'm already limping a little. But I've been waiting and hoping that I would have something to do to keep my hands full and my mind occupied, but the only other thing that I've had has been a three-wheeled cartoon of a wagon that already knows a lot more than I'll ever learn. It can find its way where I never would guess that there is one. That's what I call a college-graduate wagon."

"I've been admiring it myself," he said. "And what's the conclusion that you're drifting all these ideas toward, Joe?"

"It's a sad thing, boss," I said, "but I'm going to vamoose. I'm afraid that you've got the wrong kind of a man in me. You oughta fill up your bunch with recruits from the old folks' home, or a hospital, or something like that . . . the sort of people that wouldn't ask to be more than just mildly occupied and amused for about twenty hours a day, the way I've been. You take old people, and they get childish again, and they don't mind lying down and sleeping right through the whole of four or five hours a night."

"Old son," he said, "I see that you're giving me the best advice in the world. I thank you, and I'm mighty grateful to you. But I can't help suggesting that maybe I could shift your berth and give you another job."

"What job?" I asked. "What sort of a job on this Christmas Eve knitting party?"

"Why, there's the forking and feeding job," he said. "Pete Bramble has been pretty nearly going to sleep on his feet, over there with the Jackson fork. Why not change with him?"

"I dunno that Pete would want to change," I said.

"I've got a kind of an idea," he said, "that Pete would actually change with anybody. Even the wire cutter, over yonder."

This wire cutting was a job that I hadn't looked into much, so far, but I could hear a good deal from this fellow who was running the outfit there; sometimes the sound of him half a mile away went into my mustangs like a whip and made them jump.

Here the red-headed kid spoke up. "That wire-cutting job was made for me," he said.

The boss looked him over. "Ain't you too old for that kind of active work?" he asked.

"I'm getting kind of childish again," said the kid. "I just want

25

to stand around and play with toys like that all day."

"You know all about hay presses, I guess?" the boss said.

"No, not all about 'em," the boy answered. "I've forgot a lot. But I used to build 'em, that's all."

"D'you think," asked the boss, "that you could cut as many wires in three hours as we can use in one?"

"I think," said the kid, "that I could cut as many wires in one hour as you could use in three."

"I guess you could," stated the boss with a sneer. "I guess you could do that. I guess you're a regular dollar-a-day man, ain't you?"

"You know the way the saying goes?" said the kid. "Put up or shut up!"

"Kid," he said, "go over and do your stuff. Tell Bosh Miller that he can step down from that wire stretcher."

The boy still sat where he was and chewed on the straw and twisted it slowly from one side of his mouth to the other. "At a dollar per?" he said.

"If you can turn out as many wires as we use . . . yes!" the boss declared. "But if you spoil more than two of those wires . . . What's your name?"

"Chip," the boy answered.

"If you spoil more than two of those wires, I'll make you less than a sliver," the boss said. But he was talking to the dust that lad made as he streaked it for the wire cutter.

"Now, Joe, what are you saying?" remarked the boss to me.

"Well," I said, "if Pete Bramble is chump enough to want to change jobs with me, I suppose that I'm chump enough to want to stay on and see how the thing turns out. That kid's a whale!" So I sauntered over to the stack and asked Pete if he wanted to change to my job.

He came blinking to me through a cloud of dust. He took me by both shoulders. "Boy," he said, "d'you mean it?"

"Sure."

He said not a word. He simply turned and climbed for the spot where my buck was standing. I looked down at my shoulders. There was a stain of blood on each of them.

Chapter Four

"Theory and Practice"

It's a strange fish that can swim out of water. The trouble with the whole business was that, while Newbold knew all about cows, he did not know all about hay presses. Not half! He had a theory, and theories have wrecked greater men than Newbold. A theory is the sort of thing that takes ten dollars and sells on a margin when the market is dropping, and buys on a margin when the market is climbing, and pyramids all the way and makes three hundred and twenty dollars the first week, and ten thousand the second, and three hundred and twenty thousand the third, and ten million the fourth, and three hundred and twenty million the fifth, and ten billion the sixth—and there you are. The seventh week that theory has the multimillionaires and all that small-time crowd asking for introductions; the eighth week they beg for jobs, and the authorities vote a medal to the Napoleon of finance who kindly didn't take up the whole of Wall Street and the rest of the country into the bargain.

Right at the beginning, Newbold showed us his theory. He said: "The shorthorn who sells me this machine, he says that it bales forty-five tons a day and averages forty, because you gotta waste a little time taking it down, and moving it, and setting it up again. Now, we'll allow five tons a day of lying to that crook. Still, we've got an average of thirty-five tons a day. We've cut three thousand acres, and we ought to bale twenty-five hundred or three thousand tons . . . and we ought to do that in ninety days. Now, ninety days is a lot of time, but so is three thousand tons a lot of feed. It ought to feed five thousand weak head of cows for a hundred days of the worst winter or the worst summer pickings. You see what that would mean to us."

He always put it that way. He was always talking as though we were a company in which he was no more than the executive officer, say.

This same fellow who sold him the machine had said that the right pay was eighteen cents a ton to the bale roller, seventeen cents a ton to the feeders, and fourteen cents to the power driver. But the boss did not remember that much of the talk. Only later we found out. What the boss offered us was just half of the right rates. However, even that looked pretty fat to us. You take eight cents a ton, say, for forty tons a day, and you've got three dollars and twenty cents of any man's money. And that makes close to a hundred a month, if you don't knock off for Sundays.

Would we knock off? We would not! We lay around in our bunks, that first night, and we bought ourselves new saddles and picked up Thoroughbreds for a song, and won the Kentucky Derby with them, and took trips to New York and Cuba, and just raised heck in general.

Even the kid had done his share, and more than his share. He had hopped around from one end of that machine to the other and actually cut a lot more wires than the machine had managed to use up. He kept the wire fairly jumping off the coil and the head-twister warm, he hummed it around so fast. We used a big wire for the central part of the bale, and a smaller wire for the ends. He could make the thinner variety fairly hop off the machine of its own volition. The bigger kind he had to strain over, bracing his weight to get down the stretching lever. But he never said no, and his production was steady all afternoon.

At the end of the day he went up to the boss as fresh as paint and said: "You gotta be congratulated on having one first-class man, Newbold."

"Which man is that?" asked Newbold.

"Me," said the kid. "If you don't believe it, look at that!"

He pointed back to a fine little stack of wires that he had cut and laid out. Newbold usually had a word when he wanted one, but this time he was plainly beat. He had to turn around and walk off, and that kid got on at a steady job with a man-size salary of a dollar a day, which was real pay in those days.

But I have to leave the kid, for a time, and get back to what was happening to the hay press. The job of forking from the stack looked all right, and it sounded all right. All you had to do was to grab that three-cornered Jackson fork and plant it in a wad of hay. Then you yelled—"Hay!"—and the derrick driver started up his horse and jerked that load up into the air. When it was dangling over the feed platform, you pulled the trip line and the load dumped down where the feeder could get at it. It looked easy. You seemed to be standing around a lot of the time, doing nothing.

But it didn't turn out so easy. For a starter, the fork weighed forty pounds, and all those pounds were put in the worst places. There were four long, curved teeth, needle-pointed, and always trying to get at your legs with a down-drop or a side flip or some other dodge. The trip iron had a sharp edge and was specially designed to clamp down over your fingers. Then there was an art in using that fork. On the one hand, you had to dodge the spears of bucks as they came steaming in with all the push of two-mustang power behind them. Then, as you side-stepped, you heard the feeder screeching at you for more hay. But you had to put in the fork just so. If you didn't use the fork so that it divided the big, snarled masses a little, the feeder had to break his back muscling it apart. If you tried to help the feeder by sending up small forkfuls, you half killed the derrick horse, which had to back up all the time, and, in addition, you starved the feeder you were trying to help. Add to all this that you worked in a cloud of thick dust and chaff that filled your neck and your throat and your eyes, and it makes a pretty picture. But not strong enough for the fact. Nothing is as strong as the facts about a hay press, no matter how words are put together.

I got through that afternoon, and when I came to the end of the working day—which was about dark, and long after sunset—

I was almost too tired to wash my hands. Then I waddled into the cook house along with the rest, and, while I was looking at the greasy flapjack and sowbelly that the cook called our supper and trying to make a start in eating, in came the boss with hay burrs sticking out of his hair and chaff down his back stuck to his flannel shirt.

He had been adding up the tags of the bale roller, and he was pretty sour. Then he said: "Nineteen gol-darned tons!"

"Nineteen tearin' wildcats!" I said.

The boss sat down at his plate and looked at the flapjacks and turned his head and opened his mouth to say something to that red-armed clown of a cook. But he seemed to remember in time that he was the man who bought the food the poor cook had to prepare, and that stopped his mouth for him a little.

Nineteen tons! It was right. He showed us the books, and nobody would believe, and everybody took a look. Our bales were averaging about a hundred and eighty pounds, and we had only turned out a little more than two hundred of them. The feeders swore that they had pitched at least a thousand tons of blankety-blank hay down the throat of the what-not press. The bale roller said they lied like something else, because he, personally, had taken out at least two thousand tons, and had tied, tagged, and rolled and piled it.

Just then up spoke the kid. Those greasy flapjacks didn't bother him a bit. He ate them as though they were sponge cake and the sowbelly was honey. He floated down his food with the alkali solution that our cook called coffee.

The kid said: "You know how it is, boys. You gotta learn. If I was up there on that feeding platform, I'd show you how to build your first feed big, and then taper them off so's the last one is just a kick of your foot to knock some chaff down the throat of the old lady."

We all looked at him. For my part I wanted to throttle him.

The old man said: "You know, do you, son?"

"Sure I know!" said the kid. "I used to build these here machines. You might say I invented 'em."

"Well," said the boss, "tomorrow morning you're gonna climb up there onto the platform and show us. And you ain't going to come down till noon."

"Aw, that's all right," the kid replied. But he looked a little startled.

We dropped the beater in that man-killer at four sharp in the morning, and, sure enough, there was the kid up there with a pitchfork taller than his head. And when he had said that he knew, he was right! You could drown him with a forkload of hay that crammed the platform to the far corners, but somehow or other he would manage to clear the feed table, and, when it raised its ugly long lower jaw, sure enough, there was a full bite for its long, square throat to swallow.

He built the first feed high and thick and sloped it off and packed it on top. When the beater rose to the top of its height, he gave the upper layers of the feed a shove with the fork and started the load sliding even before the table rose. And so he poked down a starter that nearly choked the press and got the bale well started.

He could pick to pieces a tangle of hay that looked like a trail problem built up out of barbed wire. Even when the feed floor looked as bare as the flat of your hand, he seemed able to pick out another feed for the making bale out of the corners, here and there. But, all the time, he was riding me, out there on the stack, and calling down to me to find out if I was asleep, and how long had I been off baby food, and wasn't I only part of a man and when was the rest of the sandwich coming?

He not only had tongue for me, but he used to stir up the derrick driver, too. That driver was an Irishman by the name of Clive Rooney. Once Rooney started to climb up to the feeding platform to take the boy apart, but the kid stood right there and begged him to come on and told him he would straighten his crooked jaw for him and knock a whole vocabulary down his throat. This line of talk cleared Rooney's head a little, and he remembered that he was dealing with a mere kid. So he went back to his single-tree and derrick horse. But with every trip that the horse made out and back, Rooney gave one black look at the kid up there on the table.

It wasn't Rooney alone, or I, that tasted the boy's tongue. Sometimes he leaned around the corner of the press and asked the power driver if he had a team of prairie rabbits, or were they just burros. He got that fellow to raging and throwing the whip into the ponies. Still the brat had time to lean over the edge of the table and tell the bale roller a few things, and ask him if he thought he was rolling dice, and if he hoped to bale more than he could eat, and who had told him he was old enough to leave home. He even had a few words for the drivers of the bucks, and the squeak of his voice cut out clear and high through all the clangor of the press and the cursing and shouting of the men.

After a while, he stopped bothering me. I guess he saw that I wasn't to be made angry. The fact is that I was too interested in watching his tactics to lose my temper. For he was playing the gaddy and driving the whole set of us, grown men though we were. He wanted us to bale hay, and he was making us do it.

I could not help wondering how long he would last. He could not keep up the pace till noon, I knew. It was very plain that Chip knew all about feeding, and that he knew all the art of handling a pitchfork—for it is an art—but in spite of his craft and his strength beyond his years and his wild spirit he simply could not stand there in the flying dust with the temperature a hundred in the shade—heaven knows what it was in the sun fire and hay smoke where he was working—and push so many tons into the feed box forever.

We worked from four to six. Then we had breakfast. At breakfast, the kid was as gay as a lark and taunting all of us. At ten o'clock we had a lunch of stewed prunes, bread, and coffee. The kid was still pretty chipper, but not quite so gay. He didn't come down from the platform. He simply sang out: "What's the matter? You boys think you're all at school and are getting paid for your recess time?"

He didn't come down. He just disappeared, and I knew that he had flopped down flat on the table to rest there, in spite of the beating of the sun.

I finished off my lunch before the rest and sneaked a cup of coffee up to the platform. He was dead to the world, his eyes closed, his mouth dangling open. I shook him by the shoulder, and he got up with a start. He gave me one hard look, tossed off the coffee, handed the cup back to me, and said not a word. He just got up and grabbed his pitchfork again.

I went back to the cook house and threw in the cup. I said: "You'd best call down the kid from the feed table, boss. Or he'll kill himself before noon."

"Let him kill himself, then," the boss said, and Rooney and a couple more chimed in with the same idea.

So I went back to watch, and to worry. For I began to guess that I'd said more than I knew and come close to the truth.

Chapter Five

"Miss Marian Wray"

Believe it or not, between four in the morning and eleven that lad shifted fourteen tons from the feeding table into the feed box. A whisper of this went around, and even the hard hands on that crew wanted to see the kid let off. Marvel or no marvel, of course, he couldn't keep on at that rate. Not at fifteen years of age. Only, I want to repeat that he didn't look quite as young as fifteen. I want to say that for us all. We knew that we were doing something bad; we didn't know really how bad.

But when eleven o'clock came and the boy was still at work up there on the platform, I was outright worried. He had stopped all of his pestering talk, by this time. Through the rifts of the dust smoke, I could see his face set and lined like the face of an old man. He was taking his punishment and never making a murmur. I don't suppose it had occurred to him that there could be a man in the world like our boss, with a mind as small as an arrowhead and a heart as hard.

The sun went higher, and kept pouring down a billion tons of yellow-white, scalding sunshine. We changed the power horses every hour. We changed the bale rollers every two hours.

But the kid was still up there in the swelter of that furnace, never ready to say die. Poor Chip!

Then fate came along and offered him an ace from the bottom of the deck. I mean, Miss Marian Wray came cantering up on her best saddle horse. It was a good deal of a surprise, although the Wray place was no more than ten miles away, which couldn't be called any distance at all. But you wouldn't expect Marian Wray to be that far away from home—not hardly with a company of troops for an escort, to say nothing of being all by herself. For she was the real silver spoon, Back Bay, how d'you do aristocrat. She made me pretty sick, the way that she went around with her chin in the air.

I don't mean to say that she snubbed anybody. She was the opposite to that. She was always friendly and never let anybody go by without saying a few words, and the boys were crazy about her. But for my part, I never liked a peaches-and-cream, picture-book blonde. I never liked them a bit, and I liked Miss Marian Wray the least of the lot, with her democratic manner. She even used to go to the dances, now and then. But she never stayed more than thirty-one minutes. Thirty minutes to stand around and admire the decorations, and say that things were "too sweet," and the decoration committee had sure outdone itself, and that sort of rot. And then for one minute she slid out onto the floor with Tex Brennan—or somebody like that—that knew how to step, and made all the rest of the girls look like zero minus.

The funny thing about it was that the other girls didn't seem to see through it, either. The whole dang countryside, when you mentioned Marian Wray, just broke down and gibbered and practically wrung its hands over her, and the women were as bad as the men. I suppose that they thought she was so rich and lovely and beautiful and everything that's to be desired that there was no use in even envying her.

She was all dressed up like a regular range girl with a broad-brimmed hat and a loose blouse and divided skirt. The look of her blowing along in the wind of the gallop was enough, I have to confess, to make a fellow's heart jump. But when she came up close, she was a lot more Back Bay than range. She had a tailored and a manicured look, as though three maids had been working all morning to turn her out like this.

Even the boss was staggered a little by the arrival of the girl. All the other men were hanging out their tongues, they were so anxious to hear two words spoken by this queen of the May. Even the boss almost took a few minutes off. I say "almost," but not quite. He just used the interval while the power horses were being changed to chat with her, and all those grown-up fools of men craned their necks at that girl and admired her and grinned at her and looked blushing and stupid and ready to drop dead, if she ever said the word.

"I see you're a great natural innovator, Mister Newbold," she said.

"Oh, I had a little idea. That's all," said Newbold. He grinned at her, too, wide and simple as any of the rest.

I bit off a hunk of tobacco from the corner of my plug, and, while I worked it into a comfortable spot in the hollow of my face and felt the cheek muscles pulling soft and easy over the point of the load, I looked that girl over and wondered a little at what soft-heads we men are. Because most days she would have hit me just as hard as she always hit all the rest. But that day I was too worried about the boy and the perspiration in my eyes and the chaff down my neck. I couldn't have been romantic for a thousand dollars a minute, paid in advance.

I just looked that girl over and said to myself: "Bunk! Give me something with a commoner look, because you'll wear old sooner than any of the rest."

She was going around and admiring everything. It was the first time she ever had seen a hay press in action. I heard her telling the power driver how terribly brave he must be to be out there behind those dashing, crashing horses, because suppose the beam should break, what would happen to him when it kicked back? And she said to the bale roller how could anybody really do so many things at once, and wasn't it wonderful how the human hand could work as if an independent brain were operating in it? Then she came back and gave me a look, and she said what a frightful peril I was in, handling those four sharp, crooked, lance-like things. She called me Joe, too, because that was her idea. Look at Napoleon. He knew the name of all the men in his army, didn't he? Well, that was her trick. So dog-gone queenly that the meanest of her subjects was good enough to get a glad eye from her.

"You bet your boots, if you're wearing boots," I said, "that it's a frightful peril. . . ." I was about to add something else, when the dust cloud blew away from the feed platform and she saw the white face of the kid just as he sank his pitchfork into a wad of hay bigger than himself, a good deal.

"Great heavens, Mister Newbold," she sang out with something in her voice that sent the prickled chills even up my back, "do you employ children . . . at cut wages?"

Did he employ children! I thought that Newbold wanted the earth to open and swallow him, and I wished that it would and never let him out again.

Chapter Six

"One Man Down"

It was not often that one had a chance to see the great Newbold put down. But down he was now. Just then that ornery boy, Chip, leans out from the table, after shoving down the last feed on a bale, and just as the driver yells—"Bale!"—the kid sings out: "Hey, Newbold! Is this a dance that we've bought tickets for? Or what are all the skirts around for?"

I thought that Rooney would climb up and massacre that kid, when he heard the remark. The bale roller leaned his head out, after he'd jerked the bale out of the press and locked the door behind it, and gave the kid a glare.

But I understood. Chip wasn't cashing in on any female sympathy. It gave my heart a stir, I can tell you, when I saw what an outright man the boy was. I knew that he was sick all the way to the bottom of his boots from the work he had done, but he wasn't complaining. He was willing to leave the women out of the matter. You can imagine that the boss did not waste any time using the kid's lead.

He said to Marian Wray: "You see . . . fresh kid that wants to show us how to run the hay press. I'm taking some of the crow out of the little rooster."

"I know," Marian Wray said. "Some of them are that way. Gutter ruffians from birth. I suppose one ought to pity the poor little wretches." But there wasn't much pity in her, just then. She gave the kid a look that would have melted a galvanized iron roof, but Chip already had his back to her and was jamming a fresh feed down the throat of that old press. He was as game as they came.

He had given Marian Wray something to think about. She gathered the remnants of her usual smile about her—strange how pretty girls all learn to smile like actresses—and pretty soon off she went.

As soon as she was hull down, I waited for the boss to call poor Chip off the table, and I even saw the boy give the boss one side glance, but Newbold pretended to have forgotten him. There was no mercy in that heart of his. Having cashed in on the boy's pluck and spirit of fair play to get the girl out of the way, Newbold just left him up there to work his heart out.

It seemed to me that every minute would be his last one. I could see the boy wobble and shake as he staggered about. But he continued to stick that pitchfork into the hay, and he continued to heave the hay over into the mouth of the press. His last bale was as fat and firm all the way through as his first one.

Finally, the last long hour wore away from minute to minute, with the whole crew of us watching nothing but the fight that boy was putting up. The fact is that he lasted until the sun was right over our heads, and, by twelve noon, he had shoveled sixteen tons of hay off that platform. I have had a lot of grown men who knew the business doubt the thing, but I was there and saw it done, and I added up the pages in the bale roller's book with my own fair hand. It was eighteen pounds over sixteen tons, to be exact. And the boy was fifteen!

As I was saying, he kept right on until the cook banged on a pan at the door of his cook house to show that it was high noon by his stove, no matter what it was by the sun.

So the boys knocked off work, and the derrick and power horses were unhooked, and everybody started wiping chaff out of his shirt collar and dust out of his eyes. I watched the kid and saw him start down the side of the press, and then change his mind and come slowly over to the hay dump that was slanting up to the feed table, half dust, clods, and the rest chaff. He lowered himself over the edge of the table and slid down. Halfway to the bottom, his body slewed around, like a bear in a running current with nobody at the tiller, and he rolled the rest of the way. You might have thought that he had given his head an extra hard knock on a lump of sun-fried earth on the way down, but I knew what was the matter.

I ran over and picked him up by the nape of the neck and had a squint at his face. He was blue around the mouth and white around the eyes. He looked like one of those painted monkeys. And he was limp as a dishrag. So I hauled him over to the drinking water and doused him good and plenty, and dragged him into the shade under the cook house, and hoisted his legs higher than his head, and began to fan him.

The boys came around and helped. They didn't say anything. Not a one of them had anything to offer. But one man took the fold of a newspaper out of my hand and continued the fanning, and I remember how Pete took a scalded rag and squeezed out a steady stream of drops onto the hollow of the kid's throat. They were an ugly lot of men. They were ashamed of themselves, and nothing is more dangerous than a man who's ashamed of himself. He wants to get back his self-respect all in one stroke.

Big Newbold came up and said: "The brat's had his lesson, I guess."

Nobody spoke, even then, but every man jack of us turned and gave the boss a good, thoughtful look. He said no more. He cleared his throat and pretended to get interested in the making of a cigarette. But I saw a small white spot in both of his cheeks, and I knew that even Newbold, if he couldn't feel shame, could feel fear, at least.

We worked about a half hour and still nobody spoke a word, except when one man would call another a chump, with underlinings, and shoulder him out of the way to take up his share of the work. For my part, I had made up my mind that Chip was dying, and that Newbold would be dead soon after, when the kid fluttered his eyelids and looked at us in a puzzled way and then sighed and closed his eyes again.

"Mommie!" he said, and turned over on one arm and sighed again.

It knocked me all in a heap for some reason. I mean, we didn't need to see his birth certificate just then to see that he was two or three years younger than we'd been rating him. If we felt sick before, you can imagine how we felt when we heard him speak, and saw him turn and sigh like a child in his bed when his mother kisses him good night.

Newbold took hold of me with an iron hand and moved me out of the way and leaned to have a look. He didn't say anything. His face was better than a whole book filled with words.

Just then up piped a quiet, musical voice, as cold as the snow water in a mountain stream, and said: "I see that you allowed him to keep right on showing you how to run the press, Mister Newbold!"

It was the girl. Her horse had cast a shoe, and she'd come back at a walk to see what our camp could do about it, because she knew that we had a good blacksmith attached. It was the very worst thing that could have happened to us. It was the sort of a story that we would not like to have even men repeat. But as for a woman—why, it was a yarn that every woman in the countryside would eat up and give forth again with embroideries. And every time the yarn was repeated, our crew would be made to seem more and more like cannibals—child-eaters!

Above all, to have Marian Wray talking about us and starting the thing! For everything she said would be taken as an understatement. My first thought was to start right then, horse or foot, and climb for the nearest railroad and put a thousand miles of 'dobe between me and that scene.

I think that the rest had the same idea. But the first thing we knew, there she was, sitting with the head of the boy in her lap and not regarding us at all.

She just said: "The poor child! The poor little boy!" And she ran her fingers through his dusty, chaff-filled hair, and brushed it back from his forehead.

This was only a starter. Somehow, she managed to convey that there were a thousand leagues of distance between such a "poor little boy" and grown-up male brutes like us. Perhaps she was right.

Then, while the iron was hot—melting hot—she said: "You might stop pouring on the water. His temperature is already sub-normal. We might as well try to save what's left of his life." But she added at once: "Though, of course, after the shock of this he'll never be anything but a wreck of a man."

We didn't question her medical wisdom. It was a case where we felt that she had us with a strangle hold, and the less we said, the better for all of us.

I forgot exactly what she did. But I think that she asked us if we had any whiskey and begged our pardons for suggesting that we might be carrying such poison around with us. Poison? She was the poison just then. She was poisoning us all. I swear that she even kept a little smile at the corners of her lips. And every now and then she raised her glance from the boy and fixed one or two of us, slowly, carefully, as though she wanted to remember our names and faces for future reference. Altogether, it was a miserable time. I even forgot to feel any sympathy for the boy. I would rather that he had been run over in a stampede and turned into a patch of fertilizer on the ground than that he should have involved us all so deeply.

Now and then I gave Newbold a look, and after the second or third one I was amazed to see that even the rhinoceros hide which he wore in the place of a skin had been pierced, and that he was suffering a good deal. Rather more than a good deal.

Finally he said: "Miss Wray, I didn't know. . . ."

She lifted her head, with that ice-cold imitation of a smile. "You didn't know what, Mister Newbold?" she asked.

He faced her. I must say that for him. "I didn't know that I could be such a brute."

I'm sorry to say what followed. She looked him right in the eye and answered: "Oh, didn't you?"

It was the wickedest remark I've ever heard passed along from one human being to another. And I've heard some pretty active tongues inspired with red-eye, at that.

Just then the boy stirred and groaned.

"It's all right," she said. "It's all right now, poor dear."

At that, the kid sat bolt upright with a start. He gave a look around and stared at the girl. "What's all this kindergarten bunk?" he said. "Cut it out!" And he got right up on his feet.

Chapter Seven

"Boy is King"

I must say that it did me a lot of good to see the boy fetch himself up to his feet again. He made a sort of wobbling first step, but he caught hold of himself again and leaned a hand against the rim of a cook-wagon wheel.

"Gimme the makings, Joe, will you?" he said.

I knew by the green of his gills that he didn't want a cigarette. But I fished out the makings and began to roll one for him. I could see that he was making a play to kill time. The rest of the men could see the same thing.

But the girl did not understand. She followed the boy and said to him: "Don't you think that you'd better lie down again? You really are not as well as you think. Something has happened, my poor boy. . . ."

He gave her a mean look. Then he turned to the rest of us. "How does she get that way?" he asked. "Lead me away from it, Joe, because it might be catching."

It set Miss Wray back quite a few steps to hear these cracks. But she kept on. When a woman has made up her mind that she's being good and that she's on the right track, hardly anything will stop her.

"As a matter of fact," she said, "hadn't you better come home with me? My father has need of such a . . . man . . . as you are." She set off that word "man" as a concession, between a couple of her sweetest smiles.

The kid responded: "Who's your old man, ma'am?"

"He's Judge Arthur Wray," said the girl gently, so as not to swamp the poor kid with the full glory of the name.

"Judge Arthur Wray? Judge Arthur Wray?" the kid said, cocking up one eye, as though he had to think hard to remember a name that everybody in the West knew as well as they knew the Tetons. "Oh, yeah. I remember now. He's the fellow who roped and hog-tied the Injuns in that land deal, ain't he?"

It was true, some people said, that old Judge Wray had used more corn whiskey than cash to get out of the Indians some of the best rangeland that cows ever grazed. If it was not a tender point with the Wray family, at least it was plain that the girl had heard about it. She got a sunset-red into her face in no time at all. Perhaps she could have answered, but that terrible kid didn't give her time.

He went right on: "It might be that your old man wants a good hand on his place. But you tell him I'm mighty grateful, but that I don't talk Injun good enough to be much use to him. And I do talk hay press."

"Of all . . . ," began the girl. Then she stopped herself. Perhaps she remembered that she was about to say something trite. Perhaps she only cut off something always old but always new. She just took a fresh breath, however, and went ahead. As I was saying, you can't stop a woman when she thinks that that's she's carrying the flag. She'll keep on carrying it even while she's walking over a thousand faces, grinding in her high heels.

"You'd better think it over. I left my father a few miles back, but we can pick him up on the way. And when I tell him . . . well, I'm sure that he'll want to employ you. You know that there's room for young . . . men . . . to rise with him. He had to go out on a hunt this morning, but I think we'll find him on the way back."

"Hunting Injuns?" asked the boy, who seemed to be all calluses and no tender places.

The girl was patient and sweet as pie. "Hunting a thing worse than Indians," she said. "A real criminal, man-killer. A desperado," she wound up, and shook her head and smiled again, as though the courage of old Judge Wray staggered her a little.

"What might his monicker be?" asked Chip, the tough kid. "What's his name?"

"My father's name?" she said, as patient and angelic as ever.

"No. This here desperado's?" said the boy.

"His name," she said, "is Douglas Waters."

"Hold on!" the boy shouted. "I didn't know you played with a joker in the pack."

"Joker?" she stated, a little bewildered.

"You mean," Chip replied, "that your old man is out man-hunting the squarest shooter and the best bunkie and the rightest 'puncher that ever rode the range? Is that what you mean? Then if I see him, I wouldn't talk about a job, I guess. I'd talk something stronger." He turned to me. "Joe," he said, "come on over here and lemme show you something about the way to throw a Jackson fork, will you?"

"Sure," I said. I got hold of him under the elbow, and he gave me plenty of his weight to pack. So we walked right out on the well-meaning Miss Wray.

She seemed to be lagging to leeward with most of the wind out of her sails, and I must say that our boss seemed to be swallowing a smile that would have choked a sperm whale.

I didn't talk about Jackson forks. I just rushed the boy over to the shady side of the pile of bales and sat him down there, and then, with my hat, I fanned him.

He leaned back with his arms and legs sprawling, like a hopeless drunk. His lips kept twitching in and out and up to the sides, like a man who is wondering whether he can last it out or not. The first thing he said was: "Keep your eye peeled. Don't let 'em see me . . . like this."

"You're as right as a trivet," I said. I never knew what a trivet was, but so the saying goes. "Don't you worry, I'm keeping my eye peeled. If anybody shows, you'll be drawing a design on the ground and teaching me something."

His lips twitched a couple of more times before he managed to smile. Then he took my advice and began to draw lines in the dust. But he put his eye on me for a minute. "You're a partner, Joe," he gasped. "You're an old partner."

I wanted him to lie down, until the sick fit passed. But I didn't make the suggestion, because I knew that he wasn't the kind that lies down. You find men like that, one in a million, and boys like that—one in the world.

He preferred to sit up and take his medicine that way. He would rather have been on his feet, I knew. While I watched him fighting out his fight and beating the game, I looked the boy over and admired him a good deal more than I know how to say.

I wondered at him, too, and thought to myself that, after all, boys are foolish when they wish to grow up. If they're strong enough to sight a rifle and ride a horse, they can do most of what men can do. If they can do these things, they're about as good as men, take it all in all. Besides that, they have advantages all their own. They're all by themselves. A woman is a woman from the time she is old enough to take a baby doll by the scruff of the neck and call it hers. A man is a poor, weak, sentimental, sickly servant of the grown woman, their house-builder, jack-of-all-trades, supporter, and royal jester. They reward him by putting a cap and bells on his head, and they give him, as a bauble or scepter, a pretense of admiration for the muscles and the brain power that is always used merely to support the wife and the brats.

A grown man is a grown idiot. That's all. But a boy is different. That's why a boy is the only four-square-to-all-the-winds creature in the world. He goes his own way. He hews to a mark and a line and lets the chips fall where they may—and he generally hopes that they'll fall in your eye.

As I sat there, fanning Chip and admiring him, I couldn't help wondering at the ease with which he had settled beautiful Marian Wray. She was beautiful. She was lovely enough to take off the top of a man's head. One of her smiles was enough to keep a poor 'puncher awake at night, turning from side to side for a month on end. She was so charming that she had taken the crew of the hay press into the hollow of her hand in no time

47

at all. Just a look around had been enough. But she couldn't take Chip into the hollow of her hand. Not into the hollow of two hands, even. Indeed, she was helpless. What was all her beauty to him? He would rather have had a shiny new .22 than all of her, ten times over. He would have traded a gross of Marian Wrays for a three-year-old mustang with a kink in its tail and fire in its eye. So where the rest of the men had been paralyzed, he had walked right in and used his fists, so to speak, on the thin china of which she was made, and he had wrecked her, and blamed her father, and given her something to think about that would keep her turning from side to side for months on end.

Boys are a weakness with me. They always have been, and they always will be. I admire them. But when it comes to a showdown, I envy them more than I admire.

Yet, as I sat there and looked at Chip and thought of his power, and of what he had done that day and might do again, I couldn't help sighing, when I remembered that, within a couple of years, he would be like all the rest of us. The arrow would strike him in the heel; the sweet poison would run through flesh and bone; he would become the same sort of maundering sentimentalist that we all knew so well and understood so intimately, because we're the same woman-ridden, adoring, despising caricatures of Samson.

The glory of Chip was sure to pass. He would come to his mortal doom, sooner or later. But just then, he was complete, independent, sure as a fortified Rock of Gibraltar. And I looked at him as at a sort of super-creature.

Then he began to talk about the Jackson fork.

Chapter Eight

"All Set For Trouble"

The next three weeks I don't like to think about, and I don't like to write about. First, the weather got hotter every day, and the hay press broke down every day. Second, the boss fell in love with Marian Wray, and the hay press broke down every day. Third, inside of forty-eight hours everybody on that crew hated everybody else, and the hay press broke down every day. Fourth, and most important of all, the hay press broke down every day.

Taking the things one by one, I have to admit that the middle of the Nevada desert is about as hot as you can wish, but it was cool and crisp compared to the heat that we had out there on that pressing job. The last moisture was sucked out of the hay. You could break the stalks across as though they had been the stalks of straw after the harvest. And the last moisture was drawn out of the men, also. We were all dry powder, and any word was likely to drop like a spark into a mine. Gun fights were not in order, quite, but I had two fist fights on my own account. The first one was all right; but the second was with Pete Bramble, and we beat each other to a pulp. I got an eye on me that looked like a leather patch, and poor Pete had to talk and eat on one side of his face for days afterward.

But somehow the worst thing that happened, next to the hay press, was the way that the boss fell in love. "Fell" is the only word for it. He dropped about a mile, straight over the edge, and he landed so hard you could hear the splash.

You see, it appeared that old Judge Wray himself was thinking about buying a hay press, for reasons unlike those of Newbold. Wray's land was so good that his cows simply couldn't eat all the grass that grew, and so he wanted to fence off some sections and raise hay on them. There was plenty of sale for it. So he came over a number of times, and Marian came along with him.

Poor Newbold hardly ever looked at her, but you could tell at a glance what he was thinking about. He was out of his head about half of the time. I heard them, for instance, talking together one day, and the judge said: "A coat of paint would save that machine a lot. Put on a good wearing coat of heavy paint and the timbers wouldn't crack in the sun so much. I've got some heavy gray stuff at home. . . ."

"Dark gray," said Newbold, "looking kind of blue in the evening light. . . ."

"Who the deuce cares what it looks like in the evening light?" Wray answered. "The bale this turns out . . . what would you say the weight is?"

"About a hundred and thirty-five, I'd say," Newbold said dreamily.

"What?" Wray asks. "I thought you said they'd average closer to two hundred!"

"Oh, you mean the bales," Newbold said.

"What did you think I meant?" asked the judge.

Yes, Newbold was completely knocked over by the pretty face of that girl. Perhaps he was most attracted by his very sense of the impossibility of the thing. For after she knew how he had treated young Chip, her lip curled every time she looked at Newbold.

Not that Chip asked for sympathy from anyone. She was scared to death of his active young tongue and never tried anything more than a smile with him after the first day when he had let her down so hard.

But the weather and the wrangling among the crew and Newbold's stunned look when the girl was around were all nothing compared to that danged press. Never could tell what would happen.

Sometimes it would be in the red-hot middle of the day when the only way to escape wishing to die was to keep working and perspiring, so that the oven blast of the air would have something more than your hide to burn up. But usually it was in the dewy cool of the mornings or in the evenings when the sun was not so full of sledge hammers—yes, usually it was when work was almost a pleasure—that the press would give a groan, or a squeak, or a crack, and you could tell that something was sprained or a bone broken somewhere.

Twice we had to spend half a day taking out the whole side of the box so as to work on the vitals of the affair. And again, something went wrong with the gears of the power beam, and we were a whole day out of pocket. Yes, instead of averaging forty tons a day, we were averaging only about fifteen. It was sickening to think of.

But the only thing that kept us going and turning out even that much was the kid. He seemed to be able to read the mind of that machine, and he could tell in a moment just exactly what was wrong with it. He saved us time that way, and, also, he saved us a good deal by what he taught us about doing the work. Before I was through, like the rest of the boys, I had tried my hand at everything on the job, from Jackson bucking to bale rolling and power driving. The bale rolling was the hardest and the most interesting.

All you had to do, when the driver yelled—"Bale!"—was to knock open the door with an iron bar, drop the bar, grab the five stiff wires as the wire puncher shoved them through, cinch up and tie those wires with a fast figure eight—and, if you were fast enough, you took the last wire right off the needle of the puncher—and then you hollered: "Tied!" As the power driver started his team, the beater floated up, and as soon as it was clear of the table, the first big feed began to shoot down.

You had to get the bale out of the way and the door shut

before that feed started to descend, and to do this meant grabbing the hay hook off the beam overhead, sinking it in the top edge of the bale, and while, with one hand, you jerked the bale out and broke it to the right across your knee, with the left hand you caught hold of the door, slammed it, and, disengaging the hook from the bale, you used that hook to pull over the locking bar. After that, you simply had to roll the bale onto the scales, weigh it, write out its weight on a tag of redwood, and again on the page of your checking book, trundle the bale out to its place in the growing stack, and lift it into its berth, perhaps three feet high. Just as you were breaking your back to get that bale up, the power driver was sure to yell—"Bale!"—again, and back you sprinted for the dog house to do the whole thing over again.

Well, it was a pretty hot business, but it was a thing full of knacks from the tying of those infernal wires to the rolling and lifting of the bale itself. Little Chip knew all about the tricks. He could fairly make the bales walk along the ground, and nobody in the outfit could punch the wires through fast enough to keep Chip from waiting for the last one to come. Of course, he couldn't last long at it, but, while he worked, he made things hum and showed us how to do it, and how to step so that not an inch was wasted. Sometimes it almost seemed as though he had built the first hay press in the world, he knew so much about the job!

But even the kid could not ward off the bad luck that followed that machine. And every day, what between the girl and the press, Newbold got blacker and blacker and stared more and more at the ground, and not even Chip dared to sass him any longer.

Newbold used to walk out in the evening to the top of the nearest roll in the ground, and there he would stand as gaunt and melancholy as a scarecrow, staring over the surrounding acres and weeping tears of blood in his heart because he knew that he would never have enough time, at this rate, to bale all the hay that he had cut. To think of it lying there to first dry to powder and then to be rotted by the winter rains was enough to nearly kill him. He wasn't tight, I suppose, but it was a torture to him to see any wastage.

The atmosphere around that place grew more and more

charged, and pretty soon all of us knew that it was only a question of time before the sparks would begin to jump—sparks that might burn the life out of someone. The trouble was that, even if things had gone smoothly, we were cowpunchers, not mechanics. To do the same thing hour after hour was worse than a gun play on us.

That was about the time when Sheriff Murphy came out to visit us, and with his visit came the beginning of the end. It was just after dusk. We all lay around on our blankets, which we had rolled out on shocks of hay, the head end higher than the feet. Now we lay on our stomachs, our chins in our hands. Some of us smoked cigarettes. Some of the boys smoked pipes, but, for one reason or another, every few seconds there was a faint glow, and the face of someone stood out in rosy dimness at one part or other of the circle.

I remember that big Cash Logan was talking, at the time, and telling about how he once had a fight with a Canuck lumber man, a regular log-driver—and how the Canuck, being a little pressed, had pulled a knife to help out—and how he, Cash Logan, had used a trick he had learned when he was a boy, turning a handspring and whanging the soles of both shoes fairly and squarely into the face of the other fellow. So he did that thing now, and the fellow he used as an example dropped with a groan, and half woke up and thought that he had been killed by a bullet through the brain, and then felt his sore and swelling face and roared out that he had been shot all full of holes.

"That's pretty good, Cash," said Pete Bramble, rubbing his sore face tenderly. "That's good enough to be written down, pretty near. Where did you read about it?"

"Read about it? Read about it?" Cash yelled.

"That's what I said," remarked Bramble.

There might have been a fight on the spot, because neither of them was a man likely to give ground on any subject, but just then we heard the jingle and the tramp of a horse coming up to the place, and then the sheriff's voice hailed us loudly.

He made quite a sensation. For there were a number of the fellows working for the boss who preferred the misery of sticking to a job with him, rather than the wretchedness of continually dodging the police.

Chapter Nine

"The Sheriff is Curious"

It was an amusing and rather a nervous thing to see the way the boys of our outfit were shifting about a little from side to side, and acting strained, and beginning to sift back away from the sheriff, picking themselves up from their shocks of hay, and going through all of the movements of dogs, when they see a wolf in their midst. Wise dogs, I mean, that have been wolf stung once, and know enough to multiply every wolf by three or four when it comes to a fight. So these rough fellows, every one of whom, I suppose, had fallen afoul of the law at some time or other, edged away from the sheriff.

The boss, however, started right up from his place and went to meet the man of the law. That was the good thing about Newbold. He always stood by and for his men in every pinch. They knew it. That was the chief reason that they kept in their hearts some kindness for him.

Now, as Newbold fronted up to the sheriff, the latter heaved himself down from his saddle with a grunt. His horse grunted, too, as though it was dead tired. I remember how the reek of the mustang came sharply and clearly to my nostrils, and how,

54

after a moment, I heard the steady dripping of the sweat that ran down from his belly to the ground. The sheriff growled out a greeting of some sort to Newbold. Then he made and lighted a cigarette, and I had a good look at his face.

His name was Tug Murphy, and in those days he was quite a celebrity. The Tug stood for tugboat, and the nickname was a fair one, because he was a fellow of broad and noisy ways, but a great deal of steady power always applied to the business of the county. I suppose he rode ten thousand miles a year, or even more than that. He galloped a good deal of crime out of that rough country and a good deal of fear into the hearts of the crooks, so that every honest person in the district slept more soundly because of Tug Murphy, universal watchdog. He has finished his riding now. One day he leaned into a cloud of dust that had a .45-caliber chunk in it, and the lead cut through Tug and carried away all of him except two hundred pounds of useless weight. Tug is forgotten now, but at the time of which I speak he had a name that worked miracles.

He was bowlegged and wide-shouldered. He had the look of a man always grinding his teeth and holding himself in. Anger seemed to be working up to a high head in him day and night, and one waited to see him explode.

That was the look he had, red-faced, scowling, as he lighted the cigarette. The flame fairly shone on his face, it was running so with perspiration.

He said in his rough, direct, brutal manner: "Hey, Newbold, why don't you feed your crew?"

"I feed my crew," said Newbold.

"You don't feed 'em enough to keep 'em from half starving," insisted the sheriff.

"Who told you that?" asked Newbold.

"They've been going over to the Seaton place lately, and slipping away with a few of the best chickens that they could lay their hands on," said the sheriff, "and old Seaton is a little tired of it. He didn't take the trouble to come over here and complain, but he took the trouble to come all the way to town to tell me about it. Now, you look here, Newbold. You may not step over the traces yourself, but you're makin' trouble for others. And I ain't going to have it!"

55

Newbold said nothing. I thought that he was going to swallow these disagreeable remarks.

The sheriff, having made his first point, went on steadily: "I'll tell you, Newbold, that they is some that approve of lynchin' hoss thieves. But my idea is that a man that would steal a hoss is a regular hero and a giant alongside of the poor, sneakin' skunk that goes and robs a henroost. . . ."

Newbold said: "What you're doing is to call me a poor, sneakin' skunk, I think."

The sheriff answered: "You can put on the shoe, if it fits you."

"Peel off your coat and your badge," suggested Newbold, "and I'll see what your size is!"

"You wanta fight, do you?" the sheriff asked. "And you think that I'll go around wasting my time fighting with fellows like you that don't mean anything to me? If I have to come and get you, Newbold, then I'll fight you, but I won't work you over for nothing."

I was surprised by this speech. I had thought that the sheriff really lived from day to day on the sweet prospect of the trouble he could find along the way. And here he was, nevertheless, avoiding a whole harvest field of it. The rest of the boys picked up some spirit, when they heard the sheriff shutting down a little, as it were.

Pete Bramble said: "Nobody in this outfit is a chicken thief, Sheriff. You've got this wrong."

"It wasn't a fox, and it wasn't a coyote, that got into the Seaton hen house and lifted chickens twelve nights running! A chicken every night. A fox or a coyote wouldn't work that way. It wasn't any of Seaton's own men, neither. He watched them for a week, and they was always there . . . and the thievin' went on while the whole pack of them were under his eye. Now, where would the thief be likely to come from?"

"Out of the hills," said Pete Bramble. "Some greaser who's lying up in the hills and don't want to waste ammunition for his meat."

"No," said the sheriff. "This ain't a greaser."

"If you know his complexion," Newbold said with a sneer, "why don't you give us a description of the crook?"

"I'll tell you a description of him," the sheriff replied. "He's small, and he's quick. He's small enough to go through a window that a full-sized man couldn't wriggle his stomach through. And he's quick enough to catch a chicken and dodge the load of a shotgun that he's touched off with his own hand. That handful of buckshot, it ought to have blown him in two, but the crook dodged fast enough to get away, it seems, and there was no blood on his back trail. He's a small, fast, tricky feller. He's probably got a face like a fox, because that's what he is . . . a regular fox on two legs. Old Seaton has taken three shots at him, and never had no luck, and set a dozen different kinds of traps, and still he keeps right on stealin'. He's a mean, hardy feller. And you've got a whole pack of mean, hardy fellers here, Newbold."

I was a good deal interested by this account of the persistent chicken thief, and, to be sure, the fare in our cook house was enough to drive any man to drink—or chicken stealing.

"You figger that I've starved out my boys," said Newbold, "and when they passed the plate the second time, I've poured hot water into it. That's the way that you've figgered. And then they got hold of an inspired chicken thief, and they sent him out and he raided the coop every night, eh? But I'll tell you what, sheriff. You're barking up the wrong tree altogether."

"I'm gonna have a look, just the same," said the sheriff.

"Take your look, and be danged, then," said the boss. "But if this outfit started to stealing chickens, they wouldn't stop with one a night. Lemme tell you something, Sheriff. The kind of men that I keep out here, there's nothing but real men among 'em. The kind of men that I've got around here, they would eat a chicken each just to sort of get their appetites limbered up. If they got going on the Seaton chickens, they'd carry off half a dozen apiece . . . and, when they got through crunching up the chickens, they'd eat the Seatons, bones and all. You can tell Pa Seaton that, from me, and tell Ned and Harry Seaton, too. I've gotta mind to saddle and ride right over to see the Seatons now! Chicken thieves, eh? That's the kind of men I hire, is it? Chicken thieves!" He was furious.

Sheriff Murphy said: "You cool yourself off a little, will you? The fact is that I've made up my mind to it. One of your men has been doin' it!"

"That would mean," Newbold suggested, "a trip of about five miles each way. And I tell you what, after my boys have finished wrestling with this here hay press all the day long, there's dang little energy left in 'em. They don't even cuss at the cook any more. Speakin' personal, I'd rather be sentenced to a prison for sixteen years than to a danged hay press for sixteen days!"

He snorted like a horse, as he spoke, and from his circle of men there came a deep-throated murmur of sympathetic understanding.

"Let's get down to business," the sheriff announced.

"That's what I've been standing here waiting for," answered Newbold.

"How many men you got out here with you?"

"Seven."

"That doesn't count you?"

"No."

"Does it count the cook?"

"Yes."

"Lemme see them seven line up," Murphy snapped.

"You line 'em up yourself," said the boss, more and more angry. "You can see the cook over there in the cook house, working at his stove. I wish he'd cook himself, dang him! And here's the rest of the boys."

"There's five here," said the sheriff.

I counted the same number, including myself.

"Oh, that leaves the kid out," the chief explained. "And he's turned in and gone to sleep."

"What kid?" Tug asked. "Where does he sleep?"

"Right yonder. You can see his hat, there. He sleeps with his hat on. He's a tough kid for you!"

"Lemme have a look at him," said the sheriff. "Hey, kid!"

"Leave him be," the chief recommended. "He's tired. He does the work of two men all day long."

"And gets the pay for half a man, I suppose," suggested the other. "Hey, kid, stand up and lemme look at you."

Chip did not stir. The sheriff walked over to him, and I grinned to myself, thinking of the fine flow of language with which the boy would certainly drench down the sheriff, when the officer arrived.

The sheriff leaned. Then he straightened up, holding Chip at arm's length, dangling.

Not Chip, after all, but only Chip's hat, and his blanket attached to his hat, and out of the blanket streamed down the hay that the kid had twisted up inside, so as to give the effect of being a boy asleep there.

The sheriff let the stuff drop. It collapsed on the ground as he turned to Newbold.

"Your men ain't chicken thieves, eh?" he spit. "Then your boys are!"

Chapter Ten

"Counting His Chickens"

I saw Newbold turn a little to one side and then to the other. "Leave the boy be," he said. "You've got nothing on him."

"Not yet," said the sheriff, "but I'm going to have!"

"He's right around here," Newbold said miserably. "He's sure to be right around here. He was here just a minute ago. I saw him."

"You don't see him now," answered the sheriff, "and you won't see him later on, either, until he's got some extra filling inside of his stomach, I guess. Oh, he's a bright lad, all right!"

"You're wrong," Newbold insisted. "The kid's the best kid that I ever saw."

A sort of a rumbling chorus came from all of us. He was the best kid. He was also the meanest, most cantankerous, sassiest, most trouble-brewing kid. Steal chickens? He would as soon steal chickens as play marbles or go shooting. The minute the idea was suggested, we could all feel that stealing chickens would be worth a five-mile ride to the boy. Simple enough, too. He would merely catch up one of the big horses that was wandering around near the house, and he would jog away, and the rest of us would be asleep in two shakes after we had turned in. It would take a man made of steel to work all day the way Chip worked and then go off for half the night. But boys can do what men never could do. If they begin to run down, they can wind themselves up and go right on ticking again.

"All right," said the sheriff. "I've found out what I want to know. Of course, he's a good kid. He'd have to be good to steal chickens so well. So long, boys." He mounted his horse again and started off at a jog, lining out across country in the direction of the Seaton place.

"That's the dickens!" the boss said, and began to swear.

"We ought to send somebody out to cut in ahead of the sheriff and warn the kid," said Pete Bramble.

"The kid would never let you get up close enough to give him a warning," Newbold warned. "He rides like a dang jockey."

That was a fact. We wouldn't be likely to get up close to the boy. But, at any rate, I felt that I couldn't stay away from the trouble. I was nervous, and I just wanted to be on hand to see what was what. So I saddled up a horse and left the rest of them, discussing what a mean chap the sheriff was, and cut across country on his line. I hadn't gone very far, when I saw the loom of him before me.

He turned around, pulled up his horse, and waited for me with a gun in his hand.

"It's all right," I sang out to him. "I'm just your posse, Sheriff. I've come up from Newbold's camp to help you out."

"A lot of help anybody from Newbold's camp will be to me," Tug grunted. "But come along, if you want to. I wish that we could get close enough to see the little rat doing his tricks in that hen house. It's a caution." A trace of enthusiasm came into his voice.

"Seaton has been pretty worried," I suggested.

The sheriff actually laughed. "Seaton's an old-timer, a trapper," he said. "He thinks that he knows how to catch everything that walks and breathes. Well, he can't catch this kid. Maybe we can't. It's going to be a hunt and a chase. That's what it is!" He laughed again.

I never had dreamed that Tug Murphy could show such a

trace of good humor as he was showing now. It was a surprise. A thing not to be dreamed of. I played him along on this line. I told him that the boy was wild and tough, but the gamest that ever stepped, and the best sport, and the rightest kind of a lad. He listened to me and seemed to believe that what I said might have some truth in it.

We rode along at a good clip. Then the sheriff admitted to me that he was a little worried. "I never had to play against a kid before," he said. "Yes, against what we call kids . . . boys of nineteen or so that are as strong as a man and as fast with a gun, and sometimes a good deal straighter in their shooting. I've had those lads to handle, and some tough times they've given me. But suppose I take into jail a brat of fifteen or so . . . ? Well, how old is this Chip?"

"Fifteen," I said.

He let out a small-size shout. "Fifteen! And Seaton has dragged me out here on this rotten business? I'll tell him what I think of him."

"You tell him that Newbold is going to call on him, too," I said, grinning in the dark.

"He wanted to fight me, that Newbold," said the sheriff, and chuckled again. "He's all right. Anybody's all right . . . anybody that's always ready to fight when he's dead sober! You bet he's all right. Newbold is all right!"

I thought that Tug Murphy, for that matter, was all right, too. He was climbing up in my estimation all the time. I never had talked with anyone exactly like him, and the more he said, the more I wanted to hear. I told him that he was dead right about Newbold.

"Sure I'm right," Murphy agreed. "He wanted to fight me because of the kid. What's the kid to him? Nothing! No kin! But he wanted to fight me because of the kid. Anybody's all right that will fight for kids that don't belong to them."

I agreed again. The sheriff kept chuckling.

"Here I've gone and used up one of my best nags," he said. "Look at that! All on account of a dang kid." And he laughed aloud once more. He had a strange sense of humor, which this case appealed to.

"I'll bet the kid is Irish," he said.

"He has the reddest hair you ever saw," I stated.

"Sure he's Irish," affirmed Tug Murphy. "I knew it right off. Something told me. He's all right, too. The kid is all right. He's stealing those chickens every night. That's what makes him all right."

I did not understand this. I failed so completely to understand that I admitted I did not follow his line of thought.

He explained to me: "You look at here. If he stole just for stealing, he would've cleaned out the chicken house the first trip, wouldn't he?

I admitted that he would.

"And if he stole because he was just hungry, he'd quit as soon as he found out there were dogs watching for him, and men, and rifles, and shotgun traps all set to blow the tar out of him. He'd quit when he found out those things, wouldn't he? You certainly can't digest very good, when you've got a hole blowed clean through your stomach, can you?"

"No," I admitted. "You couldn't do that."

"You see how it is," went on the sheriff, getting more and more enthusiastic. "He kept going back because there was the shotgun traps and everything and everybody all set to catch him. That's why he went back. It was a game. He liked it. He even liked having the dogs run him."

"Have the dogs run him?" I asked.

"Sure they have! And he threw them off the trail. Right when they had a clear view of him. The dogs had, I mean, and they started to run with their heads up. But he chucked them. He got among some rocks, and he chucked them. And he goes back every night and plays the game again. Because he's Irish, see? That's the way an Irishman would do. I knew he was Irish right off."

He continued to chuckle and to be very pleased. It gradually dawned on me that Tug Murphy was Irish himself.

"You take a kid like that," went on the sheriff, "if he don't get hanged, he grows up and makes a real man. That's the kind of men that you need to have. The real ones. They raise a little trouble, but, when they settle down, there's something to them."

"There's something to the kid," I agreed very heartily.

"How often have you missed him away at night?" asked the sheriff.

"Never missed him at all, till tonight," I said.

"Not till an Irishman came there and showed you he was gone," chuckled Tug Murphy. "It takes a thief. . . ." He stopped himself short and hurried on, rather embarrassed: "He's Irish. He's smart . . . you never missed him away. Not for more'n two weeks, and he's been gone every night. He's a fox. He's smart. You never would've guessed, except that I came out there and gave you a lead."

Now, as we went along at a good gallop through the hills, we saw the loom of something far before us, going over a hill and disappearing into the skyline among the stars.

"That's the kid," said the sheriff. "He's going slow. He's traveling dead easy. That's a mistake. But the best of 'em get overconfident at times. And he don't know that an Irishman is after him. He don't have any idea of that. But maybe he's going slow so's he can be thinking out the way he'll turn the trick tonight."

I agreed that that really might be the idea.

We continued to gain on the rider before us, and presently we were so close that we could clearly distinguish that the rider was very small.

"No saddle," said the sheriff, who had amazingly good eyes at night. "You see how it is with him? He don't take no saddle along, because he don't want to leave no easy signs behind him. You take a saddle, the blanket of it would still be wet in the morning and give him away. He goes bareback. Yeah, he's Irish, all right." He still continued to chuckle. He seemed the most contented man in the world. But now he reined in his horse a little. "There's no use crowding the kid too much," he said. "We might as well see how he does the trick, if we can. I'll pay for the chicken he catches."

"Maybe he'll only catch a load of buckshot," I suggested.

The sheriff grunted. "You can't shoot an Irishman with buckshot," he declared. "It takes a slug out of a Colt or a rifle to stop an Irishman. No, the boy will come through, all right. He'll get the chicken again. A fellow like that Seaton . . . he never could catch an Irish kid like Chip. He has red hair, didn't you say? I sort of guessed that he had red hair, like that."

It seemed that there was to be no argument between us about the qualities and the importance of Chip. And now we came up through the hills to the gap from which we could look out and down toward the house of Seaton.

Chapter Eleven

"A Gleam of Light"

The boy was not there. At least, the silhouette of the small rider no longer appeared, and, instead, we had only the dim sweep of the hollow with two higher hills beyond, square-topped, like two raised fists. In the midst of the hollow, two lights shone from the Seaton ranch house. We made out the shoulders and the roof line of it by degrees, and then the staggered lines of corral fencing, the outhouses, and a lantern walking across the picture toward the house.

"We'd better ride straight in, if we're to warn Seaton," I suggested.

The officer of the law grunted. "Seaton be hanged!" he said. "Let Seaton take his chance! We're too late and too far behind to watch the kid at his work. We'd only scare him away. And it's a lot better if we just cut him off when he tries to retreat. We'll catch him with the goods on him. That'll teach him a lesson. That'll learn him to be a decent boy and man. . . ." The sheriff began his laughter once more.

He dismounted; he lighted a cigarette; he whistled, and he hummed to himself.

I got down in turn. It was hot there in the gap. The rocks on either hand were still throwing off the heat that the sun had poured thickly over them during the day. There was a sticky smell like new varnish in a closed house that came from the weeds that grew about us, and, now and then, there was a small rustling from the clumps of shrubbery that gave a false promise of a wind that never came.

The walking lantern reached the house and passed inside. A moment later, we heard the far-away sound of the jingling slam of the screen door.

"Now, the last man's back into the ranch house," said the sheriff. "The last man's back inside, and the trap's all set for the kid, and the dogs, and the guns, and the hunters, are all ready. And here we are, to cut off his retreat. And all on account of one red-headed brat of an Irish kid! That's the kind of men they breed, the Irish. They've got more glory and stretched more rope than any two other nations. That's the kind they are."

I could not help saying: "This sounds to me like a queer sort of law enforcement, Sheriff. But you're the boss. Only one thing I'm really bothered about. . . . Suppose that trap closes on the kid and breaks his back? There'd be some pretty angry men back there with the hay press, beginning with the boss."

"Shut up!" Murphy said. "What do you think I'm worried about, myself? But he's gotta pull through, and I . . ."

Just then, in the middle of his words, as a wave breaks over a rock at the entrance and floods all over a cave with roaring and dashings and echoes, just so out of the hollow there broke a clamor that had in it guns exploding, men shouting, dogs yelling and howling, and even the neighing of horses.

"There they go!" yipped the sheriff.

"Poor Chip," I said to myself, and hardly dared to think of what might have happened.

That uproar might have been the blasting away of a mountainside or a half regiment of soldiers. It did not die down all at once, but stretched out into a point, as it were, running in a long arm from the ranch house, and straight toward us!

"He's gone away!" I shouted.

"I told you he would!" answered the sheriff. And he struck me between the shoulder blades and bruised me to the heart.

"They can't catch the tricky little rabbit!" I said, and smote the sheriff's shoulder and felt it sag beneath the stroke.

"Not in ten million years!" the sheriff said. "Not now that he's begun to run. But look! Look!"

We could see them very clearly. It looked as though a dozen riders were galloping out from the house, the starlight fingering very faintly the sweating horses. In the dust of their raising, a fog closed over the house, and only its lights glittered through. But what made my heart stand still was the yelling of the dogs.

"They've got hounds there that'll chew man-meat as easy as venison," I suggested to the sheriff.

"They've got Butch Wafer's pack," Murphy said. "But they won't find that brat! He'll . . . he'll fade right out away from under their noses!" However, the sheriff was not as confident as his words. There was a tremor in his voice and a hesitation in his speech.

I strained my eyes into the darkness. I could see the hunter swerving a little from this side to that. Then a new note came into the chanting of the hounds.

"They've got him under their teeth," I told the sheriff. "You and your fool ideas . . . those man-eaters are right onto his heels . . . and they're running in full view. That's what they're doing. You and your ideas . . . both are not worth a cent."

The sheriff gripped me by the arm. "If I thought . . . ," he began. "Come on, son. We'll run our horses down there, and take a chance at them. We'll stop them. If they've so much as touched the hide of the brat, I'll . . ." He stopped. There was a good reason. For the dogs no longer yelled so confidently. The sound of their voices split apart and traveled to both sides.

"They've lost again," declared Tug, instantly confident. "They've lost again, and the kid has won."

"You're Irish, too," I said. "Wait a minute! But the dogs sure seemed to lose that trail . . . but then . . . they were plumb running on his heels, to hear the yap of 'em, and I've heard that pack singing before."

"Aw, they're beat! They're beat!" said the sheriff.

We could hear the hunters shouting and cursing and casting the hounds ahead, now here, now there. Presently the hounds strung out in a long line on a scent that one of them had picked up. The men whooped them on. Out of the dust of their own raising, we saw that hunt streaming through the night. Still, I could not feel that there was any real confidence in the voice of the pack. It had not the ring that keeps dwelling in the backbone of the strongest man. Then the roar struck a hollow in the hills beside us, and turned at once to a remote music and floated upward and away.

"They'll never get the kid tonight," I could not help saying.

"You've been talking like a fool," the sheriff gasped with a long, long breath. "This is the first sensible thing you've said. What've I been tellin' you all the time about. . . ." He stopped clicking his teeth together with surprise.

For a small whistle wavered up from the dark of the hollow before us, and it was answered by a whinny from among the rocks nearby. A small whistle and a small nicker of a horse, mind you. And then the sheriff began to curse softly beneath his breath. I was swearing, too. From not ten yards away from us, a mustang trotted out of a patch of shrubbery. Not ten yards away from us, mind you. And down it went into the hollow, and there we made out faintly the small form of the boy. We saw him meet the horse. We saw him carrying something in his hand. We saw him slick onto the back of the horse and go jogging away at a slant from the place where we waited.

He began to laugh, and it seemed to me that laughter was the blood brother to the sound of the sheriff's mirth that I had listened to so much during this dark ride. The very same, but a little thinner and farther away.

"Now we climb after him," said the sheriff to me.

That was what we did. We rode out of the gap, and, swinging to the left, we just kept the loom of the rider within our eyes.

He took an odd course, considering that he was due back to the hay-press camp before so very long. I mean, our sleeping hours were always too short for me, and, if the kid insisted on having his fun every evening after dark, one would think that, once the game was played, he'd strike out in a beeline for the camp. But he didn't travel as a bird flies. He was rounding away off to the right of the line and heading under a junk heap of naked hills so bare and polished by the palming of the wind that the rocks gleamed even under the stars. Under the side of these rocks, the boy dismounted, and, leaving the mustang behind him, he disappeared among the big stones.

The sheriff was worried, and shook his head. "Why should he do that?" he asked. "Why should he ride away over here to this spot to cook his chicken?"

Inspiration struck me dumb, all in a moment. "There's somebody inside those rocks waiting for him, Tug." I said.

He grunted. "Maybe so," he said. "Maybe there is a brain or two that can be rounded up inside of that head of yours."

We left our horses near the mustang from which Chip had dismounted and cut in at the spot where he had entered. We went as softly, you can be sure, as though we were walking up on the campfire of a batch of red Indians. For what might it not be that the boy was heading toward in there in the rocks? Well, we had the glint and then the gleam of fire before us after a few moments, and, after that, the stir of voices to help us along.

We had taken a good many minutes to follow the trail, but we arrived in time, after all. For when we came up through the rocks to a point where we could lie low and see the flicker and waning of the fire and then the big leap of the blaze when the breeze touched it—when we came to this point, I say, and stretched out to see what we could see, we were just in time to catch the kid come out of a dark gap between two rocks, and, with him, leaning an arm across his shoulders and looking mighty pale and thin, there was a grown man. That was why the lad had stole food every night. But the way Chip supported that tall, lank form was the strangest thing to see—even his voice had changed and turned tender.

"I heard a lot of racket down there," the man was saying. "I thought that they were after me again."

"Naw," said the boy. "They haven't got the brains to hunt up here for you. I told you that you'd be safe here, Mister Waters."

Hai! How the sound of that name jumped through me. For there was White Water, and the kid beside him, and the sheriff lying ready in the dark to take them both!

Chapter Twelve

"With a Pair of Guns"

It was White Water, well enough, but a good deal faded since I last saw him. He was thinner, leaner, lankier. And he was so weak that Chip had to steady him a little as he sat down near the fire. Still, there was the old grip about his jaws, and the look in his eyes.

"It's better out here, ain't it?" asked Chip.

Waters sighed. He stretched his arms and then let his head fall back against the rock that was behind him.

"Better? It's worlds better," he said. "By heaven, son, the shake and the flare of that little fire warms up the soul of me. And then to have the sight of the stars is worth more than I can tell you."

"Yeah," said the boy. "I bet there was days when you never thought that you'd have a look at those stars again."

"Yeah, there was days like that, all right," said the outlaw. "You know how it is, son. Lying there flat, with the fever in me, and the strength out . . . that was sort of tough."

The boy was sitting down cross-legged and was busily pulling away the feathers of the chicken. He stopped his work for a moment, and he looked at the crook.

"Jiminy, Mister Waters," he said, "I bet it was bad. And the water that I set in there beside you, I bet it got plenty warm during the end of the day, didn't it?"

"It got a little soupy," Waters affirmed. He turned his head and smiled at the boy, and there was love in his eyes. He had reason to love Chip. "But the nights," Waters continued. "They were the times when I would have given up and let go all hold, and then I would have sunk into water as dark as any ocean, Chip, and just a little deeper than the sea."

"Aye," said the boy, "I disremember when it was that I woke up kind of sick and dizzy in the middle of one night, and I was sort of choking with a bad dream. And all at once, I remembered that I was alone in the house, and that there was nobody to bring a hand to me . . . I was pretty sick, I'll tell you." He stripped the chicken white and clean beneath its feathers and began to cut it up. He was a regular little butcher. I never saw neater work done.

"But when those bad times came, Chip," said the outlaw, "I could always remember that you had been there to see me . . . and that you'd surely come the next night, too . . . and that, some way or other, I ought to fight it out . . . after all the work you'd put in on me."

"Hey! It's been no work," Chip said. "It's been fun." He chuckled as he said it. His eyes danced as he looked at the other.

"Yeah," said Waters. "You seem to like it, all right. Don't your uncle get tired of losing a chicken a night?"

"He hasn't noticed yet," said the little liar. "He's got a lot of chickens. He's got near thousands of 'em, pretty near."

"I'll pay him double for every one, Chip," Waters said earnestly.

"Aw, sure you will," Chip answered. "You don't have to worry about that. It don't make no real difference."

"No real difference," Waters muttered. "Only life or death to me. But I've wondered if you haven't been in danger, Chip, stealing this meat and getting it out to me."

"Danger?" Chip said, yawning a little. "What sort of danger would there be in picking up a chicken? Or ten chickens at a time? You know the way that it is on a big old ranch. You know how . . . aw, they roost eve.ywhere. On a fence, or on the shoulder of a stack, or on the woodpile under the roof of the woodshed. All you gotta do is to walk along and put out a hand on that farm of my uncle's, and you're sure to run into a chicken before very long."

"I imagine that you have a guiding instinct, son, as the preachers say," remarked Waters.

"Maybe," grinned the boy. He was cutting up the chicken and putting it on small, sharpened sticks. He gave two of these to the outlaw, and he took two himself. They began to turn the spits, and the smell of that good, roasting meat made my mouth water, after the fare we'd been having at the cook house.

"Tell me something, Chip," said Waters. "There were a few days, back there, when you only pretended to think I was better. You really thought that I was worse."

Chip sat up straight with a jerk and a start. "I'll tell you, Mister Waters, tonight," he said. "There was never a time when I was sure that you were going to pull through. Never a time, I mean, until tonight. You always looked kind of slipping, night after night. It used to make me sick to look at you. Aw, you were mighty sick, Mister Waters."

"Stop calling me that," said the other. "Call me Joe, or Bill, or Ed, or Nick, or anything. It doesn't matter."

The boy was lost in thought, slowly turning the roasting meat, while the fumes of the cooking arose from it.

"I might call you chief," he suggested. "I couldn't call you nothing small. You know that I was there when the three of them cornered you, and the three went down, and you got out. After that, I couldn't call you nothing small."

"Because I'm a thug and know how to fight with guns," Waters responded rather sadly, "you look up to me a little. Well, I . . ."

"It ain't that," insisted the boy. "It's just because, when the pinch comes, you don't lie down. Look at anybody else with three slugs through him, he would've gone in and given himself up."

"And be hanged, Chip?" suggested the outlaw.

"Yeah," the boy drawled, still thinking fiercely. "Hanging

ain't so bad, either. First, they get out a lot of newspaper writing. And then everybody talks of the trial. And then there's a female league of something or other's daughters, or something like that, that comes along and gets up a petition for a pardon. And the governor gets gray-headed saying 'no' ... and somebody writes a book about you ... and then there's a lot of fun before the end. And maybe it's only life imprisonment ... and then the boss of the prison, he makes you his confidential secretary and guard, and you don't do nothing but sit in leather chairs and hang your heels on the edge of a desk and smoke fat cigars and write your reminiscences, and everybody looks up to you a lot and says there goes the guy that killed eleven men ... or how many men have you really killed, chief?"

"Four," the outlaw replied, "and heaven help me for doing it. Where did you pick up all this about prisons and such?"

"You know," Chip said. "You can't help readin' the interestin' part of the newspaper and listenin' to the interestin' talk in the bunkhouses. You see me, chief? When I grow up, I'm gonna be free, too."

"Free?" asked the outlaw.

"Yeah. You know."

"No, I don't know. What do you mean by being free?"

"I mean ... puttin' up your own hoss into somebody else's barn. That's what I call bein' free."

Waters smiled, but his smile was wan.

The chicken was now ready for eating, but, before Waters began on it, he said: "I'll tell you the truth, old son. Being free means chilblains in winter and sun scalding in summer ... and one meal or none a day ... and the life of a wolf ... and no friend you can trust ... and no home, no wife, no children. Or if you have 'em, they're raised by somebody else. Being free means living on the outside of about everything that's worthwhile."

"Except freedom?" Chip questioned.

"Yes," Waters said slowly. "Except that, perhaps. Here you, Chip. You take my advice. I know about that stuff. You go and get it out of your mind. That's the only way to do."

"I'm gonna watch and make up my own mind," Chip said. "Look at me. I wouldn't be your friend, chief, if it wasn't that

I had seen you livin' free. Everybody looks up to free things. Who minds a tame duck more'n a pig in the mud? But a wild duck looks pretty fine, and the wild geese honking south or north, they give you the prickles up your backbone, and you want to break away. You know that's true."

"That's true," said Waters. Then he changed the subject. "You've gotta eat part of this chicken tonight, son," he said quickly.

"Me?" said the boy with an air of surprise. "Sure, I ain't gonna eat any of it. I'm full."

I thought of the sort of food and portions that Chip enjoyed along with the rest of us in the cook house and smiled a little.

"When I was your age, I was never full," said the outlaw.

"You know how it is around a farm," Chip stated. "You know there's always something lying around to eat. And if you get a pang, you can go and snitch something out of the pantry."

"Whatcha have for supper tonight?" asked the other.

"Me? Oh, we had venison steaks. They'd been hung a little too long, but I'm used to 'em that way . . . and they was prime and tender. And we had hominy, and corn bread with heaps of butter onto it, and ras'berry jam, and bread pudding full of raisins, and mashed potatoes, and baked sweet potatoes, too, and string beans, and pork chops for them that didn't want the venison. So I had some of both. Outside of that we didn't have nothing much but some hard candy, and doughnuts. My aunt, she makes the primest doughnuts that you ever seen. That's about all I had to eat, but what made you ask?"

I thought of the cook-house dinner and grinned again. Waters was looking hard at the boy, and I could see that he was thoroughly doubting what he had heard, but he said nothing for a moment. At last he remarked: "Chip, your job is getting me on my feet, and you're doing it mighty well. I've got no right to question you about how and where you manage all this, but I reckon that your back trail would be pretty hard to follow and pretty interesting, too. Well, here's my regards." And, with that, he started in on a quarter of chicken and began to reduce it to a white bone.

"You're looking a lot better," the boy commented. "You'll be fit to ride, pretty quick."

"I could ride right now," said the outlaw. "Only I'd like to wait a while till there's a little grip and strength in my knees. You know how it is, Chip."

"You bet I know. You'd be crazy to try to ride now," Chip agreed.

"I guess he'll try, though," the sheriff said, and stepped into the firelight with a pair of guns.

Chapter Thirteen

"Chip's Champion"

It staggered me. There was something in that scene between the boy and the outlaw that had prevented me from even thinking about the sheriff's presence. But there he stood with his two guns, looking as large and a lot more deadly than cannons.

The boy got up and reached for a stone. Waters simply stretched across and knocked the stone out of his hand.

"When a game's finished," he said gravely, "there's only one thing for it, and that's to give up your chair. I'll qualify now for all that newspaper publicity that you were talking about, Chip."

He was dead game, was poor Waters. He could smile as he said it.

I thought that Chip had colic, he was so bent and twisted with rage and pain, but the sheriff unquestionably had the upper hand.

I said to him: "Look here, Tug. The fact is that you could give a man a chance when . . ."

The sheriff favored me with a glint out of one eye. "Give a low hound a second chance?" he roared. "Give a low, sneakin' hound a second chance? A gent that goes out and lets a poor kid risk his neck every night to bring him food? He ain't a man. If he was half a man, I'd let him. I'd give him my own hoss to start him on the way, just because Chip, the crooked little chicken thief, thinks so much of him. But he ain't a man. I'd like to grind him under my heel to show him what I think of him. That's what I'd like to do."

That ended the argument on the spot, as far as I was concerned. Because I saw that the Irish was up in Tug, and, when the rage is in the head of an Irishman, there's no making him see reason, or kindness, or humor.

Then the kid came up and gave me a nudge. "You could make a play, Joe," he said. "Now you got your chance. You just trip up Tug from behind, and we and the chief will do the rest."

Yes, he would have tackled the sheriff, single-handedly. That was the Irish in him.

But poor Waters went off to jail, holding himself erect in the saddle, for the benefit of Chip. But I could see by the tremor in his shoulders how weak he was. Chip stood beside me, and watched the two ride off. As he watched them, he talked in a way that curdled my blood to hear. For a boy should not know all the words and the ideas that Chip was master of, and the description he gave of the sheriff's probable end was brilliant and entirely too incandescent. We stood and watched them go out of sight, and then we went back toward the camp and got to the hay press in a dead silence.

There was only one speech from the boy, and that was when we were about to turn in. "How much would a dog-gone good lawyer want to defend a man?" he asked. "Would he want as much as thirty dollars?"

That, you see, was about what Chip must have saved from his wages. It gave me a lump in the throat. I told him that I thought that thirty would be plenty, and, if it wasn't, I'd help him out, and so would some of the other boys.

"No," said Chip as he slid into his blankets. "He wouldn't like it. The chief wouldn't, I mean . . . if the hat was passed for him."

So I fell asleep, and they had fairly to drag me out of my blankets when the dawn broke on the next wretched day. I looked about for Chip, but Chip was nowhere to be seen. And he didn't turn up later. He was gone, and I knew where. He was gone to find, hire, or beg a lawyer to defend his hero. Poor Chip!

I forgot all about Waters, though, before the day was very old. So did all of us. I told the boys at breakfast the story of the night before, and what they said about the sheriff was not a pleasant thing to hear. Only the boss sat still, leaning over his coffee cup and stirring in the so-called sugar, and no doubt snarling silently, but never saying a word. I thought that he looked pleased, rather than otherwise. But he forgot about Waters. So did I. So did all the rest as the day wore along, and we not only saw but felt that the kid was no longer among us. I say that we felt it, because everything went wrong from the start.

When the wires were used up, the cook brought out and started in twisting and cutting at the machine that the kid had made to hum. But it didn't hum now. Those wires came off one at a time, lamely. And there was a flow of music from that wire-cutting machine that darkened the sky and yet made the day a lot hotter.

Finally, the cook came over to the dog house, where the boss was tying a bale, and that cook stood up on the weighing machine and made a speech that was worth listening to—he said that the cook house had been a lot worse than misery to him from the start, and that he hoped he'd made us suffer some, and that he wished he'd made us suffer more, and that of all the lot of greasy hobos he had ever seen we were the worst, and that the boss was the cheapest of the lot, and he hoped that we'd all go to blazes and each of us be stationed at a wire-cutting machine, but that, for his part, he was through with the outfit, then and there. In fact, he quit on the spot, with the boss's hay hook sailing after him and whizzing past his ear.

We were all sorry to see that hay hook miss its mark. Then I was dragged off the feeding table and put at the wire cutter. A wire cutter is not such a complicated machine, but this one was mean. It was second-hand, like all the rest of the outfit, and it was loose in its joints and could not be tightened. It was sprained here and had rheumatism there. How the kid had made it jump so fast was a mystery to me. I couldn't turn out wires of the same length and the same strength. Either they were stretched so much that they broke where the beater rose and let the bale stretch, or else they were so slack that they twisted like long, thin, black snakes.

But, worst of all, I couldn't make the cutting lever work well, and there were twists and turns on nearly every wire end. The wire puncher almost went mad over them, and the boss cursed me with every bale that he rolled to the pile. It was a bad day.

By the time it came for the morning lunch, I was getting so many black looks that I went off by myself and ate my prunes and hard tack and swallowed my coffee and didn't have the courage to go back for a second cup.

The wire puncher was given the job as cook on the understanding that the first man to complain would have to take his place. He said that he guaranteed complaints, too. It was a pretty black morning, and the lunch that waited for us at the end of it did not help our humor along very much.

Just to cap everything, along came the girl. I mean, Marian Wray came riding up, and first off we were glad to see her, but the first thing that she asked for was Chip. While we were waiting to find an answer, she went on to say that he was the finest boy in the world, and that her father was riding over specially to see him and try to persuade him to take up a civilized existence.

Then everybody looked at me, so I had to come out with the story of what had happened the night before. I knew that it was going to be bad, but none of us guessed how bad it would be.

When I had finished, she said coldly: "And you stood there, and let one man, one brutal so-called officer of the law, take away that poor, sick fellow?"

I stammered. I didn't find any words. I felt pretty sick and must have looked sicker.

She saw that she had sunk me with all on board, and she turned and gave her heavier guns to Newbold. Her smile was a thing of beauty.

"But if Chip has gone off to save his friend," she said, "I know that you're going to help him, and nothing can stop you."

Newbold stood up and pointed to the hay press. A wind was puffing at it and knocking off the chaff and the dust, so that it seemed to be smoking.

"If there was a silver-trimmed angel came down from heaven, Marian," he said, "and blew his trumpet in my ear, I wouldn't leave this here job until I'd finished it. That's a fact."

She shook her head. "Ah," she went on, "I know the real tenderness of men like you. You know perfectly well that poor little Chip . . . the darling! . . . will be trying to break into that jail to get his hero out . . . and he'll land in the reform school, trying to do it. But I know you won't let it come to that. I simply know."

She gave Newbold a shining look. His face pinched as though he had been hit on the chin. He took two strides that brought him away from us and right up to her. He was as dusty as the hay press. The shoulders of his flannel shirt were white with dried, caked perspiration.

"Marian," he said, "don't talk to me like that. What's this fellow Waters to me . . . or to you? You know where I stand. What's Waters to me, I ask you?"

He was serious. The rest of us looked down at our hands. We saw that Newbold was pleading with her, and it was a funny thing to hear Newbold pleading.

"What do I care about Waters?" the girl responded, quick as a flash. "Not a snap of the fingers . . . except that he's sick. Not a breath . . . except that poor little Chip loves him. And I trust a man that such a boy loves. But I know that you'll change your mind and do something about it. I've thought that you're the biggest sort of a man that I ever laid eyes on, and I know that I'm not wrong. I can't be wrong!"

Newbold pointed a finger at her like a leveled gun. "You want me to go and leave this job and pry a thug out of jail?" he said quietly.

"Ex-act-ly!" she confirmed, as precise as a schoolteacher.

"This is my job," says Newbold. "And I won't quit it. Not for Waters. Not for the kid." He had worked himself up to the climax. "Not for you!" he wound up.

She made a step back from him. "Now I understand," she stated, nodding at him. "I ought to thank you. You let me see you for the first time. I thought there was something grand and heroic about you. I see that you're only . . . a farm hand."

Chapter Fourteen

"Between Wind and Water"

I had a big brother once. I spent most of my time hating him, because he was bigger and stronger than I, and he could tease me until I was frantic, and there was nothing that I could do about it. I used to pray that something would happen to him, and one day it came about so. He was having a fight with a smaller boy than himself, after school, in the vacant lot. That smaller boy was a newcomer. He was freckled and had dusty-colored hair, and his eyes were a little crooked, and he grinned and was white about the mouth as he fought.

But he knew how to box. He was knocked down three times, but he kept coming up, and, finally, he learned how to duck under my brother's arms and gave him a fair pasting. He blacked my brother's eyes for him, and cut his mouth, and punched him in the stomach till he groaned, and on the jaw till he whined.

At first I liked it, but afterward I began to grow sick, and sicker. Finally I prayed for the skies to drop on all of us, just to end that picture of my brother's shame. That was the way I felt, for one, when I stood by and saw Newbold take his licking from that girl. She simply got into the saddle and rode off again.

But Newbold stood still, as though he had dropped anchor in a harbor of thought. Poor Newbold!

He had bullied and beaten us all at his pleasure, but still it was a horrible thing to see a fellow like him so hurt by the unjustifiable words of a mere slip of a girl. For what right had she to talk so to him? What business was it of his, whether Waters was hanged or not? What business was it of any of us?

Newbold recovered, after a time, and all through the rest of the afternoon he worked silently at his job—the hardest job of all—rolling bales. He said not a word. He was strong as two lions. And we knew it was the fire and the anger inside him that gave him the power.

But it was a miserable business. About four o'clock something happened to the beater. It stuck halfway down the box, and the power driver, after he had tried to lift it up or beat it down, gave up and yelled out: "Chip! Hey, Chip!"

The feeder stuck his head around and said with a sort of scared, glad look: "Is Chip coming? Where's Chip?"

The boss stepped out from the dog house and gave the two of them a black look. Then he climbed up there and took a look at the jam. He fumbled here, and he fumbled there, while the rest of us just sat around in what shade we could find and the drops oozed slowly down our faces and the backs of our necks.

We sort of knew that the boss could do nothing with the mess, and we knew just as well that Chip, if he had been there, could have fixed the thing in a jiffy. He would have been down there in the box, swearing a good deal, and then singing out for tools of one kind or another, and pretty soon the business would have been done. Ten minutes, and the press would have been going again. But Chip was not there. What a hole that left in our organization, and right between wind and water.

The boss did not talk. He just got big monkey wrenches and began to unscrew the nuts in order to take out the side of the machine.

We all helped him. We worked until dark, hardly making headway, although it was a job that we used to get through fast enough when Chip was there to sting us with a wasp word now and again and call us empty heads, and duffers, and what-not. Finally we got enough of the thing dismantled to see that we were all wrong. The beater was stuck on the other side!

When we discovered this, we gave up with a groan. We turned around and went off for the cook house, even though there was still a working hour left to the day. But, somehow, a general and sudden disgust struck all of us, and we just walked off.

I looked over my shoulder and saw Newbold staring after us, with an eight-pound wrench in his big grip. Ordinarily, he would have come after us like a tiger, but the tiger was gone out of Newbold. Something had happened to him—and I knew what it was. His heart was aching, and so was his soul, and his pride was burning him to a smoke, a red smoke. I made note, then, not to cross that fellow in word or deed for a month, at least. He was poison now.

Even with the rest of us gone, there was no giving up for Newbold. No, sir. He stuck to his guns, and presently we could hear how he was working away at the farther side of the machine. There he worked on and on, the two big bolts groaning and yelling out as he struggled with them. And there was creaking and jarring and crashing sounds, as he struggled.

We went in for supper. The cook banged the pan three times, but Newbold, working out there by lantern light, did not seem to hear.

I felt a pang of pity, but I said nothing. Nobody else spoke, either, except Bramble, who started to tell one of his best stories about a wrangle he got into down in Vera Cruz in the middle of a greaser revolution. But nobody even pretended to listen to Bramble. He was a good fellow, was Pete, and he talked mighty well, but the point was that we all felt something extraordinarily important was happening right at our elbows, and we wanted to pay attention to that thing.

Poor old Newbold! The memories of his hard-headedness, and harder hands, his stingy portions, his slave-driving, all began to disappear from my mind. All I could remember was that he never deserted us in a pinch, that he was a roof over us and a shield before us in a time of danger, and that he never asked from another man one half of what he demanded from himself. Well, I had all these things in mind, and I was amazed to feel the way that my heart was softening toward him.

After supper the racket out at the hay press stopped. The boys were lying around and smoking and taking things easy, when one of them sang out that the hay was on fire near the press. He'd no sooner said that than flames ran up that press from the bottom to the top and wagged their heads far in the sky above it. And not a man ran out to stop the conflagration, because we understood in one flash. Newbold had tried to make the repairs, and he had failed. And, having failed, he finally was taken by a great disgust, and he had simply doused the whole machine with oil and laid a match to it.

I ran out with the others. They looked for the fire, but I looked for a hotter thing than that. Newbold, I mean. I couldn't see him. He was out of the way. Then, far off on the rounding cheek of the world, I saw a glint of the dancing firelight that fell on the shadow of a rider, heading off away from us.

"Newbold," I said to my heart. And my heart gave a jump and a boom that I could hear as plainly as a drumbeat. "Newbold!"

I snaked out the best horse I could lay my hands on, and I sloped across that country as fast as I could go. I didn't try to follow the trail of Newbold. I knew where he was heading, and I streaked for that. He was going to Manorville, because that was where the jail stood—and in that jail would be Waters—and near that jail would be Chip—and toward the same spot the thoughts of Marian Wray would be turning.

I had cotton in my throat, I tell you, and couldn't swallow. I was dizzy. There was something Biblical about the whole affair. Like the ruin of Lot. I mean to say—an accumulation of thunderstrokes. Why, Newbold had been the pillar of the law. Newbold had fought with that hay press as if with a sword. Newbold had hated women—or not even thought of them. Newbold never had gone from his way an inch, except when one of his own men was in trouble. But now for a girl's sake he junked the press and was riding to break jail for an outlaw he despised.

I knew it from a distance. I did not have to have his voice to tell me so. So I took a short cut, and I burned up that mustang humping across the flat and soaring over the hills, till at last I got to a small hummock and could look down onto the widening main road to Manorville. There below me, coming along at a singing gallop, was a horseman so tall that he made his horse look small. Newbold, I knew.

I jabbed the spurs into the tired sides of that horse of mine and gave it pain or courage to take the slide. Down it went, and we slid out onto the road in a shower of gravel, and small stones, and sand, and I ranged alongside of Newbold.

He didn't even glance at me. No, you might have thought that he was alone, and that nothing had happened worth seeing or hearing, until we came to an up-pitch in the grade, and he said to me, as the horses fell to a walk: "Joe?"

"Aye," I said.

"What do you gain out of this?" he asked me. "What do you buy?"

"Me? Nothing," I said.

He nodded. I could see him nodding in the dark. "You go home," he said.

"That's all right," I said. "I'll stay along, I guess." He didn't argue. He wasn't a fellow to argue, except with his fists.

After a while we topped that rise, and we saw the scattering lights of Manorville with blank darkness between them, like bald spots on the head of a bleak old man.

There Newbold reined his horse to a stop, and I thought he was changing his mind. At last he said: "Look how many years I've been."

"Been what?" I asked.

"A hound," he said.

Chapter Fifteen

"On to the Jail!"

One cannot make an answer to a remark like that. So I didn't try, and we rode on into Manorville. It was a strange feeling that I had. A feeling, you see, of guilt, but of a prospective rather than present guilt. For the moment, no one could say to me that I had violated the law. Never in my life. It was a sweet feeling, too, to be able to walk along the streets and know that I was the honest peer of every man I faced. And yet, was I the honest peer, after all? No, because the guilt was already in my heart.

We decided that the first thing to do was to look things over. In case there was any action, it would be better to have our horses out of sight. So we put up our mustangs on the edge of the town that was nearest to the jail. Then we walked in. We'd left the horses in a scrub of small trees, where they could smell out the grass that grew in between, and that grass grew thick enough to content them, of course. It doesn't take much to content a range-bred mustang.

We went in past the jail itself. There was only one window

that showed light on our side, and it was a gloomy, flickering light.

The boss said: "That's a lantern, and a smoking lantern, that's inside. And it's fouling the air a good deal with its smoking old wick."

I knew he didn't care a rap what sort of a lantern was burning in yonder. He was only interested in the job that he had before him, but he took it out on small things. His heart was aching a good deal, I suppose. At last I couldn't hold in, and I said: "Newbold, you're making this play for the girl. What's your surety that she'll do anything for you, if you win?"

I expected him to grow angry at this remark, but he merely said: "Shut up and keep out of my business. I'm not sure about anything. And I'm doing it for Chip, more'n the girl. Chip . . . he's worth more than any ten men that I ever saw."

I was half inclined to agree with this remark, but still I knew, of course, that he was lying. Poor Newbold!

We wanted to pick up what information we could, and so we sauntered on together into the lighted part of town—there was only two blocks of it. I saw Pie Lafferty of the Crippled Star outfit. I never knew where they got that name for their brand. Any name would have done for the wicked scroll they used. Pie was half tight and shining like a full moon. He insisted on coming along with us, until he luckily met another friend in the next half block and switched to him.

So I went on with the boss. We passed the hotel and, just as we passed it, down the steps came . . . who do you think? Why, down those steps came Marian Wray and Chip.

When Chip saw us, he grabbed the arms of the girl, and she turned, too, and the pair of them gave us a stare. I would have stopped, but Newbold walked straight on as though he had not seen a thing. His jaw was locked hard. He was looking before him, and seeing nothing—as I knew by the way he stumbled.

Then a hand touched my arm, and it was Chip, saying: "Good old Joe. I knew that you would figger into this, somehow. You wouldn't go and leave him lay."

"Chip," I said, "what's the deal, so far?"

"Here comes Marian," Chip said. "Whatcha think? She ain't

just a fool girl. She's all right. She's about a hundred per cent. Here she comes."

She came up. And she was shining brighter than Pie Lafferty, and almost the same red. She didn't say a word, that girl. She just looked. No, sir, there was the most chipper and cock-sure girl I ever saw in my life, and the wordiest, and the most free and easy, and the most on top of the world, but all that she did was to stand there like a fifteen-year-old sweetheart and blush, by thunder, and widen her eyes, and look up, and smile at Newbold.

Yes, and that leather-necked, hard-headed, iron-hearted Newbold—why, he fairly shook in his boots. He weakened right then and there so far that I knew he never would recover. He would go ahead and be a hero and get himself busted in the face with a load of buckshot, or some such thing. But a hero he would certainly be.

Chip grabbed my arm again. "Newbold's gone nutty," he said, "and so's the girl. Look at her, now. That's the effect that a woman has even on a man like him. Kind of softening. It's a sad thing, Joe, the way that a girl with her fool smiling soaks right through the outside lining of a man and gets at the inners of him. Now, you and me have gotta plan something and put our heads together. Newbold, he'll just be a pair of hands, and no more."

I nodded. The blank look on Newbold's face promised nothing at all. I would as soon have asked advice from a flounder as a word from him. He was just looking at that girl and seeing heaven in Manorville.

Chip and I went back up the street.

"If he comes far enough to find us," Chip began, "all right. But if he don't, he'd only be a burden on us."

"Look here, Chip," I said. "You don't think that I'm going to take a main hand in this without the boss, do you? I'm only the second assistant. I'm not the straw boss, here."

"Oh, I know you, old Joe," said Chip. "You're a lot bigger hoss than you give yourself the credit of being. I know you pretty well, old son. You'd win a mighty lot of races, if only you'd enter yourself in 'em."

He had a cheerful way about him, that brat. It started a man's circulation along to hear him talk. Then he started planning what we ought to do. He had looked over the place pretty thoroughly, he said. And the best way that he could figure out was to try through the roof. For there was a tree to the rear of the jail that extended a branch over the top of the jail, and, by climbing out upon the branch, he could easily drop or slip down onto the roof, probably without making a sound. Then he could work on the skylight, and with any sort of a small jimmy he could pry the skylight loose. After that, it ought to be easy to get down to the block of cells.

"But what'll be done when you get there?" I asked. "There still would be cell doors to open, wouldn't there?"

"Sure there would," he said.

"And guards with guns, and everything?" I suggested, more blankly than ever.

"There's one guard," said the boy confidently, "and that's what I'm counting on. He'll have the keys to the cells. You and me, we sneak down in there, and I make a noise and get the guard's eye on me. He asks me what the deuce I'm doing there . . . and, while he's talking, you slip up behind and get him with a strangle hold, and I ram a gun into his stomach and ask him to come to time. He'll come to time, all right. I've seen him, and he's not one of those fellows that's got himself a big, rough reputation by shooting some poor stiff that was already blind in both eyes with whiskey. Now he lives on what he's done, and looks black, and gives three chaws to his quid before he answers a word from anybody except the sheriff. But he's yaller, or I never seen yaller."

I nodded. But I wasn't convinced.

Chip kept insisting: "What you think, Joe? If that ain't a good plan, what plan is good? You name one, and it'll do for me. But we gotta do something quick. There's a lot of interest taken in this town about the poor chief. And there's a lot of things that's been blamed on him, from burglary to dog stealin', that he never done in his lifetime. They're standin' together, the boys down there in the street, like a lot of chickens on a cold day, and they're workin' up a lot of heat about Waters. It's a handy thing to have a man ready for lynchin', in a cheap town like this. And pretty soon they're gonna come and stretch Waters's neck for him, unless we look sharp."

"We'd better wait for Newbold," I said.

"There's no use waiting," sighed the boy. "He's gone and paralyzed himself, looking at the girl. And she's gone and paralyzed herself, admirin' how Newbold has come into town. How come he to bust away from the hay press as long as this, tell me?"

"There's no hay press any more," I explained. "The boss burned it before we started for town."

"Burned it!" exclaimed Chip. "He burned that press? Why, it was a mighty good little old press, only it needed some understanding. That was all it needed. You gotta favor a Little Giant press, sometimes, but they turn out the boss bales, and the handiest in the world. You can break 'em over the knees, because they stand the highest." He was very indignant.

He was still pressing me to suggest a new plan or else to offer one of my own, when a man walked down the street with a long, stalking stride and headed straight for the jail. At the same time, there was a sudden yipping from the direction of the hotel, and, looking down that way, we could see a couple of dozen men spill out into the lighted part of the street. Every one of those men was carrying a gun!

Then I could see that the boy was right. Lynching was what the rascals intended. And the thought took my breath like a jump into ice-cold water.

"Now . . . quick!" Chip said, and tugged at my arms.

I hardly knew what to do, but I started vaguely along with him. At the same time, the silhouette of the tall man with the long step went up to the front door of the jail and banged on it.

"By Jiminy," said Chip, "ain't that Newbold?"

I stopped and stared. "It can't be," I said. "There's not even a mask on his face. He wouldn't go and tap on the door of the jail like that, without a mask on his face."

"Wouldn't he?" Chip snarled with a whine of joy in his voice. "I've seen whiskey drunks do worse than that, and a girl drunk is worse than a whiskey one. It's Newbold."

It was Newbold. I could see the labor stoop of his shoulders and the long swing of his arms at his sides.

The door of the jail opened a crack. Then Newbold jerked it wide with a single thrust and dived into the inside darkness. We heard someone yell.

In the meantime, Chip was streaking it for the danger point, and I had to lumber along behind, trying to swallow down my heart and managing to do it.

We got to that jail just as the crowd down the street near the hotel marshaled itself and let out a few whoops, and then started marching to make trouble. Every minute it was getting bigger, as men, and boys, and even women, ran out from their houses to join in the main body or the flanks. Nobody in Manorville wanted to miss fun as good as this.

But Chip and I, as we entered the jail, heard scuffling and cursing on the pitch-dark floor of the jail, and not a thing except a sense of touch to show us what was happening.

Chapter Sixteen

"Out of the Shadow"

I would not have known what to do, but Chip did not hesitate. He simply dove into the darkness of the floor as though it were water, and I heard the voice of big Newbold greeting him with a growl of satisfaction. Evidently, Chip was already helping.

I got a match lighted, and the glimpse which it gave me showed that same jailer, the one whom Chip disapproved of as a brute and a bully, with red running from several cuts on his bulldog face, trying, like a bulldog, to snap at his annoyers with his teeth, since his arms were imprisoned and anchored.

Newbold held him. Chip vainly threatened him with a gun, but the fellow was, regardless, fearless, heroic. I suppose Chip had known very well beforehand just what he would be, but had wanted to encourage me as much as he could.

A lantern was rolling with a jangle on the floor, and I picked it up and lighted it. At the same time, there was a wail and a yell of joy from half a dozen voices inside that jail. Waters was not the only prisoner, d'you see, and the others were tuning up like roosters that think the day has come.

Newbold was free now, for he had twisted a length of cord

around the wrists of the jail guard and turned him face down on the floor. "Keep your eyes shut. Don't turn your head," Newbold ordered, "or you'll be slammed!" He beckoned to me.

So I took my place there and just tapped the muzzle of my revolver against the base of the guard's skull.

"Look here, brother," I told him truthfully, "I'm not one of those heroes that won't take an advantage. You try to turn your head and get a look at me or the others, and I'll just slam a bullet right through your brain."

It was a wonderful thing to watch that fellow. I never saw more natural fighting instinct, for, as he lay there, he whined and whimpered, on my word of honor, exactly like a dog that wants to fight and is held on a leash. So I kept talking to him gently, and tapping him with that gun to keep him quiet. All the while he gritted his teeth, and his big shoulder muscles worked. He cursed and whined and cursed again. He was fairly trembling with a desire to get up and resume the fight. It was no wonder that this fellow had opened the door of the jail at the first summons. For he didn't care a rap if there were trouble waiting outside the door. Why should he? He would welcome it, and the more trouble, the more welcome. I never saw such a man. He gave my flesh the creeps.

Chip had got hold of the keys from the guard, and he was flinging down the corridor of the little cells until he came to the farthest one in the corner, and he started to try them in the lock, one after the other. I thought he was taking until the end of the world to do this, because all the time I could hear the moan and the roar of the crowd which was coming up the street. Have you ever heard that murmur of rising human tides? It's not so easy to listen to. It keeps creeping higher and higher in the throat, until the back of your tongue is glued against the roof of your mouth. But finally the right key was found, and the iron hinges of the cell door groaned as it swung open.

Through it came Waters. The lantern light gleamed on his face. One high light lay like a ghostly finger on his temple, and his sunken cheeks were marked by shadow as by soot.

Big Newbold took him under the armpits and fairly swept him through the doorway. Chip was dancing before them. And the rest of the thugs in the jail, seeing that they were not going to be turned free in the jail break, howled like rabid wolves. Hai! How their voices went through me.

I was the last to go through the door of the jail, pulling it shut with a slam behind me, and with the others before me, and the crowd breaking into a run straight at us from down the street, I circled around the corner of the jail. I knew that we were goners. Or at least, I thought that we were goners, because certainly we could not run fast enough, with Waters for a hand-burden, to keep away from the stretching hands of that rabble of manhunters.

But then little Chip, at the corner of the building, whirled around, and he let out a screech like a wildcat that's had its tail stepped on, and at the same time he snatched out a man-size Colt and let fly at that crowd. Right at them, I thought at the moment, although I was wrong. He was only shooting for the ground at their feet. However, the crowd was even more convinced than I by the maniacal screech from the boy, and I suppose that, when the bullets kicked the dust up into the faces of the leaders, they had enough on the spot.

For they stopped. Mind you, that young split of Satan stopped the whole crowd with three bullets. With three more, he scattered them yelling to either side, hunting for safety, convinced that the desperadoes meant murder.

That is how we got to the horses, and on the horses we went out of Manorville in one direction. The manhunt went roaring and shouting and gloriously whooping in another direction.

So everybody was happy. I was about the least happy of the lot. There was one thing that I 'specially hated, and that thing was the shadow of the law. I didn't want any part or parcel of it. I wanted to be clean free from it. And here I was with tar on the tips of my fingers.

By the next day, however, we knew that the lay of the land was unbelievably good. Waters and Chip faded off through the hills in one direction, and the boss and I went home in another. By noon of the next day came the story about the jail break—but no warrant for our arrest along with it.

And then over to the camp comes the girl with the final word. Yes, I've got to say that Marian Wray lived up to any unspoken promise that she had given to the boss. She came right over, where we were cleaning up happily the wreck of the danged hay press, and she went up to Newbold and kissed him—*bang!*—right in front of everybody. She came over and kissed me, too, although anyone could see the difference.

She took us each under her arm, and, while the rest of the boys gaped after us pretty enviously, she walked off with us and told us what had happened. And that was this: Everybody in Manorville knew Newbold, and, therefore everybody in the town knew that he could not have been the wild man of the jail break. Nobody dreamed of recognizing him as the great desperado.

Nobody noticed me, either, I suppose, because my part was so small. Only it was known that two tall men, and one short one—they called Chip a man!—had turned the trick. And there you are. The shadow of the law slipped right off my shoulders.

I saw before me a good break and a chance at a happy life once more, and that sun-flaming, sun-wrecked cow range, it looked to me like cool blue heaven, you can bet.

I stepped aside and let the boss go on, slowly, with Marian Wray at his side, half turning, looking up to him, laughing.

Only Chip—what would become of him and his outlaw? Nothing bad, at least. Because only good can come out of good in the end.

The Ivory Portrait

This story first appeared under the title "Chip Champions a Lady" in Street & Smith's *Western Story Magazine* (1/24/31) under the Max Brand byline. While Chip's rôle in the action of the story is paramount, his actual presence is minimal. In fact, this is the narrator's story, Joe, another character without a surname in all three stories. And just as Marian Wray in "The Fall and Rise of Newbold," Doloridas Ruan, the Mexican beauty of this story set in the Southland, is central to the storyline.

Chapter One

"Chip's Aunt"

Young Mrs. Newbold stood on the back porch of the new ranch house and sang out: "Chip! Oh, Chip!"

I was mending a bridle in the shade of the bunkhouse, and Chip was beside me, whittling transparent shavings off a stick with a knife big enough to reach the heart of a bull and sharp enough to shave a three days' beard. He canted his head and scowled, when he heard the musical voice of the girl.

"Aw, leave me be," he muttered under his breath.

"Chip!" cried Marian Newbold. "Oh, Chip . . . darling!"

"Darling?" Chip said under his breath. "Dang!" He looked guiltily askance at me, reddening somewhat.

"You better sing out, Chip," I advised, "or else she'll be telling the whole valley that you're a darling . . . to her, anyway."

His freckled nose wrinkled at me. His wicked blue eyes gleamed. "Doggone me, if I ain't stood about enough of this," he muttered.

But he stood up, rather in haste, and stepped out into the sunlight, where he could be seen. There he took off his man-size sombrero—padded along the rim to fit his head, and waved it at her. The sun flamed in his hair. Shooting fires seemed to crown him wildly.

"Hello, Marian," he called.

"Oh, Chip," she said, throwing out a hand toward him and cocking her head with a smile. "I've got good news for you! Come here!"

Chip hesitated. He drew himself up to the full altitude and pride of sixteen winters—because there was not much of summer in that flinty young nature.

"Whatcha want?" demanded Chip, parleying for time.

"I want you, dear," Marian Newbold assured, and she came down the steps and then down the path toward him, as lovely a thing as you'd want to see, all grace and consciousness. Chip made about three steps to meet her.

But she was not proud. She never was proud with Chip. She went all the rest of the way and laid her slim hands on his shoulders. "Dear Chip," she said, "everything is settled."

"About what?" Chip asked.

"About your school, of course."

"Aw, is it?" he asked.

"Yes. I've just had word from your Uncle Newbold. . . ."

"He ain't any uncle of mine," declared Chip.

"By affection he is, Chip," she corrected.

Chip grunted. "I dunno about that affection business. You know, it's all right, but it don't make uncles. What's he gone and decided about me?"

"He's found the very place for you," ran on the girl, "where you'll continue to have the splendid outdoor life that you love so much, and horses to ride, and swimming, and tennis. . . ."

"Tennis, eh?" Chip said with a shrug.

"You don't have to play tennis, though," Marian Newbold said. "You don't have to do a single thing except try to please your poor Aunt Marian for one little, single term, Chip. I certainly can call myself your aunt, can't I, Chip, darling?"

He looked at her and sighed. "Yeah, I guess you can call yourself anything you want to, Marian. But this here school business is . . ."

"It's the most wonderful place you ever heard of . . . ," she continued. "And there are big woods and running creeks and a fine natural lake. . . ."

"What would an unnacheral lake be like, Marian? But go on."

"And I have the most charming letter from the matron, Chip. I want you to read it. I know that she's a dear. And you'd like her instantly, and she'd make you feel perfectly at home."

"Yeah?" doubted Chip. "You know, Marian, it's a terrible lot of money to spend on school when you get lakes and rivers and everything throwed in and . . . and . . ."

"Oh, when you're grownup and rich, you'll pay back every penny of it," said Marian Newbold. "That's all decided. In the meantime, we're only lending a little and trying to help out."

"It's too much," Chip argued. "I couldn't take it and . . ."

"Chip!" she said.

"Don't," Chip replied faintly, for she had him close in her arms, appealing to him with her voice, her eyes—even her lips trembling.

"Chip, you will go to please your Aunt Marian who loves you?"

"Yeah, sure, but you know . . . ," he began again.

"You won't do one thing for me? One single small thing?" she pleaded. "You really don't care a snap for me, Chip. I'm not asking much. I'm only asking you for one little promise. It won't be more than three months. And you'll have horses, and dogs, too. I wrote and asked if you could have dogs of your own, and everything will be the way you want it. Say yes, Chip, please."

With this, she kissed him, and Chip winced and blinked.

"Give me a little chance to think it over, Marian," he said. "Say, by tomorrow. . . ."

"No, by tonight, by tonight." She bent her head toward him again, with her pretty lips pursed.

"Yeah. All right, all right," Chip agreed, wincing. "I'll tell you by tonight, all right. Thanks, Marian."

"Dear old Chip," she said, and gave him a bear hug. Then she went up the path to the house, singing, literally floating along.

And Chip came back to me very red, indeed, wiping his

mouth with the back of his hand, hard, and half avoiding my eyes and half daring me to laugh at him.

"It's all right, Chip," I said. "Better men than you have been coaxed by a pretty girl."

He sat down, panting. He actually shuddered a little. "The kind of trouble that they make for a man," said Chip, "it's a terrible thing just to think about it. She was gonna kiss me again, by Jiminy," he muttered in addition, looking desperately straight before him.

I swallowed my laugh. Chip had a sense of humor, but like many other wits he found it rather hard to laugh at himself. He started at his whittling again, but he was so moved that he slashed the stick right in two at the next cut.

"Where you been this last trip?" I asked him, partly to start a new subject and partly because I was genuinely interested.

"Oh, just around," he answered me.

"You've been with Waters, I suppose?" I said.

"Waters?" he answered vaguely, as though the name of the outlaw, his dearest friend, were one that he barely recognized. "It's a funny thing, Joe," he said, "how much people talk about Waters."

"Yeah, it's a funny thing," I admitted. "Poor Waters, he hasn't done a thing in the last six months, except to stick up a couple of stages and shoot up the sheriff of Inyo County. Aside from that, he's hardly stirred. But you know how it is, Chip. People have to talk about something. And when there's no war, or nothing, going on, Waters is about the next best thing."

The boy grinned at me. He had an odd, flashing smile that was apt to twist only one side of his face a bit, as though only half of his mind was amused.

"They got nothin' on him," he averred. "They got nothin' on him about the stages, for one thing."

"I thought they identified him through some stuff that he pawned in El Paso?" I suggested.

"Him? He didn't steal the stuff," said the boy. "He had just bought it and got tired of it."

"Yeah," I said. "I could imagine that after he'd bought a pearl necklace to wear around his pretty white neck he might get tired of it pretty quick."

Chip drove his knife into the ground with an angry jab. "Anyway," he argued feebly, but sternly, "he didn't have anything to do with the stick-ups."

"Nor the sheriff, either, I suppose."

"Of course, he didn't," Chip said, vainly trying to meet my eye. "Besides, what's there wrong about a free fight? And a fair fight?"

"Aw, not a thing," I said. "Waters is all right."

"He's a friend of yours, Joe," Chip said rather mournfully. "There's nothing that he wouldn't do for you, since that jail break. . . ."

I jerked my head over both shoulders. There was no one near. "Lay off of that, Chip," I warned him.

"Anyway, he's a friend of yours for life. He'd never do you no harm, Joe. He'd come a thousand miles to help you out."

"That's fine of him," I said.

He sighed. It appeared that something was on his mind, and that he could not find a handle for it. "Speakin' about women . . . ," he began again. As he paused, I helped him out.

"Have you found one that you take to, Chip?"

He did not smile, simply because he failed to see the humor in this, or the possibilities of humor. He was a little blind in that direction only—he never could look upon himself as other than a grown man with all of a man's interests.

"Me?" he said with some haste. "No, I ain't built that way. I never seem to have no time to waste. Women . . . they make me . . ." He stopped short. I was amazed by this show of tact.

"Go right on, Chip," I said. For I had heard him berate the entire female sex at great length a good many times before this.

"Aw, they're fine," said Chip slowly. "I suppose that nobody's what he had oughta be until he's got himself a danged smilin', grinnin' . . . I didn't mean that, either." He was all in a shiver. Suddenly he said: "Look at here, Joe."

"Well, Chip?"

"What about yourself?" he asked.

"What about what?"

"About yourself," he repeated. "What sort of a girl would you step out and marry, one of these days?"

I turned and looked hard at him. The drift of his thought was beyond me, but that was not surprising, for Chip's drift of thought generally was beyond me, anyway.

Chapter Two

"The Portrait"

Away past Chip, I looked across the shimmer of the heat waves as they danced on the ridges, and across the hollows, too, and out to where a buzzard was circling. Somehow, it was like looking half across the world, or clear through the heart of something, I can't say what.

My fingers kept fumbling at the bridle that I was working on.

"Well," insisted Chip, "d'you see her face pretty clear, now?"

"Whose face?" I asked.

"Her face ... the girl's face ... the one you wanta marry," said Chip.

It wouldn't have done to let a man talk to me like that, but from Chip it was easy to take almost anything. So I laughed at him. "You've got women on the mind today, old son," I said.

He broke out in a regular snarl. "Who could help havin' 'em on the mind?" he demanded. "Who could help wantin' to herd 'em all onto an island and then sink the island, and sink it deep, and wait till the last bubbles come up, and then go home and know that the best day's work in the world is done."

"You know, Chip," I said, "the race would die out after that.

You've got to have women in order to have men."

"Yeah, I know. But let the old race die, then. What's the use of having the race go on, if it's gonna be pestered and bothered all the time? There's no use. Let the old cat die, if it's gotta. It's better to let it die than to keep it dizzy always. The way men are now, about women. If you hear a door slam, it's because of a woman. There's a woman in everything, and I'm pretty sick of 'em . . . danged sick of 'em!"

I sighed as I watched Chip. It was true. I had often felt it before, when in talk with him. He was free. There were no trammels upon him. There was not even the binding grace of any great affection, except his blind and noble devotion to Waters, the outlaw. So Chip could stand, as it were, upon an eminence, from which he commanded a spreading view of the follies of man. And yet, in only a year or two, the height would be cut from beneath his feet, and he would roll in the dust among the rest of us poor mortals.

"Go on," said Chip. "You're true blue, Joe. You wouldn't dodge. You tell me the truth . . . that there's some girl that you got your heart pretty set on."

"No," I said.

"Is that straight?"

"You bet it's straight just now."

"You mean that you been in an' out a lot of times?" asked Chip.

"In and out of what?" I asked.

"Love," Chip answered, making a face as he used the word.

"Oh, sure," I said. "I been in and out a lot of times."

"Like with what?" asked Chip.

"What are you driving at, Chip?"

"Aw, g'wan and tell me, Joe," he urged.

I considered him again. I had a feeling that he was this curious for no very good or kindly reason. Nevertheless, it was always easy to talk to Chip. What one said to him was placed in a sealed book which would be opened to no other eyes.

"You want me to tell you about the girls that I've been dizzy about. Is that it?" I asked. "You wanta laugh at me, Chip?"

He reached out a hand in a sudden gesture, as though to

reassure me, almost as though to protect me—he a boy of sixteen, and I a grown man.

"No, I wouldn't laugh at you, Joe," he said. "But g'wan and tell me, will you?"

"It's like this," I explained. "The first time I was a kid just a jump older than you. It was a girl that wore a broad, blue ribbon in her hair, and she was always smiling. She had so many teeth that she had to."

"I don't mean calf love," Chip said, irritated.

"Every love affair is calf love, I suppose," I assured him. "The second was a waitress with a good-natured way. I'd ridden into a strange town on a strange range, and she sort of made me at home. But the look of her hands finally finished me. There was always a little grease about 'em, you know."

"Yeah. Don't I know," said Chip, disgusted.

"Then I got up in the world and got dizzy about a schoolteacher who knew how to look at you sideways and make your heart jump. . . ."

"Like a broncho side-jumping, maybe?" Chip asked, listening with a frown of interest.

"Something like that," I said. "The next was a tall brunette who wore her clothes pretty tight to show off her figure. But the boys were always crowding around her, and, when I saw that I'd never be more than one in a crowd, I swallowed my heartache and rode away."

Chip stifled a yawn. Yet his interest returned, almost fiercely. And he said: "That's four. Go on, Joe."

"I met a nice Swede girl from Indianapolis," I added. "We went out riding together, and it was a spring evening, and the mist in the hollow was in the blue of her eyes. And she looked sort of dewy and fresh. . . ."

"All right," Chip said, cutting in to avoid the details. "What come next?"

"There was a mighty good-natured girl down on the Staked Plains," I said, "that was as brown as you ever saw, and a good hearty laugh down in her throat like the laugh of a man. . . ."

"Did you stick to her?" asked Chip.

"To her? She went off and married a drummer. Fellow who sold farming implements, you know. That was all right. I mourned a good deal about her till I met a Denver girl with a thin back but a stylish way and . . ."

"Aw, say," broke in the boy, "to cut it all short, did you ever fall in love with a girl at first sight?"

"No," I said. "That's a lot of baloney . . . that falling in love at first sight. Don't you believe in that, Chip. It's the bunk."

"Baloney, is it?" Chip asked. "I've seen it happen, and that's all I gotta say."

I wondered more than ever what he was driving at.

He went on: "What about a Mexican girl? Ever fall in love with a Mexican girl, Joe?"

"No. "I don't want a greaser. I don't want any María Tortilla for mine."

He nodded at me, like an old man at a child. "You think of something brown on the skin and burnt in the eyes," he suggested. "But what I mean is first-class, genuine Castile."

"That's a good soap," I commented. "Kind of yellowish, though, and it don't float."

"Yeah?" said the boy.

He looked oddly at me. I felt that he was about to deliver me a blow, and I was distinctly right. I was about to have a dagger plunged into my vitals.

"Go on, Chip," I urged. "You tell me about this brand of soap that you're peddling."

"That's what I'm gonna do," he said.

I laughed a little, but uneasily. "Go on, then."

"There ain't far to go," said Chip. "Here you are."

And with that, he took out of his inside pocket a leather case, and from the case he removed a flat packet wrapped in the softest chamois, and under the chamois there was a wrapping of the finest silk, and within the silk, hulled like a body of flesh and spirit, there was a square of ivory, and on the ivory was painted the portrait of a girl who looked at me, by thunder, with such eyes that I swore she knew me, and knew that I was looking back, and was glad that I looked.

Now, I never knew enough about painting to tell whether that work was good or bad, or whether it was too rosy and olive, too dreamy in the eyes, too sweet and smiling about the mouth. I suppose that the colors were crude and the work bad. But to me, the thing was living. I took out a handkerchief and mopped my forehead.

"All right," Chip said.

I looked at him and his disdainful face. "You limb, you," I said. "You've done this on purpose. You've gone and knocked the wind out of me."

He shrugged. "Go on and ask your questions," he said, resigned. "Only, you answer me one, first."

"I'll answer anything, Chip," I said.

"You tell me straight . . . a second time . . . there ain't such a thing as love at first sight?"

I couldn't even smile. I only choked. Then I said: "You're right, Chip. You're right about everything, even love at first sight. Although how you have learned of that I don't know."

"I wished I'd died before I did," Chip said grimly. "Go on, now, and ask me if she really does look like that."

"You mean that this ain't some old master?" I asked. "You mean that this here girl is in the flesh somewhere?"

"Yeah, that's what I mean," he said.

I took the ivory in both hands.

"Give it back to me," he said.

"Go to the dickens, Chip, old partner," I said. "This here is never gonna leave my hands until I've seen her."

"Aw, you can see her, all right," said Chip.

"Boy, can you lead me to her?"

"What else did I come all the way up here for except for that?" demanded Chip.

"And why should you?" I said.

"Because the poor little girl's in trouble."

My head spun. "She looks like this, Chip?" I said.

"Lemme see," he said, critically examining the portrait.

"Yeah, her eyes is like that, but, when she smiles, it's like lightin' a lamp. You never seen the like. You can see to read by when she's around . . . there ain't no night too dark."

"And you're so fond of her that you came all the way to get me to help her out of this trouble?" I asked.

"That's it," said Chip. "She needs help, and that's why I'm here." He looked me straight in the eye, and his brow was as smooth and untroubled as marble, and his glance was as open, as pure, and as straight as the blue look of a mountain lake.

So I knew that Chip was lying with all the might of his mighty heart.

Chapter Three

"To Ride With Chip"

I studied Chip for a time. I knew that we were such good friends, and such old ones, that he was not apt to intend any harm for me. And yet, I could not but feel that his yarn was very odd, and that it might be hiding all sorts of reefs and shoals for my navigation.

"What's the trouble that she's in?" I asked.

Chip sighed. "Aye," he said. "That's the way of it. I knew that sooner or later you'd ask me that question . . . but you see, Joe, it's a thing that you wouldn't believe, if I was to tell you. And the only way that you could possibly think it true would be to hear it right from the lips of Doloridas Ruan."

"Is that her name?"

"Yeah, that's her name."

At least, he was not lying about that. I turned the name on my tongue, and, though I turned it in silence, I could hear a golden voice naming at my ear, over and over, *María de los Dolores*, and all its musical variations—Doloridas, Dolorcitas, Lola, Lolita. And with all of them, Ruan went very well at the end.

So I looked down at the miniature again, and the black magic spread through my veins. I cannot tell how it was that even then I felt that there was danger and all manner of trouble wrapped up in this thing. But know it I did. Some extra sense was working in me—that and the knowledge that Chip was lying about something, or holding back, or saying too much.

"Chip," I said, "do you think I'll go with you to help this María de los Dolores? I don't care what her sorrows are, unless I know them."

Chip shrugged. "Oh, you'll come, all right," he responded. And he grinned at me, and suddenly I knew that he was right.

"Tell me this. Is she married?"

He thought for a long moment, and then he shook his head. "I oughtn't to talk about her," he said. "That's a thing I mustn't do."

"You ought to give me a chance at the truth," I insisted. "You've got to tell me something . . . that much, at least. Is she married?"

"No," he finally indulged me. "She's not married. I'm telling you that on the promise that you won't badger me with a lot of problems and questions all the way south."

"To where she is?" I said. "D'you think, Chip, that I'll fly off and leave my job and go away with you on a wild-goose chase like this?"

He looked me flat in the eye. He had the nerve of a brass monkey. "You'll just about do that," he declared. "You know that the old straw boss job will be waiting for you whenever you wanta come back and take it up again. You don't care much about it, anyway. Nobody enjoys workin' much under old Newbold. I know that. Because I've worked for him myself."

I laughed a little, thinking of those hay-press days, when Chip had badgered us all so thoroughly and driven us like a gadfly. A gadfly he was, stinging men on to strange performances. Well, I was terribly uneasy, but every now and again I looked down to the ivory and the beauty, and the strangeness of that face went through me with a tingling shock of sweetness. Yes, that lad was right.

"How far is it?" I snapped at him.

"Ten days' riding," he answered.

"Not any train riding?"

"No. Hosses. And mules, maybe."

"Mountain work, then?"

"I've said enough," said Chip. "I told you that I wouldn't answer no more questions."

"You've gotta answer one, though," I said. "Here you've come like a homing pigeon ten days north to find me. Why did you come all this way? Why did you come 'specially to me?"

He shook his head.

"You won't tell me?" I persisted.

He shook his head again and set his teeth, and yet I could see some sort of an answer glimmering in his eyes.

"You've got to tell me, Chip."

At last he burst out: "I will tell you, Joe, if you'll promise me that it's the last question."

I took a quick, deep breath. I knew that I was a fool. I've already said that I felt danger fairly humming in this situation. But still I was tempted and all the sweet voices of romance were making music in my brain. "Well, Chip," I said, "I'll make that promise . . . though I still won't promise to go. I won't ask you another question, if you'll tell me why you really picked me out from the whole world to do the job."

"Because," he said with the utmost solemnity, "there ain't another man in the world that could do it."

There might have been a good deal of question about his other remarks before this one, but there was no doubt at all about the ringing sincerity in his voice now.

"And you know, Joe," he continued, leaning toward me, "that I wouldn't want you to risk your life, neither, if it wasn't a job worthwhile."

"Risk my life?" I said, with sudden pressure choking me. "Risk my life?" I repeated, and the hair stirred and prickled upon my skull and against my very brain pan.

"Aye, risk your life," Chip said huskily. "You're an old partner, Joe, ain't you?"

"Aye. We're partners, Chip. But what's this idea about life and death . . . ?" I made a feeble attempt at a laugh.

But Chip shook his head mournfully. "You'd have about one chance in three of pulling through," he said. "That's about all the chance that you'd have, old partner. But it's the kind of a grand game that I know you'd really like to play." He was getting fired up.

"You keep your Irish blood tamed down, will you?" I said. "You know me, Chip. Or you ought to. There's no Irish in me. There's nothing in me that hankers after grandeur and adventures. I'm willing to sit back and wait for my time to marry some hashslinger or . . ." My voice petered out. I was looking down at the picture of Doloridas, and the sight of it stopped me at once.

"You're gonna do a great thing," the boy said to me. "You're gonna do a thing that'll make you happy for life . . . and pretty famous . . . and you'll have Doloridas, besides. Why, old son, the smile that she'll give you, when you arrive, will make your ten days of riding seem just like one afternoon. And now I've gotta be sloping. Are you the man that's riding south with me, Joe?"

"Hold on, hold on!" I exclaimed. "You can't leave. You gotta see Marian Newbold again."

"I wouldn't see her again," said the boy, "for a thousand dollars a minute. You can say good bye to her for me, will you?"

"And get blamed for your going?"

"That's all right," he said. "They won't hold no grudges against the two of us."

I knew he was right, and yet I was ashamed to go in and face Marian. She could chill her manner and her words on the warmest sort of a day, and I didn't want to be frosted all over. However, I saw that he was stubborn. He was afraid of another affectionate demonstration, I suppose. So I went into the house and spoke to Marian. She gave me one of her kindest smiles. She was always kind to me, but I knew that she wasn't interested. There was only one man in the world. That was Newbold. There was only one outside person—until her own kids should begin to arrive—and that was Chip.

"Marian," I began, "Chip's decided not to go to school."

"What?" she cried. "Chip gone?"

She ran to the window. I followed after. And through the window we could see a mule with a bald and mangy rump going down the southern valley trail, and there was a small rider in the saddle, a rider slewed well around to the side—the very manner of Chip in the saddle.

"Oh, Chip, oh, Chip!" Marian said, wringing her hands. "You'll never give yourself a chance to be what you could be!"

"Listen, Marian," I continued. "What kind of a school could he go to? What kind of other boys could he find there that would stand the wear and tear of being shaken around inside of any set of walls with that cast-iron bombshell, that Chip? What sort of a school would stand that wear and tear? Why, away out here in the West, where they talk about the open spaces, things are sort of crowded with one Chip. There isn't even room on your ranch for him. You know how things go when he's around here?"

She sighed. "I love him," she said logically.

"Sure you do," I said. "You women always love a trouble-maker. And that's where he's bound now . . . to find trouble. And I'm going along after him."

She caught her breath and turned around sharp on me. She put her hand on my arm and peered into my face in a rather frightened way. "Do you mean it, Joe?" she said.

"Yeah," I said. "I mean it, all right. I'm starting now. I don't like to step out of the job like this. But you know how it is."

"I don't know how it is," she replied.

"You will, if you take another think. The only reason that the boss wants me around here is not that I'm an extra good 'puncher, but because he feels that he's my friend."

"And he is your friend," she said.

"Yeah, but he doesn't need me. He's able to do his own bossing of his men, goodness knows. So I'm sliding out from under. I'm following Chip."

"Where?" she asked.

"I don't know. Just south," I said.

She sighed again. There was a real pity in her eyes. "Dear old Joe. Do you think it's wise to ride blindly on the sort of trail that Chip, of all people, is likely to follow?"

It angered me a little, I admit, the way she sort of talked down to me. "I'm not the toughest *hombre* in the territory," I agreed. "But still, I've stood the wear and tear so far. I've worked with the boss long enough to callus up some of the tender spots. I'll take my chances with Chip on the trail."

"Oh, Joe . . . ," she began.

"Well, what?"

But then I saw that there were tears in her eyes and a tremor in her lips, so I backed out and said good bye and left at once.

Chapter Four

"Up and Down"

When I rolled up my pack and strapped it on the back of the roan, I was still feeling a little blue. It's all very well to have a woman treat one in almost any way, except one. A man will stand anything from a girl with a pretty face—anything except pity. And I had last seen Marian Wray Newbold with her eyes filled with tears of pity as she looked at me. Why? She didn't know what danger might be on this trail, although she might guess that Chip did not ordinarily ride for the mere fun of seeing landscape. But why pity me so heartily?

You see, I could ride about as well as the next man, I could handle a rope, do my job riding the range, and shoot enough game to keep me in fresh meat, if I had an hour a day for the hunting. I was man-size, reasonably well set-up, and on the whole I could pass in most crowds. The sag of my broken nose didn't make me beautiful, to be sure, but it wasn't on account of my looks that Marian Newbold had been pitying me. I knew why, too. It was because I was just ordinary Western iron, and whatever job the kid was steering us for was apt to require steel tools. Iron is a good, tough metal, too. And you can put a reasonable edge on it. But steel will cut it through like butter, almost.

Newbold—there was a fellow of steel. You could put an edge on him, and he wouldn't grow dull through a lifetime of pounding. And Dug Waters, whom Chip worshipped so—there was another fellow all steel—a finer temper, even, than Newbold, I suspected, although Newbold worked inside of the law and the other worked outside it. But I was not that sort of stuff. I was only iron. I could cut wood, but I couldn't cut rock. I could shoot fairly well with a revolver or a rifle. And I think I had average nerve. But the difference between me and a Newbold or a Waters was—simply that between iron and steel.

I reflected on this as I rode down the trail after the boy. And I began to wonder more and more. Chip knew my failings. He knew that I was no more than an average man. When he had a hero like Waters at his beck and call, why should he have ridden for ten days to get hold of me?

It hurt me a great deal. It hurt me to think that I was such a fool. It hurt me to know that everyone could see through to my weaknesses as if they were looking through a glass window into my heart, Marian, among the rest. It's not so bad to be looked down upon by men, big and important men. But it's hard to have women see one's weaknesses.

I was beginning to scowl and put on a fighting face, when I turned a corner of the trail and there I found Chip was waiting for me. He said by way of greeting: "Does that roan take to the mountain trails pretty well?"

"That roan," I said, "will walk wherever a mountain goat walks."

"Mountain goats," said the kid, "never were seen in the country where we're going."

"No?" I said.

I grinned at the freckled face of Chip. It was good to be out there on the trail with him again, no matter what was ahead of us. No matter what else he did, he made me forget about women, confound them.

"No," repeated Chip, shaking his head seriously. "Where we're going, the goats get dizzy, and even the flies make it a step at a time, and the bees go trembling along the edge of nothin' at all."

"Above timber line, is it?" I speculated.

"Above timber line?" he said. Then he laughed. "Why, old partner, them that have climbed up to where we're going forget that there ever was such a thing as a tree in this little old world of ours."

It was good, as I said before, to hear Chip stretching things again, but just the same it was not exactly reassuring. And so we went along the trail, and to cut a long story short we climbed two ranges and crossed two valleys, and we got into the wildest heart of the Mogollons. I hear people rave and rage about great and famous mountains—Alps, and such things—but the Mogollons are good enough for me. They're high enough to fall off and crack your sconce, and they're high enough to catch the rain clouds and squeeze the water out of them to the last drop. I've seen storms good enough for Antarctica or the North Pole right there among the Mogollons, and cliffs that jump a man's mind into the heart of the sky or drop it down to the bottom of the well to the hot place. And there's something wild about the Mogollons. They haven't been tramped over and camped over as much as other mountains. They're like a Western mustang, just full of humps, and bumps, and meannesses, and twists, and angles, and shakes. They're bad enough to fill a book. Not even a dude ranch can flourish out there in the Mogollons. But I've known people who loved those mountains because of their wildness, and I'm one of the people that I talk about.

There are other things than mountains and mountain forms to be seen down yonder. There are mining towns, here and there, and, when the grass is good enough, you'll find regular cattle ranches, and hither and yon will always be a bright bit of old Mexico dropped down into a sheltered corner, all white and red, like a Sunday washing of table linen and red flannels. There's a peculiarity about the Mexicans that most people don't notice, and that's the ease with which they establish their boundary lines.

The Río Grande is a mighty small stream. On the north side of it there's all the fuss and the bother, and the stamping and the dusting about the greatest nation on earth. That's enough to establish the northern side of the boundary wall. But on the south side of the stream, there's only a sleepy, good-humored, and lazy lot of soft voices, and dark eyes, and dusty streets, and the wind goes one way and the river goes another, and nobody gives a dang. But that southern boundary is as strongly marked as the northern one. You can see and feel and smell Mexico when you're halfway across the international bridge.

Up there in the New Mexican mountains it's the same way. Where the Mexicans have formed their communities—and they've made plenty of them, of course—one leaves the soil of the United States—the spirit of the Americans, at least—and passes instantly into another world, spiritual and physical. So it came to us on this day which was to pass me out of my old world and into a new one.

We dropped over a miserable trail that zigzagged like a lightning scar down the face of a cliff. So we came into a white alkali flat where birds and beasts were whitish, too, and we went over this flat that shone and dazzled beneath us, casting up a fiery reflection so strong that it scorched us beneath the chin and under the eyes, until we came to a dry draw where the water must have run strongly in the rainy season. But now the bed was filled with the last evidences of the waterwork. The boulders and the strewings of smaller rocks lay just as the hands of the currents had last let them fall, and all was gleaming and bright under the sun.

There was a staggering bridge that crossed this draw, but it looked a little feeble to us, so we took our way down one bank, up the other, and so came out again into the continuation of the trail beyond. And there, immediately beside us, we saw the shrine of a saint—I don't know which one—with the boarding that had hooded it fallen away, and the wooden face of the image lifted in suffering to whatever weather might be.

I looked at this shrine with a good deal of curiosity. It was carved rather roughly, but it had great expression, and the fellow who did that work must have found a model of suffering in his own heart. Otherwise, he never could have cut so close to the quick. With equal interest I looked at another thing. On the little platform just under the shrine there was lying a pair of old spurs, nailed in place, simply by forcing the rowels into the wood.

Those rowels were the big-fingered, Mexican kind, and they had rusted almost to nothing long ago. I wondered over them. A Mexican may treat his horse with contempt, but he usually treats his spurs with the utmost tenderness. And, here, these had been left to the work of the weather. They were an offering, of course. I could not help trying to surmise what man, hounded across country on a bitter chase, by the law, or else trekking slowly across the desert, in the moment of necessity had vowed his very spurs to this little wayside saint, if he could win through to safety. It must have been so.

From this moment, the air and the atmosphere of the United States were altered, and in their place we were riding through old Mexico with a vengeance. As we got across the valley and into the first rise of the trail beyond, we got out of the gray region of the cactus, the agave, and the yucca to the belt of greasewood and sagebrush, with the heat still increasing, because the slant of the slope held us flat in place for the sun to beat against. And here we passed a broken house of adobe. All the upper walls were gone. Most of the bricks had dissolved with rain and wind, but some lay broken on the ground, and one could see the clumsy and familiar hand-made care which had produced them. This hut had consisted of two rooms, for one could look in on the floor plan. And there had been no outhouses, apparently. It had stood there in the low-blowing smoke of the greasewood, an utter desolation. No white man could have chosen to build his home in such a place, far from good wood and water, far from good hunting, too, far from grasslands. But a Mexican will build wherever the impulse stirs in him, and only the saints can tell when and where the impulse will budge him.

The mouthful of emptiness made my brain ring like a rusty tin pan, and I went on with the boy, shivering a little. Even Chip looked askance at that sorry bit of ruin, and twisted his mouth a little.

We passed over slopes spotted with cedar; we climbed to the region of pine and fir, and got into thin, pure air, two miles above the sea. Then we dived through a twisting gorge, half blocked by the remnants of an ancient Spanish fort. Why should there have been a fort here? That again only the Mexican mind could have answered. And so we came twisting down through the peaks and at last came out into the view of a little flat bottom valley, a Mexican valley of rocks, and pines, and grassland.

Chapter Five

"Chip Turns Back"

I say it was a Mexican valley because part of the grasslands were farmed, and the farms were not checked off in square fields but were worked in long strips, such as the peon loves to set out and till. I could see men toiling in those fields, and by their bent backs one could tell from the distance that they were not Americans. For Americans may bend in labor, but they don't seem to stay bent. In a hay field, or even with a spade, your true American seems to be standing erect most of the time. But an Italian or a Mexican always appears to be bent over like a pin that never will be straightened for fear of breaking it.

Those fellows were peons, I could swear. And, besides, the Mexican atmosphere of which I speak, which had been thickening ever since we passed the shrine and the spurs, now rose in a steam, as it were, from this little half-barren valley. The very shape of the rocks were not American, it seemed to me, but were twisted and flattened and carved and chopped by nature, as nature generally is south of the Río Grande. Even the pine trees which formed good plantations here and there were not American, if I dare say it. And right across from us, I saw, well up from the floor of the valley, crowning and overflowing the top of a hill, what seemed half house and half fort. Or, rather, it looked like a house that, on occasion, had had to play the part of a fort as well.

Its bastions ran down over the sides of the hill. It had a great, broad patio into which I could look. I saw that half of the roof was fallen in. Little streams and trailers of greenery, glittering like running water beneath the sun, ran down over the walls of this ancient house, and still they ran down, trickling and twisting beside the trail that ran from the dignified entrance gate to the level of the valley beneath.

Some inspiration came to me, and a chill along with it. I pointed toward the house.

"Doloridas lives yonder, Chip!" I exclaimed.

He gave me one of his quick side glances. "Yes," he said. "How come . . . ?" But he did not deign to finish his question. Instead, he looked with mournful eyes across the valley. There was a certain hopelessness in his face that I never had seen there before. "Yeah, Lolita lives there," he concluded, and shook his head dismally.

"I thought you said that we were going to travel above timber line to get to the place?" I asked him, both relieved and disappointed. For now that we were near the goal I rather wished that we still had other days of traveling before us.

"Well, we have been above timber line plenty since we started," said Chip. Then he added: "You don't think that this here is very high. But you'll see. It's been high enough to make me pretty dizzy. It's likely to make you dizzy, too. You wanta watch yourself up here on these trails, Joe. Because a lot of people have missed their steps and taken a thousand-foot drop. That's a mighty lot of dropping to do all in one step, I'd say."

"Yes, I guess they thought so," I said, feebly amused.

"Well, there you are," he said. "That's the place that you're bound for."

"Why do you wave me on, Chip?"

"Because that's where your trail lies, ain't it?" he answered. He was irritated.

"Are you going to stay behind?" I asked, more and more alarmed.

"What should I wanta go in there for?" he asked me, as sharply and as unreasonably as before. "They'd only sink a knife into me between the shoulder blades, so's I wouldn't know the face of him that stuck me. No, no, Joe, old son. That's your job . . . the entering of the house."

I felt the color draining out of my face. My skin felt puckered with cold fear.

"What sort of people are they, then, in yonder?" I asked. "Is that a murder den?"

He started to shake his head, and then, fixing his eyes steadily and coldly upon mine, he nodded several times, slowly. "Yeah," he said, "there's been murders done in there." He paused, as though sullenly waiting for me to refuse to enter such a place.

I bit my lip. I never wanted so badly to get away from the sight of any place as I wanted to get away from this one. But two things pushed me forward. One was the ten days of accumulated travel behind me, dammed up and pressing against me like gathered water power, and the other was folded in its silken sheathing and lay nearest to my heart. Besides, there was my pride, whatever I had of that, telling me that I could not afford to shame myself before this boy. I sighed a little. I felt rather beaten.

"I thought that you were going through this thing with me, Chip," I told him mournfully.

"Aw, Joe," he said, "buck up a little, won't you? What good would it be, I'm askin' you, for me to go along with you? The minute they seen me, everything would be up, and they'd just slam us both."

"Why would everything be up?" I asked him. "What have you ever done to the people in that house?"

He groaned, impatient with himself for his last speech, as it appeared, and annoyed by my lack of resolution. "I've done enough talking," he said, "and I've answered enough questions, and that's a fact."

"All right," I said. But I found myself moistening my dry lips and still staring across at that house on the hilltop that seemed to be growing larger every moment. "I'd like to know what sort of people are inside of that house. That's all I'd like to ask you, Chip," I finally said to him.

He seemed to hesitate, doubting the wisdom of making an answer. Then he replied: "I'll tell you. They're people just the opposite of everything they seem. That's about all I can tell you of 'em."

That was as little cheering and comforting as any answer I ever have received in my life. "Chip," I said, "it's pretty hard lines. I'm not any hero, and it needs a hero to go up there into the house, I tell you. A hero compared with me, at least. But I'm going to try to drag myself along. Only . . . I expected that you would be with me."

He held out his hand to meet the one I proffered. Then, as our grips closed, he gave my fingers a great squeeze.

"I'd like to be with you," Chip said. "But bein' a hero wouldn't help a man . . . not up there in that house."

"What is it that would help a man, then?"

He rolled his eyes rather wildly. "Luck," he said at last. "Nothing but luck."

He jerked his mule around and went riding back up the trail down which he had brought me. It was a hard thing for me to sit there in the saddle and see the last of him. My heart was weakening all the time. I stared after him until, at the last corner, he turned and gave me a wave of his hat, and he was still waving when the rock shut him away from my sight.

I turned, then, and looked again at the old house-fortress in its ruin. It stood up brightly in the mountain sunshine. Its rock wall glowed; its greenery flashed like running water; and suddenly it seemed to me that the house, the valley, the trees, the rocks, the blue-headed mountains beyond, were all part of a picture that some hand had painted before, and here I was riding into the margin of a scene of the imagination. This odd thought was so strong in me that it enthralled me completely. I looked down fixedly into the valley. It seemed to me that not a laborer had stirred from the moment I first saw them, and that they were not stirring now. There was a horse and a high-wheeled cart in the near distance, off to the left, on a crookedly winding road. I stared at this cart until I saw it twist a little, as it struck a rut. Then I wakened from my daydream.

"Well," I said to myself, "shall I go on, or shall I hold back?

I'll hold back, if I have any sense. I'll go on, if I'm a fool. And a fool is what I've always been."

The horse began to walk forward of its own volition, and instantly I accepted this as a token that I was meant to form a part and a portion of that picture which I saw before me. As the roan went forward, I had a weird feeling, stronger than before, that I had ridden through the frame of the picture, and that now I was a part of it. Or, to put it another way, that now I was something to be looked at, framed, and hung on the wall, stared at by a casual, uninterested eye that might be bored, or indifferent, or, perhaps, cruelly malignant, and might choose, at just this point, to poke a finger through the canvas, or blur to nothingness this spot of the wet paint.

When I had got over some of this dreamy emotion—with the first sharp stumble of the horse—I began to use my eyes a little more carefully, and, as I got down into the valley, I saw that it was a poor place. A good place for looking, you might say, but a poor place for soil. Elbow grease and fertilizer might raise some ragged crops of oats and corn down yonder, but the land was not meant to produce. It was barren. It was as barren as the old oil paint on a canvas.

However, I could see the signs of life in actual movement as I got down into the floor of the valley. Dust I saw thinly curling up from the wheels of the distant cart, and then, from a field almost as far away I heard a wailing Mexican song. Yes, the laborers were moving at their work, and my dream was beginning to come to life, with me in the center of it.

I headed straight across the flat breast of the plain toward the house on the hill. I crossed the darting face of the creek that ran through it, chiseling through the rocks so that I could measure the shallow scratchings of the surface soil, scant inches deep. Over the hump-backed, little bridge I went and saw my crooked image dimly in the swift water beneath. I passed from the hollow sound of the hoofbeats on the bridge to the quiet of the road beyond, and so wound up and up toward the gate of the house.

I could see, now, why there was greenery along the trail, because a runlet of water made a gutter on either side. Because of that spring this site must have been chosen for the building.

And I came up to the great, thick wall, and saw the gate sagging open, made of ponderous beams and crossbars of time-whitened pine. I looked about me. There was no bell to ring, nothing to knock on. It would have been, besides, like calling aloud to the dead centuries. So I rode on through and was up the slant and passing into the patio, when I heard a heavy, booming, crashing sound behind me. I jerked about in the saddle and saw that the gates had shut behind me and were quivering still from the force with which they had been slammed together.

Chapter Six

"Spider"

I wanted to run back and jump from the saddle for the top of that gate and try to get out that way. I was fairly blind with the impulse to try it, but I kept the impulse locked back somewhere behind my teeth. The thing that had slammed those gates was watching me, of course, like a spider in its den. I was the fool and the fly!

I decided that I had better show as little emotion as possible. This was a trap; I was inside it. There was no use in jumping over a precipice just to please whatever bloated scoundrel was standing behind the scenes, watching me. A very odd thing, that. I mean, from the instant that gate slammed I felt that whatever power controlled that house had the form of something swollen out of normal human shape. It was as clear in my mind as something already seen, and then more than half forgotten.

I went about my movements slowly and deliberately. I was shaking in my boots, but I dismounted, and threw the reins over the head of the roan, and that tough little brute amused himself, picking at the grass that grew up through the cracks in the paving stones of the patio and the crevices between them. There were no nerves in that mustang; that was the reason I had selected it for this mountain work. Now I couldn't help remembering what Chip had said about heights and dizzy places. I was on one of them now. I was a mile above *terra firma*, it seemed.

I looked about that patio, while I made a cigarette. Making a cigarette is the most soothing thing in the world, because it gives the hands something to do, and, when the hands are safely occupied, for some reason or other the brain has a better chance, and the nerves will stop jumping.

There was not a soul in view from where I stood, and I seemed to see everything. The patio was apparently a big square, with a blank wall at the north and an arcade running around the other three sides. A rough arcade of stones that had been quarried not for uniform size or color, but just to fit in haphazardly. It was ponderous work, and yet it was joined together with that sort of cunning that Indian masons always have shown. Those columns seemed to budge and stagger from side to side and in and out, and yet I knew perfectly well that this heavy masonry would outlast steel skyscrapers. Why had the roof fallen in, then, over a section of the house—as I had seen from the distance? No weight of time was apt to have crushed it; the force must have exploded from inside.

There was very little to see in the patio. There were the remains of a fountain in the very center, but it had been disused for so long that the bowl was all cracked, and the green scum that had dried around the sides of it had faded to white. The only thing that lived in that court was the dull green of the moss inside the northern wall. When I raised my head from the lighting of my smoke, I snapped the match suddenly and forcefully away. For, in front of me, leaning against one of the rude pillars of the arcade, I saw a Mexican standing, his feet crossed, his arms folded, a sneering smile on his face as he watched me. He was just a round-faced peon of the lowest class, it seemed, but now he was looking me over from a height. He was complacent, as though he had felt the whip and expected me to feel it soon.

If you can guess the house from its servant, the Casa Ruan was a junk heap. This fellow wore a shapeless, white cotton shirt, white cotton trousers cut off at the bulge of his brown calf, and a tattered straw hat. His feet were stuck into the ordinary *huaraches*, and for a weapon he had stuck into his belt the machete which the Mexicans understand and love as the old French used to love rapiers.

He looked me over for a moment, while I drew down a deep breath of smoke in order to brace back my shoulders and recover a little from the shock of seeing him. Then he made a gesture to follow him, and walked through the shade and spotting sun beneath the arcade to the farther side of the patio.

I followed him and went through an open arch into the southern garden of the house. It was ten or twenty degrees warmer than the patio. Once it had been formed with care, the rock trenched, and the soil brought to the trenches. Now most of that soil had been washed or blown away, and there was only a ragged semblance of a garden, outlined in shrubs. The winding paths were half seen and half lost in the bracken. But yet this had been a garden once, and a noble one. It needed no more than its view to give it still a certain dignity, for the eye looked out from it above the great, trembling void of the valley, with the mountains heaped up incredibly high beyond.

I gave these things something like a tenth of a second's observation. There was something else to take my attention. For there, stretched out in a sort of invalid's chair, taking the sun fearlessly without a hat on his head, was the spider. I mean, there lolled the controlling power of the house. One felt it by an instinct. I would like to linger for a moment over the picture of him, partly because of what he was to do, and partly because I would like to speak of the various chills and electric currents that ran all at once, in a single pulse, through various crannies of my body, mind, and soul. Sensations of a mild fear, and interest, and loathing, and excitement shot quivering through me. To describe him as well as I may, from his wooden leg to the brown, fat hands that were folded over his stomach, would take a lot of time and many, many words. But what I think of, usually, is first of all the bloated body and face of the man that, somehow, went with the smile upon his face. His eyes were closed. He was either asleep or shamming it. No, I think that he was really asleep, and smiling when he thought of how he had digested the last living thing he had caught in his web.

Next, I noticed the golden brown of his skin, with a hearty, healthy touch of red in the cheeks, the grizzled hair that stuck up straight on his head in an unusual way, and the bald spot over one ear, the top of which was itself tattered as though a wild beast had worried it off. Then I think of his clothes, which were those of a vagabond, and, finally, of the grease that blackened and shone upon the collar of his coat.

In any other setting, he would have been put down as a fat, worthless beggar—the sort of scoundrel who sits on a street corner and whines for pennies. But here it was very different. He was not whining. There were no whines in that pursed, smiling mouth of his. There were simply teeth.

The peon went over to his master, took off his straw hat, and made a bow.

"Swine!" said the sleeper, without opening his eyes.

What had wakened him, I wondered. Apparently, the crash of the closing front gate, like the boom of a cannon, had not been sufficient. He had slept through that. So could it have been no more than the trailing shadow of the peon's hat as it brushed across his face?

The peon bowed again, and then the fat man opened one eye and looked at me. I mean, deliberately, just that. He opened one eye, not both, and the eye that was opened was not filmed in the slightest. It was as bright and clean and keen as the eye of a boy. He kept that one eye open, and the other closed, while he stared at me.

The peon, having pointed me out, started to retire, but the master said to him—in Spanish, of course: "Go get me a bottle of wine and two glasses, and be back here with them before I blink my eyes."

The peon disappeared. There was merely the shrill whisper of his *huaraches* on the stones, and I wondered if he feared the fat brute might mean what he said.

In the meantime, the master looked at me with both eyes; I would rather he had limited himself to one. He turned his fat head on his fat throat, slowly, as though there was a pivot joint that could be turned as a bird's is turned.

"How was the trip up?" he asked in good English, with a good American drawl to the words.

I could not have answered him. I was too astonished. I never saw a place where the American language seemed more out of place.

"Sit down," he went on, without waiting for me to speak. "Take that stool. The chair wouldn't hold you. Sit down and rest yourself."

I sat down on the stool, as directed. It was the cheapest, clumsiest sort of homemade manufacture—rudely shaped wood, held together by wrappings of sinews at the joints.

In this position, I faced him and had the valley view behind me, also the sun. And I felt as though the whole valley was rising and pouring swiftly toward me, like a river about to sweep me away. It was a strange and giddy feeling, but I lost it almost at once. The reason I forgot about that odd sensation was that I saw my host was looking straight at me, with wide-open eyes—and yet he was directly facing the sun! I don't think it was entirely an optical illusion. It seemed to me that I could see the terrible keen ray of the sun enter his eye as it enters the eye of a snake. But this was not the flat lens of a snake's eye. This was brown, and the light shone deep inside it, running down a narrow, luminous well. However, he was not bothered. He continued to face that volleying of a million cruel lances without trouble, and I knew that he was not even dazzled, and that he was seeing me as clearly as though he sat in the shadow, and I in that blinding brilliance.

Then he said: "You know me, son? You know me, do you?"

"No, sir," I said. Yes, like a boy I said it—a schoolboy. "No, sir," I said, to that vagabond, in his tatters, with his greasy collar and all, and his wooden leg, and his bloated stomach, round as the body of a spider that has dined well.

"I'm Pete Ruan," he said. "Pedro Ruan to the people in this little part of the world." He waved his hand to indicate what he meant by "little part." The fences he indicated were the far monstrous mountains. Inside of that range, I gathered mutely, was his domain. It was enough.

The peon came running back with the bottle and the cups. It was a leather bottle, of goat's hide, with the hair still on the outside. He held it under his arm, and he poured the red wine into wooden cups, hand-carved. They looked like mesquite wood, hard as ivory. I thought I saw the twisting grain of the mesquite root in them.

"It's a mighty bad wine," said Pete Ruan, "but you'll like it, because it's cold. It's the temperature of spring water. Take a drink of that. It's not poisoned, either. Drink that and have a smoke. I'll send for her in a minute."

Chapter Seven

"Doloridas"

He kept on smiling as he talked. He moved nothing but his lips, and his fat cheeks quivered a little. From the moment he opened his eyes, his cheeks always seemed to be pulsating a trifle, as though he breathed with their power. But what did he mean by sending for *her* in a minute? The fellow might be a wizard, a fiend. I was prepared to credit him any sort of power that could be imagined.

"Look here, Ruan . . . ," I began. I stopped.

He sipped the wine. He sipped it noisily, and smacked his lips after he swallowed it. "Horrible wine," he said. "But just the right temperature. Temperature of snow water that's run through the rocks. It's the only proper temperature for this climate. You can live on temperatures, son. Hot outside and cold inside, that's one good way. Or cold outside and hot inside. I get both degrees up here, summer and winter. How do you like that?"

I tried the wine. I was not at all sure that it was not poisoned, though I had just seen my host drink the very wine that I was sipping. It had rather a sharp, acrid taste, but there was some of the fruity taste of the grape in it, too; as he said, it was cold, exactly the right degree of coldness for a man who had been riding all the day under the brilliant mountain sun.

"I like it," I said.

"Tell me your name," he demanded.

"I'm . . . well, José, in this part of the world, and Joe . . ."

"Never mind the last name," he said. "I just want a handle for you, that's all. How was the trip down?"

"Pretty good."

"How long?" he asked.

"Ten days."

"Ten days . . . ten days," he murmured. "Mule, or horses?"

"One mustang," I said.

I was rather surprised to hear him asking so many questions. I half expected that he would know all about me and about everyone else. He sipped his wine again, as loudly as before, and drew his big cheeks in and let them unfold again, flowing down toward his big shoulders.

"Yeah," he said. "That's quite a spell. Ten days on one mustang. That's thirty miles a day. That's three hundred miles. Eh?"

"Yes," I said. "Around about that, I reckon."

"Double the trail, make it about a hundred and fifty as the crow flies, eh?" he said.

"About that, maybe."

"You been educated. You can think better English than you talk, Joe," he said.

"I been educated a little," I admitted.

"And then took your education and wasted it on a cow range, like me, eh?" he commented.

I shrugged my shoulders. I kept feeling that he was driving at something important, although I could not quite make out what it might be.

"I done the same thing," he said. "I was educated, fine. Spanish and English. I took myself out West, and I wasted myself on the range, just the way that you've gone and done." He smiled as he spoke. His complacency was enormous, and it was easy to see that he did not think that he really had wasted his time. No, he was satisfied with what he had done and what he

136

had accomplished, even if the accomplishments included a wooden leg and the grease on his collar.

"It took a good while to learn the Western ways," he went on. "You know. Guns and things. They shot off a leg for me. Fine bright boy of Chicago, he shot my leg off, son. Pretty near didn't need a doctor. He put four bullets right through, side by side. He said he'd make me a lame duck and a tame one." He put back his head. He opened his mouth. He closed his eyes. He laughed, and his brown and rosy jowls shook up and down on either side of his mouth as he laughed. It was like seeing a swine laugh.

I moistened my cracking lips and said nothing. I hardly thought, either. My mind was growing numb. A beastly fascination took hold upon me and kept my brain from moving.

"He was a good shot," went on Ruan. "He split the bone apart as clean as you ever seen. The doctor that came along a couple of days later and trimmed the leg off, he said that he hardly needed a saw, except to do a little trimming. He said that shooting was purposeful shooting. And I admitted that it was. It was a good job that boy from Chicago did on me." He had hardly finished laughing, as he said this. Gusts and rumblings of his enjoyment still were coursing through the vast hollow bulk of him, and his smiling lips puffed out his cheeks. I felt that he was smiling a good deal of the time simply to keep the fat of his cheeks back, as with two hands.

At the same time, I began to hate his smiling as much as I had hated his laughter. I wondered how much good feeling toward Americans remained in him, after that little shooting escapade that had put him on one leg for the remainder of his life.

"I said I wasted myself on the range," he continued, "but it ain't a waste, I can tell you. I learned. You learn a lot while you're lying on the flat of your back with the life running out of your leg at every pulse of your heart. It's a great thing, son, to feel the clock running down, and nobody on hand to wind it up again. You ever feel that?"

I admitted that in such wisdom I was a novice.

"Ah, yes," he said. "I see how it is. Bein' so young, you're carryin' on to complete your education some, and so you've come up here to take a look at me and my niece. Ain't that it?"

Max Brand

It was hard for me to answer. I tried to speak, but the words wouldn't come out. You can't very well walk into a house and tell the master of it—even if he wears a greasy collar—that you want to have a look at the beauty who is housed there.

But this Pete, or Pedro, Ruan, had no foolish delicacy about him. He sang out in a huge roar: "Lola! Lola!"

I heard a faint answer, a sweet, small voice from the inward of the old house.

"You can have a look at her," said Ruan. "After the ride that you've taken, you can have a good, long look at her. I see that you're modest. Modesty's a foolish thing. There's many a man might have been king, if he'd cared to go and sit on a throne. But if you keep yourself in the dust, you'll never get anything but pennies throwed to you now and then."

"Look here," I said, "you're not going to call out the *señorita* into the court just to . . . er . . . just to . . . I mean to say, Mister Ruan, that you wouldn't want me to . . ."

"Here she is," Ruan said. He beckoned. "Come right up, my dear."

I got up from my chair with frost on my temples and cold fish down my back. I took off my hat and held it in both hands and tried to smile and look polite, but knew that I was gaping and grinning like a frozen monkey.

For there came Doloridas into the garden, stepping quietly among the broken rocks and the wild brush. She was the girl of the picture, mind you, only the picture didn't do her justice. Not by a reach a mile long. She was not big. She was only about shoulder-high on me. But I never liked a lengthy woman much. A man ought to have a chance to look down, in one sense at least. As for the rest of Doloridas, I won't talk about her. I hardly dared to look at her face, although her eyes were down. I looked no higher than the hand with which she held together the filmy edges of her *mantilla*. She came straight out there to us.

Then, as she paused without looking up, Ruan said to her: "María, this is Don José. He's rode ten days to see you. Go and make him a bow."

She turned a little toward me and made the curtsey, but she did not lift her glance.

"He wanted to look you over," Ruan said, "and I reckon that you want to be looked at. There she is, Joe. There ain't much to her, but what there is, is prime. She ain't big, but she's all quality. Look at that wrist. No bigger'n a baby's. Look at that hand, all dimples and softness, and not hardly big enough to hold a whip. But it can lift a mighty weight of trouble, d'ye see? Can't it, María?"

"Yes, *señor*," she said.

Oh, the soft, tired, musical voice of her. And the stony patience in her face as she submitted.

"Put out your foot, María," he said.

By heaven, she did it, actually lifting the hem of her skirt a little, and not a touch of color came into her pale, clear olive skin.

"Look at that pastern, Joe," Ruan said. "Look at the spring of it. Small, but made for speed, is what I always say about her. Look at that ankle, round as a bell. No big bone, no big tendon. A picture, is what she is. A real picture of a woman, is what my María is! But you ain't lookin', Joe."

"Mister Ruan," I said, "I don't think it . . ."

"Don't think, Joe," Ruan commanded. "That's the trouble with young men. They're always bound to be thinkin'. But don't you think. You just start in usin' your eyes and followin' your nose, and pretty soon you'll find yourself up on a high place. That's what I've done, and just look at where I am now!" He leaned back his head again, and opened his mouth, and closed his eyes, and once more, like a swine, he laughed, and I half expected something to strike him from the sky.

"It's María's fault," Ruan continued, wiping the tears out of his eyes. "She embarrasses you a lot, not lookin' at you. Where's your manners, María? Look at the gentleman, will you?"

"Yes, *señor*," she said, and she lifted her big, brown-black eyes and looked at me. No, not really at me, but toward me, and past me, and into the big valley that makes me, I know, seem like a foolish pygmy in a great frame. I could see that she was enduring as the martyrs endured in another day, with her soul and her mind shut to all physical sensations that could happen to her on this earth.

"That's better," said the brute, Ruan. "But it ain't good enough. Smile for the gentleman that's rode all this dusty way, María!"

Chapter Eight

"A Kind Uncle"

Now that I put down the words of the one-legged pig, it's sure
hard enough for me to believe my hand that writes it and my
eyes that see it. But the scene comes pouring back on me—the
old garden, and the gleam of it in the sun, and the brown and
rosy face of that pirate, Ruan, and the smile of the girl that
seemed toward me, and for me, but was only for the world that
lay behind me.

I looked down at the ground after one glance at her. I was
pretty well done up by this submission to the outrageous orders
of her uncle. I would have given him a piece of my mind, except
that I told myself it would be foolishness to cross him. For
nothing could be gained by that, whereas, if I said nothing, I
might do something for María de los Dolores. Only I most bitterly felt, now, that she had been rightly named, both for her
beauty and her sorrows.

So she smiled when he directed, as she had looked toward
me before, and extended her foot for my inspection, as a well-
trained animal being offered for market.

This brute of a Ruan went on: "She's got a pretty lot of spirit, too. She ain't showin' herself off at all well today. But she's got the right kind of a spirit in her, the sort of a spirit that a real Yankee likes. For I never seen an American yet that didn't like to have his womenfolk kick him in the face, now and then. Oh, she's got lots of heart in her. If you seen her reining a bucking mustang, or sitting a prancing young mule on the edge of nothing at all, or dancing here to a guitar. Why not dance now? By heaven, María, you shall dance now!"

He most excitedly clapped his hands and bellowed out something, but now I said: "Mister Ruan, I've never heard a girl spoken to like this before. I've heard enough of it, too. Let her be, won't you? If there's to be a dance, I'm not here to see it."

He was not angered, when I crossed him in this manner. He simply broke out once more in his loutish laughter. But I must say that the girl, who might have given me at least a direct glance in recognition of my interference, showed no emotion at all, and seemed as unconscious of me as before.

When his laughter had died off to a rumbling, he told me that it should be as I wished. "Have you seen enough of her?" he asked me.

I couldn't say that. I could have looked at her, with a lot of pleasure, from that minute to this, and still been rooted there where I stood, I'll swear. But I managed to say something about knowing that she was inconvenienced, and that I hoped she would do as she pleased.

At this old Ruan broke out with a roar: "No, by heaven, but she'll do what pleases you! That's all! She'll do what pleases you, my friend. You've come down here to risk your blessed neck for her, and now she'll please you, or she'll answer to me for it, and she'd better answer to the point!"

He put a lot of force and emotion into this. His eyes glared, I'll swear, with a red light, and his anger and fury were so great that after he had finished the words he lay for a while panting. There was no mask on him now. He was all malevolence. He was all brute fury. What he had said I've only put down in part. Some of it was too full of cursing for me to repeat, because it makes my blood boil to think of the way I allowed him to speak in the presence of that girl—to her, in fact. One thing was clear. He hated her with his entire, piggish nature.

He went right on at her: "Tell me, María," he said, "are you here to please the *señor*, or are you not?"

"I am here to please the *señor*," she answered.

Some of her calm was gone, now. She was paler. Shadows were thumbed out under her eyes. I thought that I saw her lips trembling. Poor girl, she was suffering a good deal, and I was mightily sorry for her.

"If she's here to please me," I broke in, "she's free to go back to her room."

Ruan snorted and glared at me. Then he pointed. "Get out of here!" he said to her. "He's told you to go, hasn't he? There's one more come here to suffer for your sake. And this one is telling you to get out of his sight. Why're you staying? Go, go!"

She didn't wait. She gave him a little curtsey, and one to me, and off she went as meekly as you please.

I watched her with a tortured feeling that I should have done still more, and that I should have dressed down that swine of a Ruan. But there was another sting in me, and that was what he had said about me as another come to suffer for her sake. I could imagine that this house might be an inferno. I thought that I had seen a bit of the Hades in it. But what, exactly, had become of the others who had come here before me—for her sake? It was enough to give any man pause for thought. When she had gone, I was pretty well stunned, all things considered. I didn't know what to do or to say. I simply knew that I had been thrust into a false position. At last, I saw that Ruan, the pig, was watching me with his brown and rosy smile, as cheerful as could be, and that he was waiting for me to speak.

So I gathered my courage and my wits as well as I could, and I said: "*Señor* Ruan, I'll tell you how it is . . . it's a true thing that I rode down here like a fool in an adventure book. And it's a true thing that it was because of *Señorita* Ruan that I came. But . . ."

"But what?" grunted the pig, although he continued smiling.

"But I see," I said, "that she never could care for . . . in other words, I wouldn't be wanted, and . . ."

"I want you, though," said Ruan. "You please me. That's what is important. This ain't an American household. This is Mexican, and it's the Mexican parents that decide who their children are going to marry. You please me. And you're gonna have my niece. You hear me?"

"I'll have something to say about that," I responded. I had gathered my dignity around me, you see, and felt rather Roman and even senatorial.

Ruan only laughed in my face. "You've come here to get her," he said, "and you don't go away without her. Don't anger me, Joe, my son. My nephew, I should say, since that's what you're going to be. Now that you're inside of the house, you're not to leave until you have her, or until you . . ." He paused, and took another swallow of wine.

He did not need to finish off his last speech, because I could supply the missing word. I was not to leave until I was the husband of the girl, or until I was dead! You may say that it's not a great pressure to be forced to one's dearest wish. But I was all chills and fever.

He went on: "Sit down again."

I did as he told me.

"We're gonna be friends, my boy," he said. "As an enemy, I'm all thorns. But I can be a pretty good friend. Now wipe that fool look off of your face and talk to me sensibly and open and manly and free."

I took a breath, and settled myself on the stool as well as I could.

"Bein' friends," he continued, "suppose you start right off and tell me about yourself."

"I'll tell you whatever you ask."

"It's easy for you to talk about yourself, is it?" he asked.

"Yes," I said. "And afterward, will you tell me something about this place . . . and the men who've come before me?"

"Why, I might," he stated. "If we're friends, words come easily to me. Now suppose you tell me if you had any second reason for riding this far south."

"What?" I asked.

"Outside of María, I mean."

"No. What else could there be?"

He narrowed his bright, strange eyes at me. "I mean," he explained, "that sometimes the law is fool enough to bother men . . . innocent men, of course . . . and make them want to get into a hole-in-the-wall country, just like this. But I don't suppose that the law ever has wanted you?"

I reflected back to a certain jail break in which I had assisted. But that matter had blown away. The law knew nothing, so far, to my discredit. "No, the law has nothing against me," I offered.

"Humph!" he spit.

And I felt that he was not exactly pleased.

He went on: "A boy with your education, Joe, and with everything that seems to be inside of you in the way of politeness, he's been well raised, and there's been some money behind him, and I guess that somewhere in the background, you got some rich relatives, ain't you?"

I smiled and shook my head. "Not even a fifth cousin with an income worth leaving," I told him, truly enough.

He actually sighed with relief. His anxiety had pulled him forward in his chair, but now he relaxed deeply into it again. What evil was in him that made him glad that there was no great amount of money behind me?

"But you've got influential friends, anyway," he insisted. "I know the way that it is. You've got friends that can take care of you and push you along when the right time comes for the pushing."

I shook my head. "I don't even know a sheriff very well, except one," I said. "No, I've got no influence. Now that I say that, I see that you think I'm a fool. I've come down here like a half-wit, hunting for . . . well, for María de los Dolores, and I have no way to provide for her, even if I should have all the luck and win her. You're only right if you call me a blank fool. I see that for myself."

No, I was all wrong. He did not seem to be sorry that I was penniless and that I had no prospects in the world. Instead, he actually began to rub his fat hands together, so violently that even his brown-jelly cheeks were quivering with his pleasure. And he beamed on me, and nodded at me again and again.

"Lad," he said, "I like to see a boy and a girl begin life right from the beginning, with a good start and no money. And I'll be able to give you some advice. You can reach out and lean on me for millions of dollars in the way of advice, if you want to."

I saw the thing clearly enough now. Plainly he hated María, poor girl, so very bitterly that he was glad to see her married off to a beggar.

Chapter Nine

"A Peon On Guard"

After this, he seemed to lose interest in me suddenly. He clapped his hands twice, and a *moza* appeared, a ragged wildcat of a woman with tousled hair streaming in wisps across her face, and buried, hunted, desperate eyes. He told her to take me to a room, and, before I could get up to leave him, I saw that the beast was asleep again, his eyes shut, and his face composed, with the last fierceness of the sun beating upon it, and the smile gently curving his lips. Yes, there he was, sunk into a well of unpretended slumber, with his hands folded caressingly upon his vast stomach, while I went off behind the *moza*. I felt that I had heard one profound truth from the lips of Ruan. Even a swine could speak one truth, and say that this place was Hades.

The *moza* went up before me, running on the stone stairway, which had been hollowed by many generations of use. The ragged calico skirt whipped around her brown legs, as corded with muscle as the legs of any peon who labors in the mines or in the fields. She took me up to the floor above and led me into a corner room. It had a good prospect through two windows, one over the eastern reach of the valley, and one straight up into the

southern mountains. But view was about all that room could
offer. There was a cot with a goatskin over it and a straw pal-
let—and no other bedding whatever. There was a worn and
faded grass mat on the floor, and one stool like the one on which
I had sat in the garden below. There was also a homemade table,
very small, and a wooden bowl on it, and a bucket of water
beside it, and a coarse towel thrown over the top of the wooden
bowl. Here was the total equipment to receive a guest, and I
had little doubt that this was as good accommodation as one
could expect to receive in the house. Of course, I had roughed
it in worse quarters than this. But what I looked suddenly toward
was the picture of Doloridas, delicate, slender, frail, and all the
sorrow of her name standing in her eyes. She of all living crea-
tures to be raised up in such a house as this.

I turned back from the window toward the *moza*, who was
standing in the door. She had not been waiting to receive my
orders, but had lingered there, it appeared, to have another
glance at me. For now I saw her finishing her survey, without
hurry, and something between a sneer and a grin on her face. I
never saw or received a more evil glance than this in all my
life, except once. She did not banish her grin when she saw that
she was observed. Only, presently, she shrugged her lean, mus-
cular shoulders and withdrew, and went down the outer hall with
the springing step of a young athlete, rather than that of a matron
of some forty-odd winters.

I sat down on the casement and smoked a cigarette and tried
to think matters over. But, to save my life, I could not manage
it. For it seemed to me that I was merely more definitely than
ever committed inside the frame of a picture, and that like any
other production of the artist who had put me in it, I possessed
no authority or governance over my own actions. What was to
be done with me would be done, and I could fold my hands
and wait. Because of this inward observation, rather naturally I
could not calm myself, and I smoked my cigarette so fiercely
that I burned my lips with it before I was aware. So I threw it
away and spent a moment running over the mechanism of my
revolver. It was new, and it shot strongly and well, as most Colts
do. I was not a bad hand with it. But as I sat there in the
casement, it seemed to me that I had been the most careless

jackass in the world and that the manifest duty of every human was to spend at least an hour a day in the use of firearms.

I had not spent that hour. I had selected my opportunities. Now I should, perhaps, need to use weapons as an artist uses a musical instrument, and I should be found lacking in the moment of need. Well, there was no point at all in sitting stiff and mourning about calamities which, at least, had not yet happened. So I left my room and started exploring the house a little. But it was such a jumble that I needed a guide to make head or tail of it. I very soon got into the ruined part of it, and there it was plain that I had guessed rightly. What had knocked it about was a force that burst on the inside, for the walls leaned back, but the fragments of the roof did not lie on the floors of the despoiled rooms. The whole roof here seemed to have been blown off, and there was a blackened pit from which the explosion appeared to have come. I looked at this thing with an increased trouble. The whole house seemed filled with gloominess.

Then I followed the remnants of a broken staircase out of that blackened pit and so up to the roof of the house. This was much better. Even where the roof had fallen in, there was a broad rampart remaining at the sides, although the surface of it was much broken, of course. One could make the big circuit of the house itself and all about the walls, even the walls of the patio to the gates. That was the walk I took, and found the gates still closed, and, outside of them, I looked down at a ragged shepherd who was squatted on a rock, but instead of a crook he was leaning on an old rifle. My shadow from the wall brushed across him, and he looked up quickly. Like all the others who were connected with the place, when he first saw me, he gave me a sinister and foreboding grin. Then, slowly and deliberately, he took off his straw hat and saluted me; but he did not rise. There was a good deal of mockery, I thought, in that courtesy of the peon's.

"If you wait long enough down there," I said to him, "a deer may walk up and wait for you to shoot it."

He grinned back at me. He showed me his long rows of white teeth, and his nostrils flared a little, as the cheek muscles pulled at them. "Even a bear might come, *señor*," he said.

"Yes," I agreed, "even a bear. That's pretty strong meat, but there's lots of it."

"Or a mountain lion might come," went on the guard.

"Yes, or a mountain lion."

"And jump even this wall, *señor*?" he said. His eyes flashed significantly at me.

"Jump the wall to steal chickens?" I asked.

"*Hai!*" said the man, more excited than ever. "You don't know about the mountain lions that we have here?"

"No. I don't know about them," I said. "You tell me, my friend."

"Yes," he answered, "as I am your friend, I must tell you. It is this. The mountain lions all around us in these hills, they have a strange appetite, *señor*. The flesh that they like the best is the flesh of *gringos!*" His sneer was filled with the most deliberate malice.

"They must be very thin cats," I said sarcastically.

"No," said the peon, "they are fat . . . but the diet makes them mangy!"

I felt like climbing down and punching his round, brown face for him. There's nothing that can be as insolent as a Mexican, when the humor strikes him. However, I saw that there was no use trying to get down that wall, and still less use in inviting him to come up and argue the point with me. Americans were not popular in this corner of the world. That was simply all that there was to it.

"You know, *amigo*," I said to him, "that every hole is not a rat hole?"

"I have heard that," he said.

"And," I continued, "while you sit there and watch for the mouse, perhaps a snake will come out and taste all of you at one bite."

He rubbed the lock of his rifle with affectionate hands as he heard me say this. Still he sneered, and grinned, and looked despitefully up to me. "I have killed snakes, too," he said. "I always blow their heads off, because the fools cannot help pointing themselves down the gun barrel."

I could not help laughing a little. I mean to say, this man's malice was so open and his hatred of the *gringo* was so sincere that it stopped being offensive. It was a caricature. When I laughed, he actually opened his mouth and gaped at me. He seemed amazed by my mirth. But, after a moment, he shut his mouth again and began nodding his head, as one who understands.

"The sheep are that way, too," he said again.

"What way?" I asked.

"Happy even in the slaughterhouse," he explained.

It was a little more than my nerves could stand. I glowered for a moment at him. He was grinning once more, triumphant at having caught me so easily. Then I got my dignity together as well as I could and marched off from him. I circled back on the rampart.

The view straight down, on all sides except that of the gates, was a pretty dizzy thing. In one place, I dare say, that the almost sheer drop amounted to something like a hundred yards down to the floor of the valley. This great height made the big, old house seem smaller, perched rather lightly on its crag. From the added height, too, I had a good view of the entire valley and could mark every twist of the creek. It was running rose and gold now, until it carried all of its color and brightness into the blue mists at the foot of the valley, where a gorge slit sharply, like an axe cut, through the mountains that were ranged there. It was an odd thing to imagine the milliards of years that trickle of water must have consumed, cutting through such a mass of solid rocks!

The mountains, now that I was held up among them, took more of my attention than the plain. A wild lot were those peaks. They had a raw look, as though their bare heads had just been heaved up from the sea level the day before and they were still glittering with the salty water, although they had picked up some forests upon their shoulders in rising. From the western peaks, flags of clouds streamed out in long pennons that snapped off at the ends and kept shooting volleys of little fog puffs across the blue. I watched them with fascination, for the sunset was coloring them all, and each one differently.

The wind was growing colder rapidly. A damp chill was in it, and I felt that it was the breath of the oncoming night. I had a foolish thought of how far night had to creep up from the dark world before it could master this height, and, as I turned from looking upward toward the bright sky, I saw that Doloridas was standing there before me, precariously near the verge of the rampart.

Chapter Ten

" 'There's a Lion' "

Now, when my eye was taken so suddenly from the hugeness of the mountains, and the sweep of the clouds in the wind, and brought down to the single form of the girl, she seemed to me a child, and I most certainly a fool and a brute for coming here to pursue her. I got off my hat and went up to her, and, although I thought that I could see her wincing away from me a little, there was so much fine courtesy in her that she met me with a smile and a little inclination of her head and body that was almost another curtsey.

I said to her: "*Señorita* María, will you listen to me a little?"

"Don José," she said, "I came up here to talk to you, if I could." She blushed a little, as though there were some guilt in this. And then she went on: "There's no other place where we could talk safely together, but here the wind will blow our words away as fast as they are spoken."

It was an odd way of putting it. One might have thought that words were concrete substances, likely to fall like leaden bullets, or images which could be picked up and afterward read by others.

It put a good deal of honor in me to have her begin in this fashion, so I said: "Your uncle goes about things in a very harsh sort of a way. I don't want you to understand me as being of a mind with him."

The fear seemed to be quite out of her. She looked at me rather with pity and curiosity.

I went on: "You know, María, that I came down here . . . to . . . er . . ."

I stuck on this. The girl astonished me by coming to my help.

"You came down here because you saw a picture of me, and you saw that I had a pretty face," she said. There was no boldness or immodesty in her saying. Instead, she was not even coloring. She put up her slim hands to the sides of her head, as though she were measuring and making small the face of which she had been speaking.

"Yes," I said. "That's the reason of it. But you know, María, that a man thinks that he can see something besides prettiness in some faces. I don't want to rush along into compliment and make a fool of myself before I know you. But that's the truth, and . . ."

She lifted a hand to stop me. "There's no reason to apologize for saying anything to me," said the girl. "My uncle will have us dead or married inside of twelve hours, I think. If he can drag us to it."

That silenced me.

She went on: "And there's nothing that either of us can do about it. You cannot get away, now that you've been closed into the house, unless someone shows you how to get out of the place. And there's only one person who will show you how to manage that."

"Who is that?" I said.

"I will do it," she said.

A good hot wave of romantic hope jumped up in me. "You want to escape from the house with me, María?" I said.

She smiled shyly at me. "What good would it do for me to try to run away? He could catch me."

"Your uncle has a wooden leg, after all," I said, "and we might be able to go as fast as his hired men."

"My uncle?" said the girl. "No, no! I'm not speaking of him.

154

I mean that other one, who can climb these walls as a squirrel climbs a little tree."

"What other?" I asked.

She gaped at me, and, putting out her hand, she rested it on the top of the wall and seemed to need that support. "Good heavens," she said, "do you tell me that you came down here without knowing about him?"

"Not a word," I said. "I know nothing. I only know the picture of you, and yourself and your uncle as I've seen you. That's about my limit of knowledge, María. I've tried to guess a good deal, but I haven't managed very much."

She looked about her in a desperate way, as a person does when there's a great explanation to offer, and no words in which to put it. "Tell me this, *señor*," she said. "Was it a friend of yours who showed you my picture?"

I thought back to Chip. He was a queer boy, but I would have banked his friendship, or his good faith, at least, against a million. "Yes," I replied, "a friend."

She cried out: "You're wrong! He's a lying friend, and a man who wants to see you dead, or he never would have sent you here."

I was falling into a panic again, rather naturally, but there are limits past which most of us won't be driven in fear, at least, in the daytime. Now I shrugged my shoulders. I said: "Look here, María. It seems that somewhere in the mountains, there's a lion of a man. . . ."

"Ah, yes," she agreed. "A lion!"

"And he's going to come in here and eat me alive. Is that it?"

"What can keep him from it?" she answered, putting out both her hands, palms up.

That answer was sufficiently naïve. It was sufficiently convincing, too. But I remained logical. "There are the walls," I said, "for one thing."

"He will climb them as if they were a low board fence," said Doloridas.

"And then there is your uncle and his servants, who seem a tough lot," I went on.

"They will run from him as mice run from a cat," she said.

155

"Besides, I think they love him. They serve my uncle, I don't know why . . . but they would serve that other, because they love him."

"Then," I said, "supposing he's come through everything else, and he lands here, there's still me, isn't there? I'm not a great hero, but I can put up some sort of a fight."

She watched me, and nodded. "You are brave, *señor*."

"Not so brave, either," I responded. "But will you tell me, María, if I have some sort of a hope . . . if there's a hope possibly in front of me, supposing I should win through this fight, with whoever it may be?"

"A hope of what?" she said, frowning, and a little bluntly.

"Of you," I said equally bluntly.

"No," she said, and slowly shook her head.

This bluntness of hers angered me a good deal this time, and I said: "There's always that hope remaining . . . that your uncle will drag us together, as you say, and marry us off."

She did not even flush. "You would be dead within an hour afterward," she said.

"I don't think so," I said. "Another thing, María. What makes you so sure that no one could have a chance with you? Let me have the right to ask you if you've promised yourself to any other man?"

"No."

"And then what locks you up so?" I asked.

"I never shall marry."

"Say," I responded, "that's a pretty young way of talking. You're a man hater, then. Is that it, María?"

She smiled away from me in a singular manner, at the mountains and the moving, rosy sky.

"No," she said. "I hate no one. But I've seen enough of men!" She broke out at me, then: "Don't you suppose that I have a reason for what I'm saying? Do you think I'm talking only to draw you on, further and further? Oh, I tell you that I've seen reasons as red as the best blood in your heart, *señor!*"

She pointed down. I could conjure up dead men at her feet. Her face was pale and tragic. I must say that during this little talk she seemed to have drawn a great distance away from me. I felt that she was a very superior being, and that I was barely worthy of kissing the ground at her feet. But I also felt that there was nothing in the world half so worth having as herself.

"You won't ask for reasons any more, *señor*," she continued. "You understand now that I mean what I say, and that you are to forget me? And tonight, I'll come quickly after darkness and show you the way from your room. Are you a brave climber? Are you not afraid of great heights and climbing with a rope?"

"I should say that I'll go," I admitted sullenly.

"You will say so," remarked the girl, very sure of herself. "You are not so young as some of the others," she added gloomily.

"I should say that I'll go," I said. "But the fact is that the more you convince me with your talk, María, the giddier I'm getting in the wits. I ought to do as you say. You don't care a whit about me. You probably never will. But all the same, I can't pull myself away. You starve a cat long enough, María, and it'll sneak into the kitchen and stay there, no matter how hard you beat it."

This girl came suddenly up to me and threw well back the hood that the wind was sweeping about her, and let the flow of the air press her clothes about her as closely and smoothly as though she had been suddenly drenched in water. She held out her arms to me, and raised her face in a way that I never can forget, and she said: "Look at me, *señor!*"

"Heaven knows, María," I said, "that I am looking with all my heart."

"But you're not seeing the truth. You're only seeing this instant, and you don't know what will be left of me five years from now, or how I'll be scored and marked and bent and writhen. Oh, Don José," she said and began to cry like a child, "I'm not what you think. I'm not proper for you to look at, as you're looking now. You had better take home a curse with you than to take home me!"

I don't know what I should have done or said—except that I must have told her that I would welcome a thousand times over a curse wearing her face. But just then a loud voice that had both a boom and a ring to it shouted up from the center of the house, as if out of the bowels of the earth: "Doloridas!"

She shrank. She snatched the cloak about her as though to

hide herself. "I must go!" she said, her frightened eye lingering on me a last and desperate instant. "Heaven, give you wisdom. Heaven give you strength. Pray for us both, as I shall pray."

And off she went, and the bull-bellow of Ruan rose and roared and rang again, calling for her.

Chapter Eleven

"Pierce Collins"

I had supper with Ruan, outside the house, in a corner of the patio. The gate had been thrown open, and we could look out through it toward the end of the day. As the dusk grew thicker and thicker, big torches—the most primitive kind, made of resinous pine wood—were brought out and kindled. Four of them flamed and snapped and cast out dazzling yellow sparkles, while the black smoke went shooting up above their heads. They made a wild company, from my point of view. And they cast a proper kind of light over the brutal face of Ruan.

The girl was not with us, and, when I asked after her, he said with his smile that she was tired, after her chat with me.

"You take a woman that has to talk ag'in' a high wind like that," said Ruan, "and it tires her a lot, eh? Particular when all her talk goes for nothing. I've got a little disappointment of my own to tell you about."

I asked what it could be, and he said: "Why, the good, honest, fat brown *padre* . . . he looks enough like me to be my brother . . . ain't coming here tonight for the marriage."

"Ill?" I asked.

"Likely," Ruan answered. "He ain't to be found, at least. He's gone and disappeared. That's what our mountain lion has managed, this time. But then, he always has his little tricks. Always a trick here or a trick there. A cat's a mighty smart beast, son, and it takes a wakeful man to beat it."

I could agree heartily enough to that. I said: "What's the name of this fellow . . . this lion . . . this wildcat that everyone talks about so much?"

"Oh, he has a lot of names," said Ruan. "He has so many names that it likely wouldn't do any good if I was to tell you about 'em. You eat your supper and go to bed early, and have a good sleep. The morning'll be the time for you and María. She done her best to talk you down, I reckon?"

I avoided his face. I could not bear to see his grin as he spoke to me of the girl. "She did her best," I said. "Nobody could do more than she did. What my position ought to be, I don't know. I'm pretty well baffled."

"I'll tell you your position," Ruan said calmly. "Your position is between the devil and the deep blue sea. The devil is the pretty face of the girl that you want. The deep blue sea is conscience. Conscience is always putting up a fight for us . . . to get us into heaven . . . and conscience is always losin' the fight. You go up to bed, and don't you bother no more about your worryin'. You'll do what any man would do, when the time comes. You'll take the girl, and spend a week or two thankin' fortune that you've got her. Besides, the fact is that she don't know much about men, son. You take that fact in mind, and you'll see that kindness and all that would pretty soon make her fond of you. Them that marry out of love are in the worst way. There's no place to go except downhill. And that's the fastest and the worst way to go. But them that marry just by agreement, why, they've got no place to go except up . . . which is fine for the view . . . or straight ahead on the level, which is the easiest way of all."

He seemed in a humor to talk a great deal, but I had had enough of him for that occasion. I left the table, as he had suggested, and went up to my room, where I sat gloomily by the light of a bad-smelling, homemade candle. The candle soon melted down into its little stone basin, and the wick, hanging over the lip of the basin, continued to burn, or rather, to fume—

giving only a treacherous glimmer of light in the room. I knew very well that I could not sleep, so I lay down and tried to think things out, and find something worthwhile in my thoughts. But all I could do was to repeat, like one hypnotized, the words of Ruan, when he said that I was between the devil and the deep blue sea. I was between the devil and the deep blue sea. And the devil, as he had suggested, was more than reasonably sure to win. While this was going on in my mind, I forgot even the words of Ruan, and lost myself in watching the waves of shadows as they washed back and forth across the ceiling of the room.

Well, I was about as unhappy and worried as a man can be. I was worried because I felt that I was being drawn into a dastardly rôle, and I was frightened because of the unnamed fellow who, like a wildcat, roamed through the mountains and, it seemed, could not be kept from leaping into the house and carrying away living men like mice between his jaws. I wriggled at the thought, and, as I wriggled, I heard something between a sigh and a groan in my room. I could not even sit up. I was frozen too stiff for that. And then I remembered that, like a jackass, I had left my revolver upon the chair and not taken it with me when I stretched on the bed. I was helpless. There was not a weapon within my grasp.

I heard the same sound repeated, and then it seemed to me that it was not actually in the room, but just outside—at a window—no, at the door, perhaps. I heard it again. It was the same moaning sound that I had listened to before, and now I felt a return of courage. Things that sigh and moan were not what I would essentially fear. I got up from the bed, caught hold of my revolver, and tiptoed to the door, listened, and thought that I heard the faint whisper of breathing just outside of it.

"Who's there?" I said.

"Pierce Collins, about all in. Open the door and give me a hand, will you?"

This might be a mere ruse to get my door open, of course, but the gasp of the speaker was sufficient to reassure me. It's the sound that comes out when a man is sick with pain. I pulled my door open, and, by the shaking light from my room's lamp, I saw a long fellow sprawled upon the floor of the hall. He was struggling to his hands at the moment, and I leaned over him.

"Get me into your room," he said. "Get me onto a bed and covered up. The cold of the stones is biting through me like teeth. I thought I was gonna die here like a fish out of water. Take me in for mercy's sake, will you? I came here to do you a good turn, and now it's like to be the death of me."

I could not help believing in him. I leaned over, got a good grip under his shoulders, and pulled him like a sack into my room, and dragged him onto my bed in the same fashion. Then I hurried back to close the door to the hall, for it seemed to me that all sorts of dangers were running with a tiptoe whisper of speed to get at me through that opening. I closed and locked and bolted the door, and braced the stool against it. Then I came back to Pierce Collins.

He lay exactly where I had left him, his arms flopping clumsily at his sides, a faint pucker between his eyes, and his lips working a little. Yes, he felt pretty sick. There was no doubt about that. I thought he was a mighty good-looking fellow, of the thin-faced and long-drawn-out type. But he seemed to be cut clean, and cut right. I put a hand over his heart. It went fast and fluttering, but there was no real stagger to him, and I guessed that he was not so badly off as he thought. So I said: "Look here, Collins, you're better than you think. You're gonna be all right."

"Thanks, old son," he said, in something better than a whisper. "I guess I'll be better. When I slipped and fell in the hall, I thought that the strain had busted the wounds open again. Feel under my coat. Is there any blood running?"

That gave me a bit of a jar, all right. But I felt under his coat, and it was all dry across his breast. I found where the broad, thick bandage went right around it. "Somebody got you pretty close to the wick," I suggested to him. "But there's no blood running now. You're dry as a board."

"Thank heaven," Collins said. "Yes, I was trimmed. I was pretty nearly put out. But that's all right, too. I feel better, now that I know the blood didn't start. My God, partner, how it takes it out of a fellow to think that the blood has started."

I could see that Pierce Collins was no hero. But neither am I, so it didn't matter so much.

He went on: "Bend a little closer. I want to save my strength all I can. I have to get back down that hall pretty soon to my room. I've come here to give you a tip, old son. Will you take it?"

"I ought to," I said, "after you've spent so much trouble to get here. What's the tip about?"

"Doloridas," he answered.

I grunted, the name hit me so close to home.

"Yeah," he said, seeming to recognize the sound that I had made. "I was that way about her. Until I got tapped with a Forty-Five-caliber slug. And that let out all the romance, I tell you."

"You came here because of her?" I asked.

"Yes."

"Did a kid go and fetch you?" I asked.

"A kid? What kid? What sort of a kid would go and fetch me?" he asked, puzzled.

"It's nothing," I said. I was relieved to see that Chip was not a mere rat-catcher. "You came here account of María . . . and this is what happened to you. How thick were you with the girl?"

"Not with her at all," he responded. "I fixed it up with her father. That's the Mexican way, you know. I fixed it up with him, for me and Doloridas. Everything went along pretty well. . . ."

"What did the girl think?" I interrupted.

"They don't think much, Mexican girls," said Collins. "They let their families do the thinking for them. It's not a bad way. They get on pretty well, afterward, it looks to me. Only this time, nobody counted on the other one."

"What other one?" I asked.

"El Blanco," he answered.

"Who is that?" I asked.

"Who . . . is . . . that?" he said, letting his voice rise with each word a little. "Why, El Blanco is the original fiend. That's what he is! And he's a fiend that wants María de los Dolores, and he jumped the wall of this here house, when he heard what I was after . . . and this is what happened to me. And that's why I come dragging down the hall to let you know. He'll jump the wall for you, too. And you won't turn out as lucky as I did."

A door banged in the distance. I jumped halfway across the room, when I heard it. Then I hurried back to my wounded man.

"He'll murder any man who wants María?" I asked. "But he didn't murder you!"

"No, because I knuckled under," said Collins. "And I swore to him that I'd never look at her again. And now you come, poor chap, and you're between El Blanco and Ruan . . . and heaven help you, and heaven help the girl, too."

Chapter Twelve

"Under the Brow of Peril"

Even before this, I had not been feeling particularly chipper. Now I felt a good deal worse, naturally. At last I said to him: "Did the girl ask you to do this?"

"What?" he muttered.

"To come here and tell me these things?"

"Yes," he admitted. "She's pretty decent. She's like you, between the fear of El Blanco and Ruan, her uncle."

"What makes him want to see her married off?" I asked.

"Don't you know that?" asked Collins.

"No, I can't imagine, except that he's such a fiend that he doesn't want her around the house with him."

"The house won't be his until she's married. That's the terms of the will his brother made when he died."

"Was her father worried about getting her married off?" I asked. "Why, she could find a husband in every block of a big city."

"A white American husband, though, is not so easy to come at, down here," Collins said. "They have to be fetched in, you might say."

"Just how were you fetched in?" I asked.

"Oh, I was down here doing some prospecting. That was all. I just happened to see her and her uncle together, when they were out riding. Everything flowed out of that like water running downhill. You know how it is."

I thought of the beauty of the girl, and it seemed to me that the whole world would follow if it saw her.

"You'll not be a fool, man," said Collins, urging me on. "You'll let the girl show you out from the house tonight, won't you?"

"This fellow, this El Blanco," I pursued, "is he as much poison as all that?"

"There's no more poison in the world!" Collins said very heartily. "He's all out for himself. And a cold-blooded devil, too. If he found me here in your room, he'd cut my throat along with yours and . . ."

Collins had talked himself into a thoroughgoing panic by this time; he seemed to feel that El Blanco, like a cat, was walking right into the room. I had a good deal of the same feeling myself, but his terror, instead of being contagious, sobered me and steadied me a little. I told him that I was mighty grateful for the warning he had given me, and that now the first thing was to get him back to his room. So I took him under the armpits and helped him into the hall. A gust of wind came down it with a rush and a chilly whisper, and Collins wilted in my arms and moaned. But I managed to hold him up until he had made the two or three turns necessary to get to his room.

It was a duplicate of mine for barrenness, but it was long and narrow as a tunnel, with one window, like a single eye, looking down through the length of it. Collins peered about fearfully at it as though he were seeing it for the first time. Finally he nodded, as though to admit that it might be his apartment. I got him over to his bed, and he lay down, shuddering and groaning and muttering that he wished he never had seen the cursed house of Ruan.

I could have seconded that wish, except for Doloridas. So I went slowly out of that room and down the hall toward my own room. Enough moonlight to show the way slanted through the windows, but in spite of that I lost my direction—I think it was because I must have gone down, instead of up, a certain flight of steps. At any rate, all at once I walked straight out into the old, ruined garden.

I had a cold feeling that my fate had brought me there. It was like being pushed onto a stage before an audience that I could not see. It seemed to me that the moon was pouring down the sweet, thin odor of jasmine. As for the garden itself, between sun and moonlight, it was transformed. The wrinkles, one might say, had gone out of it, and it presented a young and lovely face.

I went over to the parapet that looked east down the valley. To the west, the plain was as clearly printed out as at noonday, but here to the east the moon mist clouded everything from side to side. Sometimes the river flashed a bright curve through this luminous fog, and sometimes the rocks were glinting, but on the whole there was little to be seen here.

I remember thinking that, after all, a man's life was something like this, and even the brightest parts of it were clouded over, let's say, with too much light, and the true facts of it came flashing through in mere bits and moments. I grew more and more the fatalist. If I were to die here in the house because of Ruan, why, I would die, and that would be an end of it. I took a good grip on the handle of my Colt, and that made me feel better. As for El Blanco, he was only mortal. If I could hit a rabbit—now and then—I might also be able to hit a man. I was being logical, you see, and there's nothing in the world so dangerous as logic; it leads you into pits a mile deep.

Now I saw something flutter from the corner of my eye, and I turned about and saw María de los Dolores coming toward me. Not that I knew her at first, for she wore a wide-brimmed riding hat and the rest of her was swallowed up in a big cloak. But when a woman once has touched a man's heart, she cannot come near without stirring it like music again. So I knew her even before I could penetrate through the thick black of shadow that fell across her face. She paused by the dead fountain, and her gesture in drawing her cloak closer about her shoulders made me sure of her.

I went over and met her. I said: "Look here, Doloridas, you ought not to be wandering about alone at night in this house."

"But you see, *señor*," she said, "I am not alone."

And, with a charming gesture, she indicated me, and drew me into her company and her intimacy. It jumped my heart over a mountain and brought it down singing. I moved a little closer to her and made sure that she was actually smiling a little.

"Doloridas," I said, "you've come out here to see me. About what?"

"To take you out of the house," she said. "To take you out before he comes!"

"El Blanco?" I ventured. "I don't care, if he comes riding a dragon. I'm going to stay here. I was doubting myself a while back, but now I've seen you smile. And I'm staying here. I wouldn't budge without you."

"Look," she said, "I am dressed for riding."

I caught her by the arms. I turned her toward the moon, and she bent her head back a little and let me see her smile.

"By the eternal jumping thunder, my dear," I said, "do you want me to guess that you care a little about me?"

She said nothing. She only opened her eyes and looked up at me. And that was enough to make my head swim. I held her until I could feel the warmth of her body and the beat of her heart. Then I leaned and kissed her lips. They were cold, and a small shudder went through her, but she did not draw away. I asked myself if the shudder were on account of my nearness; but then I decided that this could not be, for she made no effort to escape. It was a miracle that she could care for a common, plain-faced man like me. But no matter what a pagan a man may be, when it comes to love, he puts his trust in heaven and is willing to believe in miracles. I believed in this one.

"If you will ride with me, Doloridas," I said, "I'll go now, and I'll keep on riding to the end of the world with you. Shall we go now?"

"I'm ready," she said.

"Then lead me as far as the horses, and, after that, I'll gladly lead in my turn."

She turned away from me without a word, but looking back over her shoulder toward me with that faint, cold smile that had half maddened me with joy before. Oh, women are fools when their smiles grow too broad. All that they need to do is to touch a man with a single glance.

We did not cross through the patio at all. Instead, we went back from the garden and down a few twists of stone steps, some of them moist and slippery, until we reached, in this way, a place that seemed far underground. Here we found a complete stable with nine or ten horses and mules tethered. My roan was among them, and, when it got the wind of me, it greeted me with a whinny that sounded like a growl from a dog. However, I was mighty glad to see it again. I asked the girl what she would ride and what I should saddle for her, but I was surprised to see that she was already leading out a mule, already saddled and bridled.

It gave me a slight shock. It seemed to imply, in a stroke, that she was entirely sure of her power, and that, before she so much as spoke to me, she had made all of her preparations for the flight. But I was not in a humor to be too critical. Whatever she wished to do would be well done in my eyes.

She pointed out a sliding door that must be opened. So I pushed it out, and it made a faint, thunderous rumbling that chilled my nerves.

She passed through, and, as she passed, looking up at the sheer height of the wall of masonry, I heard her say: "Heaven forgive me!"

"Forgive you for what, María?" I asked her.

But she did not hear me, or at least she did not seem to hear me, and I, in the meantime, was closing that sliding door again, and thanking heaven that we had got clear so easily. All of those armed guards, set to keep out the wildcat attacks of El Blanco, had not been able to prevent our departure—wild and careless crew that they were. But still we were under the brow of peril.

The door had opened at the base of the hill on which the house of Ruan stood, and now we had directly before us the moon mist of the eastern valley.

As we rode out, down the easy pitch of the slope toward the plain, I looked back for a farewell glance to the lofty old house and its immense bastions, and, as my eye ran up the line of the wall, I saw in an open casement, like a picture painted in black and white, the face, the thick shoulders, and the folded arms of Ruan himself!

No one can tell what a shudder the thing cast through me. If he had had a rifle at his shoulder, ready to fire, that would have been nothing, compared to the vast, placid, evil smile on his face. The mere folding of his fat arms seemed to tell me that, no matter how far I went, how hard I rode, I still would be simply executing the will of the master of the house, and would never get beyond his power.

Chapter Thirteen

"Danger in Front"

The girl was a little in the lead. I hurried to catch up with her.

"He's watching us, Doloridas," I whispered to her. "Ride faster."

"Oh, fast horses or sure-footed mules will do us no good now," said the girl, wonderfully steady. "Ride straight on, José. There is no danger behind us. All the danger is in front." She waved before us.

I was utterly amazed by her calm. I asked her: "Do you know a safe place to make for?"

"There are friends I can trust in the town of San Jacinto," the girl said. "If we can get there, we are perfectly safe. There are such friends in San Jacinto that not even El Blanco will dare to make trouble." She tossed back her head in a way that I was to remember later on, and there was a sort of fierce triumph in her voice. "There are such friends in San Jacinto that they would tear out the claws of the tiger, one by one!"

She made a fierce gesture, while I watched, amazed at her emotion.

"He has walled me up in that horrible old house. . . . Even my uncle was no match for him. But now I trust that you will match him, José."

She reached out and laid her head on my arm, and she leaned somewhat toward me with a smile that might have opened gates of iron—to say nothing of my poor soul.

I said: "Did your uncle consent to let you go tonight? He told me that you would stay, and I would stay until . . ."

"That was what he always was saying," she answered, "until I pleaded with him. And I swore that one day El Blanco would jump into the house and carry me off like a mouse between his teeth. And then what of all the plans of my uncle? El Blanco has laid his power like two great arms around our house. Half of our servants are his spies. He has corrupted the people who work in the fields. Everyone works for him. There was no one to trust." She gave a shivering moan. Then, sweeping her hand to this side and to that, she went on: "We lived on a wretched little island in the midst of a great river. That was the power of El Blanco. And then came that weak man . . . that *Señor* Collins . . . that coward and fool!"

I gaped, when I heard her. "Oh, but after all," I tried to explain "Collins wanted to help you all he could. You're pretty hard on him, María." As I said this, I could see her eyes burn at me.

"He surrendered to one man," she went on. "Only a dog would do such a thing as that. He surrendered to one man. He begged for his life. What is the life of such a creature as that worth, I ask you, José?"

I found that this was a little bit hard to answer, to tell the truth. For, you see, there was a ring and a force in the voice of María de los Dolores that staggered me. I thought that this force gave strength and character to her, no doubt, but I also thought that it loaned her a touch of hardness, and I could not help remembering that there are bull fights and other cruelties in Mexico. But, after all, one must not criticize in the individual the faults of the race.

"Doloridas," I said, "you may rate Collins low . . . but I might have done exactly as he did. I'm no hero. And that's not modesty, either."

She turned her head and watched me, and said not a word. I

grew mighty uncomfortable in the pause, I can assure you.

"You would do more for me, José!" she said at last. "Now is the time for us to ride. Even my uncle felt that there might be good fortune lodged in you. You must ride now." She set the example by striking her mule with her heels, and that mule began to run as I never had seen a mule run before. Usually, they have a short, jerking gait. They are made for walking or for a short-stepping jog trot. But this animal could gallop freely.

The roan, of course, kept up without any trouble. But, after twenty minutes of stiff going, the roan was feeling the pace more than the mule.

Doloridas rode very well. All her people have a gift for work in the saddle, and she was not an exception. The cloak blew streaming from her shoulders, the wind of the gallop pressed against her, but still, over rough or smooth, she was able to turn and give a long regard to the distance in which the house of Ruan stood.

At last she said: "There it is! Look, José!"

I looked back, and in three places on the highest part of the Ruan walls I could see fires burning.

"They give our direction, José," said the girl.

"We'll switch directions, then," I said suddenly.

"It's no good trying," she answered. "San Jacinto has to be our goal. There's no other, now that we've come this far. Otherwise, they'll have us running from point to point all night, and in the morning they'll round us up like two poor cattle . . . and there's death for you in that, José, and something worse for me."

I understood her perfectly well.

We reached the stream in the center of the valley now, and Doloridas insisted that we should not go out of our way to ride to the nearest bridge, but that we should attempt to ford. It was almost the end of both of us. The water was shallow and the stream was not wide, but it leaped at us like running volleys of spears. When the current was no higher than the knees of the horses, it washed up in curling ripples as high as their bellies. They staggered, and finally the roan, that was working upstream of the mule to break the force of the water a little, pitched his head under and was rapidly whirling down the current in a trice. That should have been the end of both of us. For there were enough pointed rocks, a little farther down, to have eaten us like shark's teeth.

But Doloridas saved us. She had gotten her mule into the shallows, and, uncoiling a rawhide rope from the pommel of her saddle—I had not noticed it there before—she threw it with an aim as good as that of any *vaquero*. She snared the head of the roan, and the pull the mule gave fetched us both into the safe shallows. The roan was half choked, and I was more than half scared to death, but at least we were safe, though shuddering with something more than cold.

Doloridas did not seem in the least alarmed. She sat her mule on the top of the bank, calmly recoiling the rope, and laughing down at me, as I came up the bank on the roan, like a wet mouse on a wet rat.

Then we straightened our animals across country, and Doloridas pointed out to me the gap between the mountains, which was the entrance to that gorge in which San Jacinto lay. It looked very close now. Not even that mist of the moon shrouded the mouth of it, which was guarded by two long, sloping hills, like couchant beasts, rudely cut from the rock. Like guardians they looked to me. For inside of them we ought to find our safety.

I said to Doloridas, as we allowed the animals to walk up a slope: "There's no danger, my dear. There's not a thing in view. There's not a sight to be seen. Everything's well with us to-night."

"José!" she cried back at me impatiently, angrily. "Oh, be a brave man and a wise man. Danger is sure to jump up in our path before long. It's not a common man we have to handle. It's El Blanco himself. El Blanco himself!"

I grinned a little as the roan jolted into a canter again, down-hill, but I was beginning to see that Doloridas, sweet and gentle and frail as she was, nevertheless, had a will of her own, and that, after she was my wife, she might make things hum for me, now and then. Well, what could be better for me than a strong-minded helpmate? What could be better? Nothing that I could think of. Certainly I had drifted in a most foolish fashion about this world up to the present moment. Now I would do better. And Doloridas would be my panacea.

The Oath of Office

We were getting forward at a good pace. We were coming on toward the mountains at such a rate that they seemed to break up, separate, and all flow toward us, growing huger and huger, with the moon striking brilliancies from the rocks, making them seem metal, and the forests as dark as plumes. So we entered the San Jacinto gorge, and saw the two long, sloping hills that guarded the entrance slide past us upon either hand. I heaved a great breath of relief, for I felt that we were through the gate of safety.

But Doloridas, it was plain, was not relaxing. She rode crouched in her saddle like a jockey—or a cat. And ever and again her head was turning as she looked for danger about her. Yet nothing appeared. We had seen no living thing in all our way from the house of Ruan, and now the only noticeable sound about us was the groaning of the tired mule, and the snorting of the roan to clear its nostrils.

The thunder struck from that clear sky.

I saw the mule stumble, lurch forward, and then continue lurching, with its body falling faster than its weary feet could take up the ground. It struck heavily. It rolled head over heels and lay still. Doloridas was hurled from the saddle and struck through a path of brush ahead, and rolled from there onto the ground. I threw myself out of the saddle and ran to her, the rein of the mustang hooked over my arm, but she was already on her knees as I came up. Behind us the rifles were clanging, and the bullets thumped the rocks about us, or went with a brittle rattling through the brush.

I caught up Doloridas and swung her with one effort into the saddle of the roan. I had given one look to the mule and knew by that glance that he would never rise again.

"Go on!" I told her. "Go fast. I'll check 'em here, if I can. Get help from San Jacinto and rush them back . . . hurry, Doloridas . . . !"

"To leave you . . . ," she cried.

"For heaven's sake, or we're both gone!" I begged.

She looked behind. She saw the rush of the dark riders, and with no other word she bowed her head and flogged the roan into a full gallop.

175

Chapter Fourteen

"El Blanco Himself"

Impulse jumps us into strange situations, but never was there one stranger than this of mine. I turned about, and I saw that by a mere gesture, so to speak, I had placed myself in the boots of a hero. They were much too large for me. I saw that at once, but there I was, standing in them. The terrible, bold bright moon was glaring in my face, and through the moonshine, lunging up the narrow of the gorge, was that evil flight of riders, charging me.

At least, I had sense enough to see that I had no time to run, either to the right or to the left, and hide among the rocks. So, with my back to the wall, I lifted my rifle and tried to split that charge as though it were composed of Indians. I fired high, and I fired low, and those plunging, lunging fiends in full flight made no answer, but seemed to hold their fire, in contempt and ready to blast me from the face of the earth. For I could see the gleam of their weapons, held ready, and I could even make out some of the savage faces.

I felt that I was already dead. I stood with my finger crooked about the trigger unable to fire a third time, because I saw that there was no use in firing. Another instant and I would be riddled. I would be beaten shapeless under foot by the striding of half a dozen horses, and the same wave that destroyed me would wash swiftly up the valley and overwhelm poor Doloridas. This would be her last flight. Now, in one instant, under the very walls of San Jacinto, he would sweep her up.

Someone in the cavalry charge was laughing in a wild, triumphant voice, and I swore that was the man. But now, when the forefront of the wave was looming before me, I heard a voice that shrilled and squeaked above the uproar and that screeched, in perfectly familiar English accents: "Don't fire! Don't fire! It's Joe!"

Why, it was the voice of the boy, the voice of Chip, confound him! It was that same little scoundrel whose machinations—for what reason I could not guess—had brought me all this distance to the Southland, and plunged me into this very pit where I stood. In answer to that screech came a deeper, roaring voice of command, in Spanish, and it was something to the effect that he would brain the fellow who harmed a hair of me. Ah, well, there you are.

I should have died that instant, but the cry of Chip was the insect's sting that numbed the hand about to strike me, and the roaring voice of command turned that charge better than a shower of bullets could have done, so that all in a trice they had swirled away to this side, and to that, and they were sheltered among the rocks, while I, a single man, stood out there in the naked open of the sandy bottom of the little gorge, held up as in the palm of a hand to the full silver stream of the moonlight. Why, I was dead, and again dead, and a thousand times dead, if they chose to do the killing.

The barking voice of Chip squeaked and rattled at me: "Joe, Joe! Get out of the way! Throw your rifle down, or you're a goner. . . ."

I did not throw the rifle down. I was too stunned to react in time and stood there stunned, a fool, with the gun still in my hand.

"Let me shoot the *gringo* dog, *señor!* Let me shoot him, El Blanco!" I heard a Mexican screaming, in a fury of hatred and of battle lust.

177

But the same ringing voice which had commanded before now said: "It's too late. She's right under the gate of San Jacinto! She's saved!" He added, lowering his voice a little: "Joe, will you make a truce, confound you?"

Out into the moonshine, without waiting for my answer, stepped the leader, the celebrated El Blanco, the man-slayer, the wildcat who jumped the wall of a city at a bound. I saw before me none other than Dug Waters—White Water we used to call him—sauntering straight toward me, with one hand resting lightly on his hip.

"Dug Waters!" I gasped at him. "Dug Waters, of all men!"

"You've gone and turned yourself into a hero, since I last saw you, Joe," he said very calmly, but with bitterness enough in his voice.

"You!" I gasped at him, still more than half overcome. "You! El Blanco?"

"Yeah," he said, drawling as always. "El Blanco is what they call me in this neck of the woods. But, white or black, always the same, and your friend, Joe, since the night you helped to pry me out of the jail, and out of the hangman's noose."

He came close up to me and held out his hand. I took it, and I wrung it, I was so glad to see him again. Particularly at that instant.

"How could you help doing it, Dug?" I said. "How could you help blowing me to blasts out of your way, when I . . . ?"

I finished by pointing up the gorge, and, as I pointed, deeply booming and welling down the valley I heard the clangor of the alarm bell of old San Jacinto there behind us. It was like an answer to my gesture. It was a weird, a sudden, and an awful thing at that moment, as though the mountains were giving utterance.

That sound, mind you, was dull with distance, but the hideous clangor of it, the crowding, multiplying, echoing and reëchoing notes put a madness in the mind.

"Joe," said Waters, "I'm one of those simple fools who learns one thing at a time, and not many of those things . . . and, first of all, I learned always to stick to a partner. Which you were to me, one day, and which I therefore am to you forever! She's gone out of my hands, now and forever, I suppose. But I couldn't blast the rock out of the way, not if the rock wore your face, old-timer."

His men were coming out from the rocks with their horses now. A more savage crew I never saw in all my born days. They came up to me exactly as cats would come up to a bird. In spite of Dug Waters as a friend, I was frightened still.

"Only," said Dug Waters, "I'd like to know what made you do it? What brought you so far just for the sake of downing me, old son?"

"Downing you?" I said. "I have here wrapped up inside of my shirt what brought me all of the way to this place. I never thought about you at all."

"Just what brought you, then?" he said.

I took out the ivory plaque which I had had from Chip, and I unwrapped the silk that hulled about it and bared the face to Waters, as reverently as a mother bares the face of its sleeping child to a stranger.

He saw it, and then he started with a grunt. He whirled on his heel, calling out: "Chip! Come here!"

For an answer, there was a glimpse of the boy bounding onto the back of a mustang and then scurrying down the gorge.

"Catch him, some of you!" shouted Waters. "Take my horse, Pedro. Catch him, and bring him back the way a bird dog brings a bird. If you hurt him, I'll cut your throat. If you get him, I'll give you ten dollars."

I think every man of them shot into the saddle to try to win the glory and the cash reward for that service. Off they went like a roll of thunder that walks halfway down the arch of the sky while you count three. And before we could much more than count ten, they stopped the chase and started back for us, with the boy tethered and held fast among them.

He was dragged up before the chief, and then he was flung down to the ground just where we stood. It was that same Pedro who had been favored with the horse of his chief who had achieved the reward. He was the most beautiful villain I ever have seen. A great streak glistened like a mark of oil across half of his face. It was the sign of a frightful knife-cut in some brawl. He smiled, and it was like the horrible, brainless laugh of a fool—the scar tissue so pulled and twisted the face.

179

"Thank you, *señor*," he said, as he took the money. "I would as soon have done it for nothing, and I would rather have caught him with a rope than with my hands. I would rather have dragged him back at the end of the rope than carried him. You pay me for my own pleasure, *señor*."

I thought that Chip would twist himself in two, like the imp in the fairy story, he was so angry, when he heard this. He said: "You pie-faced, lantern-jawed, squint-eyed, half-nosed, raw-eared, half-wit. There never was a time when you could catch me, if somebody didn't give you a hoss too good for you. And there never was a time, after you caught me, that you could've handled me, if it hadn't been that you had a crowd with you. I'd meet you alone in day or dark, you skunk, and take off your hide in ten minutes by the clock, and you know it!"

This was a good deal to say to anyone. And it was a great deal too much to speak to hot Mexican blood. That Pedro didn't stop to reflect. He simply pulled a gun and made leap for Chip, and Chip looked to me halfway down the jaws of death. He stood straight and still, facing the rush, but at the last instant he collapsed as quicksilver from a bag. He dropped in a lump right at the feet of Pedro.

It's a good trick, but one of the very hardest that any fighting man ever learned. Pedro was reaching for the throat of the lad with his long, moon-bladed knife, and, just as he reached, his target disappeared, and Pedro found himself stubbing his toe against a rock. He tumbled head over heels, and landed with a grunt and a gasp, the wind flattened right out of him.

Young Chip, cool as you please, walked over and picked the knife out of the numbed fingers of the outlaw's hand.

"This has a pretty good point," he said, stepping back and trying the edge with his thumb. "You take my knife in exchange. It's good enough for the likes of you."

With that, he pulled out his own hunting knife and threw it straight through the throat of Pedro. No, not through the throat, though it seemed so at first, but right into the hard-packed sand at the side of Pedro's neck. The cold of the side of the knife blade sent a shiver through the whole body of Pedro.

The Mexican got up with a howl, and I think that he would

have charged Chip again, but the chief stopped him with a word. "You've got ten dollars and you've exchanged your knife, that's all," he said. "If you try that again, Chip will cut your throat for you, and if he doesn't . . . then I will."

Chapter Fifteen

"Forgiven"

This flurry seems not so much in the telling, but it made my wits spin to see it. It showed me the hand and heart of that mob of tigers, as it were. I wondered at a fellow like Dug Waters, who could live among these fellows and rule them so easily. He seemed perfectly at his ease, but the look that Pedro gave him, after receiving the rebuff, would have kept me awake for a month.

Now the attention turned back to Chip.

Waters said: "Tell me, you little miserable sneak-thief, chicken-lifter, and gunfighter, you worthless thug and train-wrecker, you . . . tell me what became of the picture that I used to own? The picture of Doloridas, I mean?"

"Why," Chip said, "you long-drawn-out son of a north wind and a black night, why the deuce should I talk to you, any-ways?"

Waters took him by the collar.

Chip answered with a neat wrestling hold that shook and almost tumbled Waters—but not quite. It was a strain and a tug, but he mastered Chip, and held him with an arm twisted behind his back.

Chip snapped over his shoulder like a dog biting at flies: "The next time, or pretty near the next, I'll put you down, Dug, you skinny four-flusher."

"The next time, I'll break your back for you," Dug Waters said. He was hot and half meant it. But I knew that this pair loved one another. They had proved it a thousand times.

"Now," said Dug, "will you answer me what I'm asking you?"

"Not if you break my arm out of the joint," said the kid through his teeth.

At that, Dug turned him loose.

I was amazed. The boy turned around, rubbing the shoulder that had been twisted, and Dug moved slowly away, with his back turned to him, thoughtfully scuffing at the sand.

"Hey!" Chip yelled.

"Well, partner," Dug said, and stopped, but didn't turn around.

"Am I still that?" asked the kid, with a shake in his voice.

"Aye, always that . . . in spite of men," said Dug.

"Or women?" asked the boy.

Dug waited a moment. I could see the black fiend in his face coming and going. But then he said: "All right. In spite of that, too."

Chip came up and went around and faced Waters.

"Look at me, Dug," he stated.

"Yeah, I'm looking at you," Dug replied, staring down at the ground, instead.

Chip dragged in a deep breath. "What I mean to say is this," he said. "I swiped the thing, but I done it for you."

"You swiped it from me . . . for me?" Waters said.

"That's it."

"You be the teacher and explain," Waters proposed. "It's pretty hard for me to follow that kind of algebra."

"All right. I'll try to explain," Chip agreed. "You're gonna hate me, Dug."

183

"Maybe not." But he was holding himself hard. That was plain to see.

"But I'll come clean," the kid said, shuddering as he said it.

"All right. You come clean, then," Waters replied.

"And then?" asked the kid.

"Then we can shake hands . . . and say good bye," explained Waters.

It froze Chip. It turned him to stone. His round face was marble white with the moon shining against it. But he half whispered: "Yeah. I'll come clean, and take my licking. I'll tell you what, Dug."

"What?"

"I seen that it wouldn't do."

"What wouldn't do?"

"These here international marriages."

"What are you talking about, Chip?"

"I mean, suppose that you hook up with Doloridas . . . blast her! . . . it ain't any good. It don't pan out. It don't work. It never does work none. I've seen it plenty, too. You take 'em by themselves, and the Mexicans are all right. They're fine. I don't say nothing ag'in' them. Only, you see how it is? I've watched twenty of 'em get married to Americans, and most generally it's a bust. They got different ideas. They're raised different. Mostly their religion's different. It don't work out hardly never. I been told so, and I seen so, too. D'you foller that drift?"

Waters took out a bandanna from his pocket and mopped his forehead. He still was holding himself pretty hard, and he was perspiring.

"Well, I'm trying to foller along," he said.

"Dug," explained the boy, making his points with a forefinger in the palm of his hand, "it's like this . . . you see Doloridas, and she knocks you off your horse. Ain't that right?"

"That's right enough," Dug Waters affirmed.

"She knocks you off your horse," the kid went on, "and you land on your ear and you see stars, and you think that she's one of 'em. Am I wrong?"

"Go on."

"What's gonna be done about it? Nothin'! Old Ruan, he wants her married, but not to your kind. Anything else will do for him, because you've given him a bad raiding before. Ain't that right?"

"Yes, that's right."

"And if anybody else comes along, you'll give him a slug of lead for a present to help him along in his courting. Ain't that right?"

"Yes, that's right, too," admitted Waters. "Go on, kid."

"I'm making it all straight," said the boy. "It's like this way. I say to myself . . . if Ruan won't let the chief have her, and, if the chief won't let anybody else have her, there's just gonna be general heck poppin' all the while. And pretty soon there's a grand bust, and nobody gets any good out of it. And so what's to be done?"

"Go on," Waters urged through his teeth.

"So I says to myself," continued the kid, "that there's only one thing to happen, and that's to get Doloridas married off . . . not to Dug, but to somebody else that Dug can't handle."

"Like whom?" Dug asked.

"Like a friend of yours," the boy responded. "Because I know that you'll never put hand on a friend of yours. I know that a friend of yours may stop bein' a friend, but that he's always sacred to you."

"By Hector, I begin to see!" Dug exclaimed.

"So I slide away, that time . . . you remember when I was gone three weeks?"

"Yeah, I remember," Dug said, gritting his teeth.

I began to feel a considerable chill, for my part, when I saw how the thing was shaping up. I began to see my own part coming into the headlines, so to speak.

"Well," went on the kid, "all the time I'd been thinking. How many friends did you have in the world? They ain't so thick."

"No," reflected Dug Waters. "I can step around between them without crossing myself none."

"Then I remembered," said the kid.

"You remembered what?"

"I remembered about old Joe, my partner, that had helped in the party when you were pried out of jail. I knew that you'd never forget what he'd done, because what he done, he had nothing to gain by it. You were nothing to him. It was just out of the heart that he done it."

"By thunder!" Waters cried, and stared hard at me.

"That was why," Chip continued, his voice getting tense again. "That was the whole reason. Will you believe it?"

"Go on! Go on!" said Dug Waters.

"So I thought that I'd get him interested in the girl. And so I swiped your picture of her on the ivory. And I rode away and I found him and I showed it to him. And he come along down here on a string. If you know what I mean!"

"Aye," said Waters slowly and bitterly. "That's a string that would pull a whole fleet along."

"And down he came, and right away quick," said the kid, "he gets to work and starts out like a real man, and he takes the girl away from the place, and then you come after and you're about to swaller him, when I sing out his name to you, and you stop. And so that's why we're standing here, and she's safe, up there in the town. Now you know everything. And I guess that it's good bye, partner."

Dug Waters took a pace up and down, and he thought about the thing a little, and after a while he stepped up to me, and he said: "Joe, what did you guess in this here job?"

I said: "I guessed nothing. I saw that picture, and I started the way that a horse starts when it smells oats."

He laughed a little with his teeth shut. Did you ever hear a man laugh in that way? It's not so good to listen to.

Then he said: "I believe you. I believe everybody. But here I am, dang it, after making my play, and nothing to show for it, except ten dollars that I've spent to get this rat by the neck again!" He turned back sharp on the boy.

Poor Chip threw up his hands, as if to parry a punch. And then he dropped his hands and stood straight and still, like someone facing a firing squad. He stood there, marble under the moon, and he waited, and Waters stared at him with a glimmer of bad fire in his eyes.

I tapped Dug on the shoulder. I tapped him pretty hard.

He whirled about on me, and I drew him one step away. I whispered in his ear. "Waters," I said.

"Well?" he returned.

"Ain't the kid worth about everything?" I said. "And who was he working for, and riding three weeks for? Himself?"

He gave a grunt, and that grunt was from the place where the stomach hurts the more when it aches. And he said to me: "Right!"

He went back to the kid. He took him by both shoulders.

"Kid," he said, "I loved her."

"Aye," responded the kid. "You're danged right that I knew that!"

"But," said Dug Waters, "I've had your life, and you've had mine, and there ain't any woman that can come between us. I can't say that I'll forget it, but I'll forgive it."

And they gripped their hands together.

Chapter Sixteen

"Three Friends"

Right here it ought to be remembered that Chip was only sixteen, and that he'd been under a pretty big strain and had been facing the loss of a man that meant more to him than anyone else in the universe. Dug Waters, he began to talk in a loud voice, and he ordered everybody to their horses, and, when he couldn't think of anything else to do, he coughed and hemmed and cleared his throat, and I began to curse at the dead mule, and kick at the sand, and act like a fool, generally, anything to make a loud noise—because I'd heard something like a whimper from the kid, and I knew that Chip was crying. We covered it up pretty well, and not a one of those Mexicans ever knew that Chip had acted, for a minute, like a plain ordinary boy.

He mastered himself pretty fast, and we all got to horse, and Dug Waters, he rode alongside of me and he said: "Look at here, son. This girl . . . what's she mean to you?"

"Everything," I admitted.

"Well," he said, "she don't mean everything to me."

"No," I agreed. "You've got a head on your shoulders. The kid means more to you."

"Yes," he stated. "You're right that he does. But about this girl . . . you want her pretty bad?"

"I want her pretty bad."

"And she wants you?"

"She asked me to run with her," I told him.

"Humph!" he grunted. "And she's a straight-shooter?"

"Never none straighter, I guess," I replied slowly.

"Then you ought to have her," he said grimly.

"I mean to," I said. "In spite of everything."

He looked straight at me, and then he laughed a little. I didn't mind the laughter very much. Because I saw what was in his mind. I wouldn't have had her, if Chip hadn't played my hand for me.

"Come on, Joe," he said. "I'm for the men, and not for the women. You're my friend, and I reckon that a friend is more to me than a wife ever would be. You wanta go to San Jacinto. So you come with me."

That was what we did. We rode up there through the gorge with the moonshine glimmering and twinkling along the rocks, and a little creek came out of nowhere and began to sing at the feet of our horses, but we didn't stop to drink, or to let the horses drink. We just went out, and, pretty soon, we came around a turn, and the valley widened a little, and there were the big, bulging, crumpling walls of 'dobe that surrounded San Jacinto. It had been walled against Indians in the first place. It was kept walled against the thugs, the cattle rustlers, and the yeggs of a later time. Still the people in that little place knew how to turn out when they heard the alarm bell begin to clang. When we came out, about a dozen rifles clanged on the walls and sent wasps singing through the air.

We pulled back into the shadows of the gorge.

"Listen, Waters," I said. "They'll shoot at twenty, but they won't shoot at one. I'm going to ride in alone, and you'll see them open the gate for me."

"I'm gonna wait," he said. "I dunno what I see. But if I see you dead, I'll hang twenty greasers for the sake of you . . . or fifty, if you say the word."

"No," I replied. "There's no chance. They won't shoot at a single man."

Max Brand

And they didn't. I rode right in under the walls, up to the light that burned by the gate, and, when I got there, I didn't have a chance to speak, for a voice sang out: "Don José?"

"That's me," I called out.

"You have come for the lady?" asked the voice.

"I've come to see her."

"You can see a letter from her."

And right away, a letter was thrown down to me. I opened it. There was a touch of perfume in the paper. I held it to my face and breathed of it. I kissed that paper, in fact, because I was pretty far gone. And this was what I read by the red light of the lantern at that gate, like the gate of an old castle of the Middle Ages:

Dear José:

You have saved me, and you have lost me. From the first, I never wished for you. I wished for another man. He is here with me. He sits beside me, and watches me as I write these words. And he stops me, for he kisses the hand that writes them.

He is the man I love. I have waited these years for him. At last I have escaped my uncle, and I am with him. And I have escaped because of you.

What shall I say? That I am unfair? No, because whatever is done for love is not really unfair.

If you curse me, curse all women. For my sin is only their sin.

Dare I ask you to forgive me?

Remember the river, and the flow of the water, and the rope that saved you. And, remembering that, I dare ask you to forgive me.

And I wish to say, also, that I never would have dared, except for a word from the boy, because after he spoke to me, I knew that you were safe from El Blanco.

But you did not know. You thought that you were facing a foe, and not a friend.

If you read this letter, it is because the boy was right, and El Blanco would not harm you.

In any case, heaven be kind to you, heaven reward you!

From me, and from my husband, you have our love forever.

Is that enough?

Ah, my friend, remember that love is a fire that burns whoever touches it. I have touched it, and my brain is flaming. May yours, on a better day, burn for a better woman than for me.

Adiós, with a thousand hopes for your happiness.

María

I read that letter once, and I was stunned; and I read it again, and I was staggered, and I read it a third time. Then I leaned a hand against the wall of the town, and I laughed, and I laughed for a long time.

"Hai, señor!" called the voice of the man who had thrown me the letter.

"Hai, señor," I replied. "Are you the man?"

"I'm the man," he said.

"Then put strong locks on your doors," I warned.

"To keep out thieves?" he asked.

"No, but to keep them in," I answered.

So I rode back to the gorge. I was not very sick of heart. Because I had begun to see things that made me laugh. I felt, almost, as though I had thrown off a fur coat on a hot day. In the shadows of the gorge, I found that the Mexicans had ridden on ahead. I could hear the jingling of their spurs, far off. Only Chip and Waters waited for me.

So the three of us fell in, side by side, and we rode down the dimness of the valley, and not a word did we speak, and only the creaking of one saddle spoke to the creaking of another.

But I knew that a great thing had happened. For a woman had come, and a woman had gone, and she had made us three friends forever.

The Oath of Office

Retitled "Chip Traps a Sheriff," this short novel by Frederick
Faust was first published in Street & Smith's *Western Story
Magazine* in the January 31, 1931 issue under the Max Brand
byline. It contains several unusual elements. First, Chip is fea-
tured prominently in this story, in contrast to the two previous
stories. Second, it has no heroine, in fact, no female characters,
whatsoever, which is most unusual for Faust's fiction. Finally,
its setting is Nevada where Joe has gone to eke out his living
by mining, and it opens with what only can be called a love
song to this area, adeptly styled in Joe's charming first-person
narration.

Chapter One

"The Perfect State"

Every man has a special country that is fitted into his heart so snugly that it fills every corner. I know fellows who talk pretty nearly with tears in their eyes of the seashore, and the white curving of the surf, and the boom and the step of it, but they never can outtalk the lads from the high mountains, where the head and shoulders of things is lifted up so high that it almost breaks loose.

Then I've heard the real Kentuckian mention blue grass and big hills that never stop rolling from one edge of the sky to the other. Yes, I've heard 'em mention blue grass, and horses, too.

Up there in New England things are smaller and put together more closely, but summer mugginess and flies and winter chilblains and wind can't stop the New Englander from talking. He'll tell you about a second-growth forest, and the smell of the moldering stumps in it, and the autumn colors slashed through it like paint flung off a brush. He'll talk of the brook where it runs, and the brook where it stands still and lets a couple of silver birches look down into it to see how much sky is there.

Then you'll hear people even rave a lot about sagebrush, and the smell of the wind that comes off from it, when it's wet, but for me there's only one land that I feel God made when He was working in real earnest. The other parts of the world—He just made 'em for practice, but finally He got really interested, and then He made Nevada. Yes, I mean that. Maybe I'm not talking about the part you know, because a lot of people are loaded right down to the waterline with wrong information about that state. There's sort of a general impression that there's some silver mining and sage hens in it, but they've got to scratch their heads to remember anything else.

There's too much Nevada for the people who live there to talk about. There's about a couple of square miles of space for every *hombre* in that country—yes, man, woman, and child. When you realize that mostly everybody is raked together in a few towns and mining camps, you'll see that it's possible to bump right into a lot of open space out in that direction. I've bumped into it, boys. I've ridden it from the Opal Mountains to Massacre Lake, and from Goose Creek Range to Lake Tahoe, and wondered how there could be that much real, fresh, sweet cold water in the world. I know the ranges that sink their claws into the hide of Nevada, like the Monitor and Pancake and Hot Creek and Toiyabe and Shoshone and Augusta. I know that whole state. I know the dry feel of it on the skin, and the red hurt of it in the eyes. And I love it. There's salt in my throat when I think of Nevada, but I love it, and I hope that I'll live there and die there, God bless it!

But now I've got to particularize a little. You may have sage flats in your mind, but that's not the part of Nevada that I mean. No, sir, I mean the place where God really turned Himself loose and did His best. He didn't waste any time picking and choosing. He just reached out with both hands, and He piled up all kinds of slates and limestones and quartzites and granites, and for color He piled in some volcanic rocks that are some of them as blue as the sky, and some of them as red as fire. He worked with this stuff and threw it up into great ridges, and He chopped out the valley with the edge of His palm. He made things ragged, and He made things grand. He didn't want to dull the outlines He had drawn with forests and such things. He wanted no beard on the face that He'd made; He preferred it clean-shaven, so He reached over to the westward, and He ridged up the Sierra Nevadas. There's quite a lot of people in the state of Oranges and Hot Air—California, I mean—that think that the Sierra Nevadas were built up for their own special satisfaction, a kind of a wall and a turning of the back on the rest of the world, but really the only reason that the Sierras are up so high is to catch all the rain winds out of the westerly and pick out the mists and the clouds so that only a pure, dry air can blow over Nevada. God didn't want those Nevada mountains and valleys to rust in the rain.

When He'd finished off the main outlines, He says to Himself that He might give a few finished touches, so He paved the valleys with fine white sand, and He polished up the mountains so that they'd shine, night and day. And then He says to Himself that this is the finest spot of earth, and what will He put into it? Well, He finally picked out the jack rabbit, that was biggest and fastest, and it could clear a mountain in its stride. Then He hunted up some coyotes that could run the rabbits down. After that He got the wisest beast in the world, a big frame and a loose hide, and an eye like a man's eye, and He put the gray wolf into the picture and yellowed and grayed it a good deal to make it fit in with the landscape better. Here and there He let a four-footed streak of greased lightning step through those valleys on tiptoe, and those antelope are the fastest and the wisest of their silly, beautiful kind. On the ground He laid rattlesnakes to catch fools, such as you and I, and in the air He put the sage thrasher and the Texas nighthawk, and the mourning dove, and in every sky He hung one buzzard.

Now He wanted to get some people in there to see all this picture, but He didn't want many. So He just sifted into the rocks of His mountains some gold and silver, here and there. It wasn't much. It was just a trace. Just enough to make your mouth water, and not hardly enough to swallow. But the prospectors got the wind of it, and they came ten thousand miles across the world to have a look. Mostly they turned back on the rim of the picture—it was too black and white for them, and all the white was fire. The thermometer was ranging a hundred and fifty degrees in the year, and some had their hearts burned out, and some had their feet frozen. But a few went on in. They climbed up onto the shoulders of those mountains and thanked God for a piñon, now and then, even the greasewood, and the creosote bushes and the sage seemed like company out there. They found their leads, and they sank their shafts into hard ground and banged and hammered all day long. They got mighty little, and they knew, mostly, that there wasn't much hope. But still they felt mighty contented.

Why? It might have been because of the mornings, before they started to work and let their eyes go sinking over the white valleys, or the mountains beginning to tremble and blush in the early light. Or it might have been because of the evenings, when they sat dead tired and smoked their pipes, and looked at the evening rising just like a blue smoke out of the bottom of the rifts.

That was what I was doing.

I was just sitting there in front of my claim and figuring out that I had used up my last can of tomatoes, and sort of cussing a little, quietly and comfortably, all to myself. But my brain didn't hear what my lips were muttering, do you see, because I was too really busy taking gunshots down one ravine filled with that blue smoke, and then down another choked with fire. The white of the valley floor was still pure, and very little clouded, and away off on the vanishing edge of things I could see a slowly moving cloud.

It was a dust cloud. It was raised by wild horses. I had seen them that morning, looking through that glass-clear air. During the night they would pass me, but on the following morning I would be able to see them again, traveling on at their unfailing lope in a two-day run to the water holes of the Shoe Horn Valley, away beyond. I remember thinking of the wild horses, that I'd like to be on the back of one of them, the wildest stallion of the lot, and go flowing on with the dusty stream of their march, and stay with them forever, contented. I mean to say, I felt that I was only sitting still on the bank of the river, looking, but those horses were in the river, they were in the picture, they were a part of it.

While I was thinking these things over, a voice says behind me: "Why, hello, old Joe!"

I just pulled myself a little closer together. I looked up, but I was afraid to look behind. *I've got them!* I said to myself.

I mean, when you're out all alone for too long a stretch, sometimes the brain wobbles a little, and you'll find a prospector turned as batty as a sheepherder. For surely that voice I heard could not have come from any human lips. That boy Chip was likely to be anywhere, but he simply couldn't have materialized there at my back. I laughed a little, with a quiver in my voice. "I've certainly got 'em!" I said aloud.

"Look around, Joe," said the voice again.

So I turned around and looked, and, by thunder, there was the freckled face and the fire-red hair of Chip, sure enough. My heart jumped at the sight of him. Also, my heart fell.

Chapter Two

"What the Broncho Brought"

"You little sawed-off son of salt," I said to him. "Where did you drop from?"

He hooked his thumb over his shoulder to indicate the mountainside that leaned back into the sky. "Aw, over that way," he said.

We shook hands. He had the same hands that I remembered so well. They hadn't changed a bit. There seemed to be the same dirt darkening them around the first joints, if you know what I mean. No, all of him was just the same. He had seventeen years of growth on him now, and a thousand years of meanness. All mixed and rolled and stewed together. Nobody ever talked down to Chip. Not more than once, I mean. One try was usually enough.

"Sit down," I said. "You just walked out here a few hundred miles and found me, eh? No trouble to you. What did you do? Learn the buzzard language and ask the birds which way to go?"

He sat down on the ground, laid his back against a rock, and folded his arms under his head. He was facing partly away from me, so that he could look at the same picture that I was seeing.

"Make me a smoke, Joe, will you?" he said.

I was about to throw him the makings and tell him to roll his own, when I saw that he was dead tired. There were violet shadows thumbed out under his eyes. Besides, just the asking for a cigarette was enough to show that he was beat. He didn't smoke them often. So I rolled him tobacco and wheat straw, and stuck it in his mouth and lighted it for him. He didn't budge a hand, but just lay there with his eyes half closed and looked at the picture in front of us.

The poor kid was almost all in. I said nothing for a time. I simply watched him, do you see? He smoked that cigarette to a butt and jerked it out, and he breathed deep three times before the smoke was entirely out of his lungs.

Then I said: "You've gone and got yourself a whole flock of new clothes since I saw you last."

"Yeah," he said, "you know the way Dug is. He's always trying to dress me up."

"Yeah, I know," I replied.

"That's the trouble with Dug," said the kid. "He's kind of a dude."

"Yeah. He's kind of a dude," I agreed, "but he's all right."

"Yeah, sure he's all right," said the kid. "But he's a dude. He's always fixing himself up and dressing up. You know what he did down in Tahuila?"

"What did he go and do there?" I asked.

"He done himself up in Mexican clothes. All velvet and such stuff. And he went and got a big plume to curl around his head. He thought he looked fine. He was always standing around and spreading his legs and looking at himself in the mirror and curling his whiskers with one hand."

"I bet you handed him something," I said.

"Yeah. I handed him something," said Chip. "But he didn't care. He's getting so he don't care what I say to him."

"He knows you kind of like him," I said.

"Think that's it?" he asked.

"Yeah. That's it," I said.

"Well, maybe," said Chip.

I swallowed a little. He and Dug Waters were closer than brothers. I was pretty thick with them, too. But what they meant to each other was real blood. They'd owed their lives, each to each, I don't know how many times.

"What did he do when he got all dressed up?" I said.

"Aw, he goes and crashes into a dance," said Chip.

"Did they try to throw him out?"

"Yeah, they tried," Chip said, and yawned heartily. He went on: "He stayed quite a while, though. The furniture got sort of busted up, and his fine clothes were spoiled, but he kept the music playing, and he kept right on dancing. I gave him the sign when the cops were coming, and then he left. But that's the trouble with him. He's always dressing up. You know how it is. You always get in trouble when you're dressed up."

"How'd you lose half of those suspenders?" I asked him.

"That was a shack," said Chip. "He reached for me as I was getting off the back end of a caboose on a grade. He got half the suspenders, but he didn't get me."

"That's good," I said. "How about the sleeve of the shirt? What happened to that?"

"A funny thing about that," said Chip. "The railroad cop, when he grabbed me, he grabbed so hard that, when I popped out of my coat, I had to tear that sleeve right out of the shirt, too, before I could shake him. You never seen a guy with a grip like that cop had."

"Where was this?" I asked.

"Aw, in a railroad yard. This was one of them mean cops. You know the real mean ones?"

"Yeah. I know."

"He comes cruising up to me in the dark," said Chip. "He makes a pass at me, and all his fingers are fishhooks, what I mean to say. He grabs me, and he holds me. I have to peel out of the coat and the shirt sleeve. The talking that cop done as he heeled after me, you'd've laughed to've heard it, Joe." He himself smiled faintly, a little wearily, at the memory.

"That was hard on the shirt, all right," I said. "You got a pretty bad rip in those trousers, too."

One side of them was almost torn away and had been loosely patched together with sack twine.

"You know how it is about a window?" said Chip. "I mean, the nails that are always sticking out around a window? That was what happened. I was clean through and ready to drop for the ground, and nobody had heard a thing, and then I got hung up on a nail. It makes me pretty dog-gone sore, Joe, the way carpenters make a window. Dog-gone me, if I was a carpenter and called myself a carpenter, and set up for being a carpenter, I'd *be* one, and I'd hammer in my nails, and I'd countersink 'em . . . around a window, anyways." He was very indignant. His anger helped to take his weariness away.

"Yeah," I said. "Carpenters are no good. Who'd want to be a carpenter, anyway? But what window were you climbing out of?"

"Aw, it was nothing," he said carelessly. "It was just a bet I had on with Dug Waters. He said I couldn't break into a house. I said I could."

I began to perspire a little. "What did you get, Chip?" I said.

He turned his head quickly and glanced at me. "Whatcha think?" he said. "I ain't in that line. I never ain't going to be in it, either, what's more."

"That's right," I said. "You're a good kid, Chip."

"Aw, go on. I ain't a good kid, either. But I ain't a thief. I don't go around stealing. That's all I don't do."

"Just a chicken now and then?" I said.

"That's lifting. That ain't stealing," said Chip calmly. "You oughta know the difference between lifting and stealing, oughtn't you?"

"Sure," I said. "There's a lot of difference. How do you feel now?"

"Me? I always feel good," he replied. "How about you?"

"I'm all right. I'm just kind of down now because I've used up my tomatoes."

"Have you?" said Chip. "You're gonna get some more."

"When?" I asked him.

"*Pronto*," he said. He held up one finger to make me listen. I heard it, then. It was the thin, silver music of a bell, beyond the shoulder of the hill.

"What's that?" I asked him.

"That's my hoss and mule," said Chip.

"Oh," I said. "Then Dug Waters is coming after you, is he?"

"No," said Chip.

203

"Who's with 'em, then?" I asked.

"Nobody's with 'em," he answered. "They're by themselves."

I looked at him pretty hard, but he paid no attention, as though there were nothing really worthy of attention in what he had said. He merely looked off across the blue and red of the evening, toward one great polished face of granite that took the light and gave it back as a mirror would.

"Maybe you've worked a charm on 'em?" I said. "And they can't help following you?"

"I got a charm, all right," he said. "I got the meanest mustang in the world, all right. He's a charm! But he'll follow me. He'll follow me around like a dog, because he gets pretty lonely without me. He don't feel nacheral at all without somebody in the saddle that he can annoy a little. If it ain't bucking, it's reaching around and taking a bite at my foot . . . and, if there's a cliff handy, he likes to walk right out onto the edge of nothing and bite a couple of chunks out of it, and he don't turn back until the cliff is crumblin' under his feet, and even then he don't hurry. Then he likes to give me a rub against a handy boulder along the way, that cayuse does. And if he ain't bucking, he's always humping his back like he was about to begin, so's your nerves never get good and settled down.

"He's so fond of makin' me miserable that he can't do without me. I'm his kicking post, and he certainly likes to kick. He's lammed me three times on this trip, and he's gonna lam me three times more . . . and I've seen the air around my head all full of his heels. That's the kind of a mustang that he is! He can't do without me. So I know that he'll follow me, because he's got a gift of scenting like a wolf, and so I hang a bell around his neck. When I get tired of fighting the cayuse, I hop off and take a walk ahead, like now, and he's sure to come after me. First he balks, and pretends that he ain't coming, but, when he remembers what a lot of fun he's had pounding me, he always gives in and comes along after."

When Chip got through with this explanation, over the shoulder of the mountain, between two runty piñons, I saw the procession coming, the little mustang first, and a long-legged, knock-kneed, potbellied mule behind him.

That cayuse came up, and my burro began to bray, it was so

glad of having company. Right up to Chip that mustang came, and reached down and took off the battered old felt hat that Chip was wearing.

"Aw, quit it," said Chip, without turning his head, and sort of tired. "Quit it, and go off and lay down, or I'll get up and slam you one."

It amused me a good deal to see the mustang drop the hat and go off to the side to pick at some bunchgrass. It amused me, because it seemed as though he had understood. He was the meanest-looking horse that I ever saw, with a Roman nose, and a red look about the eye. There was that hump in the back that always means a hard gait and a mighty good bucker.

"How'd you come to pick out that horse, Chip?" I said.

"Out of a hundred," said Chip. "I could have had my pick of the whole bunch . . . but, while I was looking, there was a fight started in the corral between a great big sixteen-hand bay, with quarters like a dray horse, and this little runt. And they just backed up against one another and let drive. Every time the bay kicked, I looked to see the runt exploded right off the face of the earth, like gunpowder. But every time it kicked, its fool heels flew over the back of the cayuse, and every time the cayuse kicked, its feet went into the big fat quarters of that bay like a clapping of hands. After a while the bay had enough, begun to squeal and run away, and this little wildcat run after him, and took a chunk with its teeth, while the bay was running. 'Shoot that blankety-blank hoss-eating mustang!' yelled the boss. 'No,' I says, 'sell it to me!' So that's how I got him."

I got through laughing, and I said: "Where are you bound, and what for, Chip?"

"I'm bound to you from Waters," he said. "Take off that saddlebag and you'll see why."

I went over and navigated around the broncho until I got the saddlebag off. I brought it back and opened it and dumped out the contents on the ground. What I saw was a whole stack of packs of cards, except that they were bigger than packs of cards, and at the ends of them I could see the figures. All at once I threw up my hands and let out a howl, because I knew that all that stuff was United States greenbacks, lying there on the rocks before me!

Chapter Three

"Followed by Tug"

Sometimes I had daydreamed about how good it would be if I could run into a flock of money like that—sort of have it poured down before me by the dropping of the tailpiece of a government truck, or something like that. I had always felt that the joy would run up through my veins as bright as silver. But I was wrong. At least, out there in the center of the Nevada desert, the first thing that I did was to throw a look around over both shoulders, and the second thing was to go and grab my rifle and shove some cartridges into it. Even then I didn't feel very easy, because my hands were shaking, and I was as cold as ice all around my mouth. My voice quaked when I came back to Chip and stood over him.

"You little son of torment!" I said to him.

He only grinned at me. "Gimme the makings, Joe."

"You don't smoke till you've done some talking," I said.

He grinned again. He settled himself back against the rock as though it were a pillow and folded his arms under his head, with his skinny elbows sticking out on either side.

"Go on," he said. "What d'you wanta know?"

"Everything," I said.

"That's easy," said the kid. "Once upon a time there was a bank, and inside of the bank there was a president that knew how to suck the gold out of people like a spider does blood out of flies, and inside of the president's office there was a safe all bright and shining and new and guaranteed, where the president laid up the gold. And now there's the same bank, and the same president, and the same safe. But there ain't any door onto the safe. Leastwise, there wasn't the last time I saw it. And a couple hundred thousand dollars' worth of lining is gone, too, right out of the president's safekeeping."

All the rocks and the mountains shifted and wavered a little as I heard this. I looked down at the little pile I had turned out of the saddlebag.

"Two . . . hundred . . . thousand!" I said.

"Yeah. Or nigher onto a quarter of a million," corrected the kid.

I looked at the loot again. It didn't seem to me like stolen money. It seemed different—I can't say why. Because there was so much of it, that it seemed almost right and good to have taken it. I thought of a lump of gold weighing eight hundred pounds. It would load down two mules solid. And that was what that little stack of paper meant. It was a treasure. That's what I thought of it.

Murder came hot up in me. I want to be honest and tell the horrible truth about it. I had half a mind to tap the boy over the head with the butt of the rifle, and then all of this money would be mine. I took my knuckles a good hard swipe across my forehead, and then my brain was clear, and I was able to think and see right again.

I found that Chip was stretched out there in just the same position, looking up at me with a funny little smile.

He nodded. "Yeah, I know," he said.

"Do you?" I said, and I stared down and saw that his bright, wise eyes were full of information and understanding.

"Yeah," went on Chip. "I had the same idea. When I started away, I was a mind to cut and run, and never see Waters again, if I could help it. But then I remembered, and didn't."

"Remembered that he'd track you down?" I asked.

"No. I remembered that he wouldn't try," said Chip.

I let this idea go through me with an electric jump, and I saw that it was true. After all that Chip had done for Waters, Dug never would lay a hand on him, no matter what else he did. Not for a quarter of a million in hard cash.

"How did he do the trick?" I asked the boy.

"How did he do it? Oh, that was easy. He just chloroformed a watchman and cut his way in and cut his way out. It was an easy job. That bank had plate-glass windows, and you could look through them into the lighted insides of the bank, day and night, and see the safe. And the light was still shining inside the bank all that night . . . but Dug, he just washed a couple of the panes of the window glass with soapy water, and after that everything you could see from the street was a mist. And he worked inside as easy as you please."

I nodded. I could see Waters, cool and easy and calm, doing his work inside the bank, with no other screen to protect him than a film of mist through which the passers-by could half see. I thought of the cleverness of it, too—people who wandered down the street that night would never give the soapy windows a thought. But a curtain or a shade drawn would have been a different matter.

"Go on," I said.

"To what?" asked Chip.

"To where you start and Dug stays back."

"They guessed at Dug, and he knew that they'd guess at him," said Chip, "and just then they didn't have anything on him, but they were pretty sure to lay a slick job like that to his door. So he sat still and let them grab him and third-degree him, if they wanted to. And while they were working over him, there was me, all dressed up in a new suit of clothes, and with a good saddlebag crammed with the stuff, hiking it down the railroad. I lost some of the clothes, but I come through with the loot."

"How did you find me?" I asked.

"Well, I dropped in at Newbold's place. And Marian Newbold, she went and cried all over me. And she was going to reform me and get me sure jammed into a school this time. But I managed to find out that you were off in this direction, so I slid out at night and barged along, and the next day I bought me this outfit and hit the desert up this way. I happened onto the place where you bought your own outfit, and they gave me enough of a lead to follow along for quite a ways. The rest was luck."

I considered this for a moment. I mean to say, I thought of the nerve of Waters in trusting that fortune in the hands of the boy, and the dangers that the kid had gone through, beating his way a thousand miles, I suppose, to find me. But here he was, true as a homing pigeon, arrived at me.

It was an amazing thing. It was so amazing that I went over and unsaddled his horse while I thought it over still longer. He got to his feet to help me, but I saw the waver of him though the dusk, and I told him to sit still. He could be the guest, tonight, and I'd take care of things. I did. I dragged in the packs and the saddles under the hoarding about the mouth of the shaft, and under the lean-to where I lived, although there wasn't much room in that.

Chip had brought along all the supplies in the world. There was no reason why he should have bought both a horse and a mule. But he said that he really did not know how long he would have to cruise before he found me, and so he had prepared for a voyage of any length. With his pockets full of cash, he did not spare his funds, but he laid in the best of everything. There were the cans of tomatoes that he had promised. And I don't know anything better than canned tomatoes on a trip. They put seasoning into even the toughest old sage hen, and they make you a drink that beats beer, even—there's a good, sour bite to it. He had jams, and the finest bacon you ever saw, and plenty of coffee, and the little runt actually put in some pickles, too. He sure was a regular food caravan, that kid.

We ate a supper that nearly burst us both, and then we laid back, and I stoked up my pipe and pulled off my boots and wriggled my toes in the cool of the night breeze, and saw the stars drifting and drifting up over the mountain heads, until it seemed as though they were rising out of the ground and setting into it again like undying sparks from a fire.

"Now you tell me why you're here, son," I said.

"Because it's a long time since I seen you, and I had to go somewhere," he said.

I shook my head. I looked across the deadness of the firelight to the face of the kid and the bright glint of his eyes.

"You liar, you come clean with me," I said.

"Yeah, I'm coming clean," Chip said. "The fact is that everything looked pretty good. And then I heard that Tug Murphy had hooked into the traces and was going to work on this job."

Tug Murphy! Dug Waters! It was not the first time that they had tried wits against one another. And it was not the first time that Chip had thrown his weight decisively into the scale. That Irish sheriff was not the cleverest fellow in the world, but he was a bulldog on a trail, and he was likely to get by persistence what smarter men missed, in spite of their brains. It gave me a stir to hear that name. I could see the red fighting face once more. I could hear the rasp of his voice against my ear.

"What has Murphy got to do with this game?" I asked.

"He's on the trail," said the boy. "I didn't mind the others. I would have stayed put. But Tug Murphy is different. He's got brains, and he knows where to look for the most trouble. So, sometimes, he might give me a look. And a whole saddlebag full of stuff ain't so easy to hide."

"He's a mean man to handle," I admitted, "and he's a hard one to get away from. There's no doubt about that. Still, old son, I don't quite know what brought you out here."

"It's like this," said the kid gravely. "There was Dug Waters all surrounded night and day, with the dicks watching him and every move that he made. I couldn't get to him to ask him what to do. And when I heard that Murphy was taking the trail, then I knew that I'd have to get close to somebody a little older and with more sense than me. And, of course, I thought about our partner. I thought about you, Joe. So here I am."

"Hold on," I said. "You thought about me?"

"Why, of course I did," he answered quickly.

"But look here, son," I said. "I don't have any share in deals like this. I don't work . . . in this line."

"Yeah, but you're a friend," said Chip.

I stared at him. I saw his meaning. A friend is a friend, no matter what the strain.

"But, suffering Moses, Chip!" I said. "Don't you realize that Tug Murphy knows that I'm a friend of yours and Waters's? Isn't he likely as not to come for me, if he hears that you've disappeared in this direction?"

Chapter Four

"Wide Awake"

This idea of mine had not occurred to Chip, it appeared. He scratched his head for a time and then nodded across the dimness of the firelight.

"It was a wrong steer that I had," he said. "I ought to've remembered that the sheriff knew you were in with us in the jail break, when we got Waters loose. I just forgot, kind of. I was a fool, Joe, I guess. But tomorrow I'll start along."

It made me feel sorry to see the boy repentant. That was a humor one didn't often spot in him. Generally he was fighting back, if you tried to corner him.

So I said: "Look here, Chip. It's all right. Don't you worry about the thing. I'll manage it, all right. After all, this is a tolerable big country for even the sheriff to find us in."

"Aye," said Chip, "but I've blazed the trail out here the second time. And just supposing that he should turn up." His shoulders twitched. I saw him shudder.

"Well, it's all right," I said vaguely.

"It ain't all right," said Chip. "Because if he seen you with that saddlebag loaded with coin, what would he be thinking?

Nothing at all, except that you were in on the deal."

"Oh, I can easily prove that I was out here when the robbery took place," I assured him.

"Yeah, but there's receivers of stolen goods, and all of that," said Chip.

"Yes," I said. "There are those, all right." I added: "You know a good deal about this stuff, it seems to me, Chip."

He sighed, and then he answered: "You know how it is, Joe. I hear a lot from Dug Waters. And I hear a lot from his pals, too."

"What pals has he got now?" I asked. "He was playing a lone hand, mostly, when I last heard about things."

"You know how it is," said Chip. "When a gent has played the game for a while, he gets sort of careless. I mean to say, he gets to thinking that he will always be able to beat it. And that's the way with Dug. He's nearly always beaten the law. And now he thinks that the law is a pup. He used never to trust nobody but me. Now he begins to trust everybody, it seems. He's softening up a good deal, I guess."

I could have sighed myself. It was a wonderful thing, the way that boy had stuck to Dug Waters. They loved each other. They would have died for one another. And Dug Waters kept the hands of the kid clean, all the while that he himself was going from gun fight to robbery to knife brawls. He watched out for the lad all the while, and the lad watched out for him. I was mighty fond of Dug. He was a little elegant, and had his eyebrows in the air a good part of the time, but he was the real stuff, and a friend that never forgot you. And that last thing is the most important in the world, I think.

So I stared through the dull of the firelight toward the boy, and I wondered what would come of him, and how he could possibly live that life of companionship with Waters without eventually becoming as outlawed as Waters was. Waters was having a free spell. He had been cornered. He had stood trial. And one of the smartest lawyers in the Southwest had freed him. It cost Waters a fortune, but now his record was smudged. The herring had been pulled across the trail, and he could come and go with all the other legal-minded people of the world. It was all right for Waters. But what about the boy?

I said: "What are you going to do about settling down, Chip, one of these days?"

"Settling down?" he questioned.

"I mean going to school, and all that," I suggested.

"Oh, I dunno," he answered gloomily. "Don't be so dog-goned sour, Joe, will you?"

"All right," I said. "We won't talk about it."

"I think about it plenty," he went on. "But I can't cut away from Dug. He needs me. He gets pretty crazy, when he's left to himself. He gets to acting like a lord, or something. He orders his ham and eggs on a gold plate, you might say. There ain't any sense in that. And Dug needs me. I sort of straighten him out. He'll listen to me . . . a little." He sighed again.

"You go to bed, son," I said. "You've been up a long while, and you've had a long march."

He nodded, stood up, stretched, and rolled down his blankets. But before he turned in, dead tired as he was, he went off and found the mustang and rubbed its nose with his fist. "Good night, you old son-of-a-gun," he said. "I'm gonna be braining you one of these days." Then he came back and turned in.

But I sat up a while. I was bothered by several things. One was pity for Chip, and wondering what was to come of him. One was thinking of that saddlebag loaded with a fortune. And one was Sheriff Tug Murphy, somewhere out in the desert, most likely, and very apt to be headed my way. It was a bad business, it seemed to me. But finally I turned in myself, and lay there for a while until the stars grew misty and dull—that was the moment I went to sleep.

I woke up with something tapping the sole of my foot. I didn't open my eyes. I just said: "Don't be a dang fool, burro. Get out of here!"

He used to have a way of doing that, that fool burro I had with me. I mean, he'd come and paw at my foot, or maybe at my hand, in the middle of the night. Just for meanness, or for company—I never could make out which.

That tapping at my foot kept on. So I opened my eyes and looked up to the sky, and there I saw the moon riding well above the eastern mountains, and the cold of the night air was on my face and eyes, so that I knew I had been sleeping for quite a time. Then I looked a little lower, and I saw the sombrero and the shoulders of a man standing below me. I didn't need another tap at my foot. I woke up *pronto*. I sat up, too, and saw a burly fellow standing there with the moon over his right shoulder.

"Hello, Joe," he said.

I recognized the voice. I recognized the iron rasp in it, I mean to say. It was Sheriff Tug Murphy.

"Hello, Tug," I said. "This is a lucky kind of a surprise." I stood up.

"Yeah, I guess it's kind of a surprise," said Tug Murphy. "Just mind your hands a little. Don't make no funny moves."

"I won't make any funny moves," I said, and added: "What's up? You're not trying to hang anything on me?"

"I dunno that I'm gonna hang anything on you," said the sheriff. "I'm just hankering after a little of your conversation."

"That's the way with bein' bright," I said to him. "People enjoy your talk so much that they just can't get along without it. They gotta ride a coupla hundred miles across the desert to hear some more of it. Sit down and rest your feet, Tug. I'll wake up the fire and get some coffee started for you."

"You just step into your boots," Tug said. "We'll let the fire and the coffee take care of itself for a while."

I dressed. All the time I was looking out of the corner of my eye at the shine of the leather of the saddlebag that lay beside the dead embers of my fire. And in that bag there was enough to soak me into prison for ten years, I guessed. I looked a little farther to the left toward the blankets of the kid. The blankets were there, but the kid wasn't. There was no sign of him. He must have heard a noise and waked and got away. I took it pretty hard of him that he hadn't given me a sign, or taken away that danged saddlebag, at the least.

I dressed, as I say, and then I threw some wood onto the fire, and it began to fume and smoke. I filled the coffee pot with water out of the bucket. That water in the bucket was standing so still that a star had dropped down into it, I remember. After the water got through slopping around, the image of the star came shuddering back again, all split and shattered into pieces, but settling down into its old self. I was pretty thoughtful as I raked that fire together and put the pot on top of two rocks, where the flame started to lick at it and curl around it.

"A funny thing about a coffee pot," said the sheriff. "It draws the fire to it, sort of. Ever notice that?"

"Yeah," I said. "That's a funny thing, but I could tell you a lot of funnier ones."

"Like what?"

"Like you being out here," I said. "What kind of a brainstorm have you got, boy?"

Tug Murphy laughed. "You mean you're too dog-gone virtuous to be suspected, eh?" he said.

"Well, you know me, Tug," I said.

"I know you all right," he said.

"And what have I ever pulled except a wad of tobacco out of a hip pocket?"

"That may be a true thing," he seemed to agree. "I dunno. That may be a pretty true thing. But you know how it is, old son."

"What way?"

"I mean, you know that rocks don't melt very easy."

"Yes," I said. "I know that pretty well."

"But still, there is fires that can melt 'em."

"Go on, Tug," I said. "I'm getting sort of tired of all this. What are you talking about, anyway?"

"I'm talking about two hundred and fifty-three thousand dollars!" said the sheriff.

I whistled. "That's enough for me," I said. "I'll take that much. But what are you driving at?"

"That money's missing from the bank," he explained. "And I'm out here after it. You see that I'm playing my cards all on the table in front of you, boy?"

"Yeah, I see that," I said. "That's a compliment that you're paying to me, Tug. I've gone and wished a quarter of a million out of a bank and laid it up here. Is that it?" I grinned across the fire at him, but he was still as serious as could be.

"I know that the kid trekked in this direction," he said. "And I know that he must have been heading for you with the cash. Now I'll tell you this. Turn over the boodle and there's not a word more said. The bank wants it bad. Turn it over, and there'll never be a word said to you about the job, son."

Chapter Five

"Out of the Bag"

It gave me a jump to hear him talk, and that I'll admit. I mean to say, there was the saddlebag, still in the corner of my eye, and if the sheriff should open it—out would come penitentiary for me. And if I turned over the stolen goods, there was an end of the trouble. I tell you that I was tingling to tell him and just point out the saddlebag. But then I thought of Dug Waters. He had been true blue with me. Down there, in my trouble when I fell in love like a fool with the Ruan girl, he had had my life in the palm of his hand, and he had let me go. He had saved me. You can't forget things like that. And there were other things between us—a lot of them. It's true that I never had worked with him on any of his crooked jobs, because that's not my line. But, nevertheless, there had been a good deal between us, and I was mighty fond of Waters. There was the kid, too. What would Chip do, if I let the saddlebag slip through my fingers into the hands of the law? He would never forgive me, and that was plain.

During about a tenth part of a second I thoroughly sifted every one of these questions, and then I decided that, law or no law, danger or no danger, friends came first, and I couldn't blab.

"Tug," I said, "it's a sort of inspiriting thing to hear you ask me for a quarter of a million. It shows the kind of faith that you have in me. There may be a quarter of a million in these mountains, but my luck is so bad that it would take me a thousand years to get it. Right now I'm taking about four or five dollars a day out of this here ground, and breaking my back, at that."

When he heard this, he laughed a little. "You know what I mean, old son," he said. "I'm talking about cash from a bank. And the kid must have brought it here."

"You mean Chip?"

"Who else would I mean?"

The coffee was beginning to simmer and to throw up the nose of its steam straight out of the spout, and the fragrance spread around over the place and smelled pretty good.

"Chip's not been here," I stated.

He lurched his shoulders forward and stuck out his jaw. "He's not been here?" he echoed.

I looked straight back across the fire into the eyes of the sheriff. I could see the savage twist of his lips and the evil in his eyes. A mean man was Tug Murphy when his blood was up, and it didn't take much to get it up.

"Have a can of coffee," I said. "There's no poison in it. Here's some sugar, too." I handed the things over.

He stirred in the sugar, still staring at me as though he could eat me. "What you doin' with sugar this long out?" he said. "How come it lasted so long?"

"You know," I said, "that I've always had a sort of sweet tooth. So I take along a good supply. But the fact is that this isn't my sugar."

"No," he said. "I'll bet that it's not your sugar. It's the stuff that Chip brought."

"Chip? You've got Chip on the brain."

"I got reason to have him on the brain," he snapped. "He's laid me the trickiest trail that I've ever followed . . . and I've rode after Indians, son!"

"Yeah, Chip could lay you a hard trail to follow," I agreed. "But I guess you won't find him here, Tug."

He shrugged his heavy shoulders. The coffee was very hot,

so he sipped it noisily. Then, breathing on it, he sipped it again. He was not a pretty man to watch, I can tell you, and he was staring at me as though I were red meat.

"Old son, Joe," he said, "I reckon that you're lyin' to me."

"All right," I said. "You go on reckonin'. And the real crook will be getting miles away from you."

He only grinned. "You out here all alone?" he asked.

"Me?"

"Yeah. They told me back yonder that you'd come out all alone."

I remember the rumpled blankets of the kid, and I answered: "No, I'm not alone. I was alone when I started, but I'm not alone now. A funny thing happened. You know old Chris Winter?"

"Yeah. I know old Chris," he said. "I used to, anyway."

"Well," I said, "old Chris, he got it into his head that he'd strike out in this direction, and, when he heard where I intended to prospect, he came along and found me, and we teamed up. It's pretty good to have somebody to talk to, you know, even if it's no more than old Chris."

"Sour old sinner, ain't he?" said the sheriff.

"Yeah. He's sort of sour, but he's all right."

"Where is he now?" asked the sheriff. "Does he smell sheriffs a long distance off and get restless and go walking?"

"You know how it is," I said. "He's got insomnia."

"No, I don't know how it is," he said. "He's got in what?"

" 'Somnia," I explained. "He can't sleep very good."

"Can't he?" said the sheriff. "Maybe he ain't got the words, but he certainly can play the tune. I recollect makin' a trip through Inyo County in California, and old Chris Winter was along, and dog-gone his heart, if he didn't make the mountains tremble all night, he snored so loud. I never heard such snorin'."

"It must've busted down his nerves," I suggested. "Anyway, he's a pretty light sleeper now."

"Dog-gone me, but I'm glad to hear it," said Tug Murphy.

"So he gets up," I said, "and he goes off for a walk in the middle of the night, when he finds out he can't sleep. It's hard on the old feller, all right, but he don't whimper much."

"How long has he been out here with you?" asked the sheriff.

"Quite a spell," I said. "Let's see . . . yeah . . . it's quite a while now, that the old boy has been out here with me."

"That's a mighty interesting thing," said the sheriff. "Does he look kind of nacheral, too?"

"Why, sure he does. That face of his couldn't look any way but natural. It would break, otherwise."

I thought this was a pretty good joke, so I laughed a little, but I couldn't help noticing that the sheriff did not seem to be in the least amused. Then he said: "There's a lot of interest in this for me. I've always been pretty interested in ghosts and spirits and things."

"What do you mean?" I asked.

"Why, man," he responded, "ain't Chris been dead for three months and more?"

It was a hard jolt for me. It was a punch on the point of the chin, so to speak. I got my breath and my wits back as well as I could.

The sheriff went on: "Chris was workin' on the Morgan and Rister crew, and he goes and falls down a shaft. Now, wasn't that a fool thing for an old hand like him to do? But I'm glad to see that his ghost has come out here to carry on with the drill. He was always a wonderful good hand with a single jack, was Chris Winter."

I let the sheriff carry on. I was trying to think. But I couldn't make much progress. He was grinning and chuckling all the while.

"Tug," I said at last, "the fellow who's out here as my partner is not Chris Winter, although I wish that name had gone down. He is a light sleeper, though, and he don't want to see you."

"I'll bet he don't," said the sheriff. "In a word, you might as well admit that it's the kid."

I shook my head. I grinned at the sheriff. I poured out another can of coffee for him, but all the while he was studying me with a lowering look, and presently he said: "You know, Joe, that you're stepping pretty deep into this business. I don't want to do you no harm. So far as I know, you've always been straight. But if I have to take you back to town with me, they'll slam you into the pen for a pretty long term. The judges and the juries around here in Nevada are getting pretty mean. You gotta fish and drag about fifty or a hundred square miles to get yourself a jury, in the first place . . . and all that riding the jurymen have got to do, day after day, it riles them a lot. They vote you guilty because they're saddle-sore. Now, Joe, you straighten up and tell me the truth, and it'll be all right. But if you don't, I start trouble right *pronto*."

I admired to hear the way that the sheriff put the case. It showed that he was a pretty straight fellow at heart. I liked Tug Murphy before. I liked him better than ever now. But what could I do? I already had thought the thing back and forth. He had proved me a liar, on the jump, and now what was I to do?

Finally I shook my head. I said: "Tug, suppose that everything you think were true . . . which it isn't . . . still, I wouldn't help you any. You ought to know that I couldn't."

"Because the kid's your friend, and Waters is your friend," he said.

"Put it any way you like."

"Then . . . stick your hands out!" He took out a pair of handcuffs and held them in his left hand.

"Aw, come along, Tug," I said. "D'you think that I'm going to try any gun play?"

"I don't like to put irons on you, Joe," he admitted. "I've seen you to be too dang decent for that. I don't want to do it. Will you give me your word that you'll sit tight and make no move while I take a look around this here camp?"

"I'll do that." I answered.

"Not make no move at all?" he insisted.

"No, I'll sit tight."

He hesitated, and then he nodded. He dropped the things back into his pocket, and I was glad to see them go. Then he stood up and looked around the camp. There was not much to it, I know, but the mischief told him where to go. He walked out, first, and found the mule, and rubbed his hand along the side of it.

"The pack saddle came off this mule no later than tonight, Joe," he said. "I can tell by the salt that ain't rubbed out of the hair yet."

I said nothing, because there was really nothing to say. I felt like a fool because I hadn't rubbed the mule and the broncho down.

Then Tug came back toward the fire, stubbed his toe against the saddlebag—and opened it up. He just pulled one handful out of that bag and stood there looking, not at what he held, but across the fire toward my face.

Chapter Six

"Headed for Jail"

To make a pretty long story short, we started on the march for jail. We only waited for the morning, and then we lighted out together. The sheriff had come out with a change of horses. He had two good, tough mustangs, rather lumpy in the heads, and with hips like the hips of cows. But they could keep going through fire. That's the sort of horse one wants for riding through Nevada.

Tug Murphy was pretty decent to me. He just arranged a rope that ran from one of my wrists to the other, and left about a foot of play between my hands. That way, I could make a smoke, light a match, and even do my share of the work around camp, when we halted. It was only, as you might say, a short hobble for my hands. The sheriff apologized for it. I'll never forget his apology. He said: "Look here, Joe. I could take you in with irons on, which would make you feel like a dog. Or else I could put nothing on you at all. But that would mean taking your word of honor first that you wouldn't escape. And I've got no right to take your word on that. If you have a right good chance to bust me over the head and make away, you go ahead

and do it. It's your right. Because, sure as tarnation, I'm takin'
you in for a long stretch up the river. But now I've got that rope
on you, it makes me easier . . . it makes you more comfortable . . .
and it's better all around. Only, it makes me feel pretty mean
to rope a man like a calf, and a he-man, and a real man, like
you, Joe."

I appreciated that compliment, coming from the sheriff. He
didn't drop many like it in his conversation, you may be sure.
Of course, I couldn't blame the sheriff. I only wondered what
the deuce would become of me, and now and then, inside my
mind, I certainly danged that boy Chip. For he had known that
the sheriff was on his trail, and yet he had led him right out to
me. Well, now the thing was ended, and I was due for prison,
and I groaned as I thought about it.

What shall I say about that inland voyage? I'll only say this—
that all the beauty went out of Nevada, as I rode along. All the
beauty went out, and the ugliness came in. The blue went out
of the sky, and the color went out of the distances. For one
thing, just as we started, the Old Nick stoked up his furnace and
turned on an extra blast. Perhaps I was not so used to the heat
of the valleys, I had been working such a height up the side of
the mountain, but, when we dropped into the bottom, it was like
dropping into a white road. The glare shot up through the eyes
and came out at the top of the head.

I knocked along pretty much like a mule with my head down.
Sometimes a hot wind came shooting at us, and the mustangs
put their heads down and just shuddered and endured it. But
they could not take a step until that wind had gone by, in a
whoop. One of those blasts would take every drop of moisture
out of the clothes and off the face, and just leave salt traces
where the perspiration had been. When the horses were dripping
with moisture, they would be wiped dry in ten seconds, and the
salt lay all over their hides in little lines, like those the waves
leave on the shore. I've seen it hot in other places. Perhaps
humid heat is worse. But I've never hankered after living on the
hot side of an oven, and that was what we were riding through.

The sheriff didn't mind it so much. I wouldn't have minded,
either, if I'd been in his boots. He was pretty sure to get at least
a ten-thousand-dollar reward from the bank, unless the bank was

a set of pikers. Besides, there was the fame. Tug used to talk over the possibilities of what he would get. It was his favorite theme all the way we rode together.

The first night we camped out in the naked flat, a dry camp. Tug wanted to shoot the burro and the mule. He said that he would charge the expenses off to his personal account. But I wouldn't let him shoot the burro. That mean little beast had been company for me too long up there at the mine. It had seen me through some lovely spots, and I liked the cock of its long, wise ears. That burro could carry his own weight on a cupful of water and a ham sandwich. I've heard the camel praised for powers of endurance, but the camel is a regular parlor exhibit compared with a real, hundred-percent Mexican burro. As for the mule, that belonged to Chip. I couldn't tell the sheriff that— no matter how sure he was—but I gathered that it wouldn't be a good idea to put a bullet through anything that belonged to that boy. I said so, and the sheriff saw the light.

"He's Irish," said the sheriff. "He's Irish, like me. And you can never tell where an Irishman will put his heart. Might put his heart on a woman, a horse, or a stone. But when he does, that woman, that horse, and that stone he's ready to die for. No, I guess that I'd better not shoot the mule. It might be Chip's favorite."

It was a strange speech to listen to, that. So we slogged along right out into the flat middle of the desert. That was not a dry camp, thank goodness. There was a little pool of alkali water. It was scudded around the edges, and it was bitter as aloes. But it tasted good enough, when it was made into coffee. We drank our coffee, and ate our flapjacks and bacon, and felt the heat still rising from the ground like steam. Great Scott, how hot it was!

Then the night breeze wakened and came softly about us, flowing like water, and we took off our clothes mostly, and let it blow. As we were lying there on the blankets for a while, cooling and trying to forget that the next day's march would be a lot worse than this one, the sheriff said: "We'll have decent water at the end of that march. I know where the pool is. It's fenced all around with rocks. It comes up and starts to flowing, and it gets about twenty feet and then goes down under the sand again. But it flows enough to keep it sweet, and it's cool, too, and there's a couple of specks of blue that fall into it out of the sky . . . but all the rest of the face of it is kept dark by the shadow of the rocks. It's the kind of a water hole that a man could dream about."

"Shut up, Tug," I said. "I'm dreamin' about it already. I'm thinkin' how it will wash the road down my throat. That's what I'm thinkin' about. And the alkali . . . there ain't any alkali in it, you say?"

"It's as sweet," said Tug, after a moment, "as heaven! As sweet as heaven with stars in it. And that's what I mean. It's a doggone honest spring, that's what it is."

All at once, I felt the whole lining of my throat go dry and crack with yearning, but I didn't get up to take a drink from our pool of this evening. I knew a little too much for that. The more you drink of alkali water, the worse off you are, and the sicker. It only keeps you from dying of thirst, and that's all.

The sheriff said: "Maybe they'll make it twenty-five."

I knew that he was thinking about how big his reward would be. I said nothing. Just then, the mule gave a snort, and then started into a loud braying.

"What's the matter with that fool mule?" said the sheriff, and sat up. "What's it seen?"

"Nothing," I said. "You know the way it is with a mule, Tug. You know why it starts in braying once in a while, like it was crying for help?"

"Yeah. I know what you mean," he said. "You tell me why?"

"Sure," I said. "It's because even a mule gets so dog-gone tired of its own mean nature that it wants a change. When you hear a mule bawling like that, it's just up and asking heaven for a second chance."

Tug Murphy lay back again onto his blankets slowly.

"Maybe you're right," he said. "I never knew a mule very well without beginning to pity it finally. They're just sons of torment, Joe."

"They are," I agreed. "And that reminds me of a story about the . . ."

"They might even make it thirty," commented the sheriff.

I saw that he was back on the question of the reward again.

I said nothing. I'd heard enough on that subject.

"But then again," said the sheriff, "you take a mean man like President Ranger of that bank, and he's as likely as not to say that I done no more than what I was paid by the county for doing."

This time I put in my word. "Yeah, as likely as not."

The sheriff grunted. "It's a cool quarter of a million," he said. "By rights they oughta pay me ten per cent, if they got any heart."

"Uhn-huh," I grunted.

"And even if they make it only five percent, that's twelve thousand five hundred."

"Uhn-huh," I said.

"But they wouldn't be short sports. They'd have to make it a round figure. Say, fifteen thousand."

"Or ten," I ventured.

"Yeah. Or even cut it down as far as ten," said the sheriff. "You talk like a regular banker, Joe. I bet you'd do fine behind the rails of a bank, collecting interest, and things."

"Uhn-huh."

"Well, that ought to be rock bottom," suggested the sheriff. "And on ten thousand, a man could do a lot. Pig Weller has set himself up with a pretty good layout, all that a man would ask to have . . . and his whole outfit, land, and stock, and all, it only set him back eight thousand."

"He didn't get much stock for that," I said.

"No, but he part paid on 'em, and they'll turn into hard cash for him."

"Uhn-huh."

"The old woman, she'd like to settle down," he stated. Then he sat up again.

"What's the matter?" I asked.

"That fool of a mule," he said, "where's it walking to? And it's got the horses right along after it."

"Maybe it smells good grass."

"They're stepping right out," he said. "And yet I hobbled 'em pretty short. They're stepping right out, for hobbled stock. . . ." Suddenly he jumped up to his feet. "By the eternal nation" he muttered, soft as you please, so that it sent a chill down my spine, "them hobbles have been cut."

That got me to my feet, too, and I was in time to see some figure—it looked small—jump on the back of the sheriff's best mustang and start off at a trot, and then at a canter, with all the rest of the livestock on lead ropes behind, and the burro last of all, pulling back hard on its line.

Chapter Seven

"Thirst"

I heard the sheriff groan. Then he grabbed his rifle and started pumping bullets at the disappearing caravan of horses, and mules, and what not. But he had no luck. You could tell, beforehand, that he would have no luck, the cause being that moonlight is the worst light in the world for shooting. Everything seems clear but at a little distance, and no one in the world can judge the distances. I knew that he would miss, and he did miss. And I saw our transportation wander off into the distance.

"Indians!" I yelled. "And this is why people that steal horses are hanged."

"Indians, your foot," said the sheriff, strangely calm. "It's Chip. That's what it is."

"Chip?" I shouted. "Chip leave me stranded like this? Never in a thousand years!"

"Who does he like better?" said the sheriff. "You or Waters?"

"He may like Waters better," I confessed, "but he'd never do a trick like this to me . . . never in the middle of the desert."

"You don't know him," Murphy said. "But I do. Because he's Irish, and the Irish blood is all red and black. There ain't any blue in it. I'm Irish, too. But we'll win through to Freshwater Springs."

You can imagine that we didn't wait. If we had to hoof it through those shifting sands that slid back six inches under every step, there was no sense in waiting for the sun to come up and broil us. It was better to start tired than to start hot.

We sifted down our packs to almost nothing. We just kept one rifle, some food, and the saddlebag that had the quarter of a million dollars. Then we started across the gloom and silver of the moonlit desert. I can't tell you how the loss of our horses had widened the desert. The place had seemed big enough before, but now it seemed a lot bigger, I can tell you. It was multiplied by ten.

Off we went, and I listened to the sand gritting and sliding under my feet, and I listened to the sand gritting and sliding under the feet of the sheriff. He was very calm about it. Now and then he would break out into a short speech, but mostly he saved his breath.

"About fifteen years in jail," he said several times. "That's about all that he'll get. And I hope that they make him perspire from morning to night for fifteen years, the way that I'm doing now. I hope that they keep the whip on him. Damn his miserable hide!"

I nodded. I was very fond of Chip, but, if he really were guilty of this business, I hoped that he would get plenty of punishment, and not have to wait for a future life to receive it, either.

We slogged along. I don't know how many of you have walked across blow sand. I hope for your own sakes that not many have. It's lighter than water and a good deal more slippery. There's no way of planting your feet that gives a good purchase. The best way is to turn your toes out and your foot on a bias. That way, you get more to push against. Even at the best it's a bad business. It's wading and slipping and sliding. Every pound that you carry counts for ten in blow sand.

Pretty soon, we talked no more, but just buckled down, and laid into the work, and set our teeth, and hoped that Chip, or the Indian, or whoever had stolen our horses might land in the hot place.

Then the sun came up. It didn't waste any time warming up. It just slugged us in the head with about ninety degrees for a beginning. The instant that it got its eye above the horizon mist, it was blazing hot, and it kept right on blazing. You have no idea how the desert sun starts its business with the first signal and keeps right on until it sinks. It shoots from the hip, without a wasted motion, and it keeps on shooting all day long.

Our canteens lasted until the middle of the morning. Then we made a halt in the lee side of some rocks, and the sheriff swallowed a couple of times to ease his throat, and he said: "We'll make the Freshwater Springs, all right. But it's going to be tough."

He was right. Particularly about this. We slogged along through that blow sand with the sun getting hotter and hotter. It seared through a man's shirt and burned the shoulders. It blistered the rims of the ears. It scorched the end of the nose. Now and then I raised my heavy, broad-brimmed sombrero, and tried to get some air on my head in that way. But it was no good. It let the steam off, but it didn't let any air in. I went along and endured it. Once you've got used to desert travel, you can remember other times when it seemed eternal, and yet it ended, sometime. But the worst part about the Nevada deserts is that there's often a blue pile of mountains off somewhere on the rim of the horizon telling you about cold running water, and shade under trees, and winds blowing, and all such things. I dreamed of palaces of ice. I could have eaten the whole danged palace!

Then we hove over a rise, and the sheriff laughed in a horrible, soundless way, and he pointed and said: "There's the Freshwater Springs. Down there, where the rocks are shining."

Suddenly my feet were light, and my heart was light, and I stepped along free and gay and bold and could almost have sung, except that my throat was hurting me too badly. We stepped along pretty briskly on that stretch, and then, as we came closer to the rocks, the sheriff he gave a queer, choked yell, and then he broke into a run. I watched him. I thought that the heat and the thirst had driven him a little crazy.

But then I saw something that made me start running, also. For those rocks didn't look the way rocks should look. They

231

were scattered and turned every which way, and their pale bellies were turned up to the sun.

I ran as hard as I could, but I couldn't keep up with the sheriff. He was a heavy-built man, but that day he fairly had the foot of me. When I came up, puffing and groaning, he was standing with both hands spread out, as though he were making an explanation silently to someone who could understand silence.

Then I saw for myself. Freshwater Springs had been blown up! Yes, there were the rocks, as I have said, scattered about, and now one could see that they were scorched and blackened, here and there. But the main thing was that the water was gone—all gone! The rim markings of the pool were there. The sand was still almost damp enough to chew, if you know what I mean. But the water was gone. Some fiend had dropped a charge away down the throat of the springs and had blown it, and the flow of the water had been stopped.

What could one do? The next prospector who happened along might drop down another charge of powder and blow it again, and then the water would likely start running. But now it was lost, and we had no powder.

I looked at the sheriff, and the sheriff, he looked back at me. He grinned, and his smile was a bad thing to see.

"Chip!" he said.

"Not Chip," I said. "Chip would never do such a thing. Not Chip! Chip's a partner of mine."

The sheriff said: "Am I Irish?"

"Yes," I said.

"Do I know the Irish?"

"You ought to," I admitted.

"Did I say that Irish blood was all red and black?" he asked me fiercely.

"You said that."

"And no blue in it?"

"No," I said.

"That's Chip," said the sheriff. "He's all red and black. The red in him is the way that he loves his friend, Waters. And the black is the way that he feels about everybody else."

I shook my head. "He's only a kid," I rationalized. "He couldn't do it. He couldn't have the heart in him to do it."

"Aye, he could," said the sheriff. "He's got an Irish heart!"

I listened to him talking, and it seemed to me that there must be some other answer, but still my mind turned back again and again to the same thought. It was Chip. He had the reason to want to plague the sheriff, and if he plagued me at the same time—well, what difference did it make? Anger came into me like steel, and I gritted my teeth, and wished that I had the neck of that boy in my hands. I would give it a twisting that would end Chip's days of mischief.

"Chip done it," Murphy said over and over. "Chip went and done it. He never stopped to reckon the time when I was pretty easy on him. I mean the time when I pinched Waters and could've pinched Chip, too. But I didn't. I didn't want to send an Irish spark like that to the penitentiary. This is the way he pays me back."

It was an interesting thing to hear the sheriff talk like that, slowly, quietly, with a voice rusted and grating with emotion and thirst. I listened to him, and I watched the bulldog working in his face, and I almost forgot my own thirst, I was so keen to see what was in the sheriff's mind.

After a time we thought the thing over, and we talked it over in just a few words, because not many words were necessary. The nature of the deed stood up and looked us in the face. We had to get from Freshwater Springs—the very name was a torture now—to the next water hole. And that water hole was a good seventy miles away.

Seventy miles, and sand to trudge through! Seventy miles! We would have to go slogging all through this day, and all the night we would have to keep marching, and most of the following day. And, at the end of our march, we'd come to a few swallows of muddy alkali water, if we were lucky. I wanted to lick my lips, but I didn't. I just pressed them a little, and made the saliva flow a bit.

We sat there in the scanty shadow of one of the overturned rocks, and we decided what direction we would have to take. I knew that country pretty well, and we picked out the valley where I knew of a water hole that was said never to go dry—perhaps. Then we got up and buried the saddlebag and started off.

Chapter Eight

"Away From Temptation"

When I put the saddlebag in so casually, I meant it. It didn't matter to the sheriff, either. All that mattered to us was seventy miles of desert sand—and how were we going to last out? We both had been through the grind before. We knew the desert. We weren't romantic about it. But a few touches of that dry, hot wind would simply soak up the blood from our bodies, and we'd die. It wasn't so much body, either. It was mind that the heat worked on. It was well enough for the sun to scorch the body, but it was a different thing to let the thought of it start to campaigning in the brain. That was what drove men crazy.

So you can believe me when I say that we put away a quarter of a million dollars under the broken rocks of Freshwater Springs and gave it not a thought. We marched on without once looking back. The rifle was there with the saddlebag, too. We had no use for that weight. We carried with us some salt, and a little jerked beef; and the sheriff kept his hunting knife on, not that he wanted it, I dare say, but because he would have felt undressed and strange without its handle to fumble as we went along. Two hundred and fifty thousand dollars lay there under

235

the rocks, and we would have changed the whole sum, believe me, for a single runt of a mustang to ride by turns, and to hang onto, to help us forward over the terrible stretch that lay ahead.

We had only one thing to be glad of, and that was that we had company. I think, for my part, that, if I had been alone, I would simply have stretched out there in the shade of the rocks and waited for death. Or perhaps I could have helped it on the way a little. But with a companion, a man doesn't give in. The last thing that remains to us, it appears, is pride and a sense of audience. The sheriff was my audience. I was his audience. And so we just headed away for the cleft in the distant mountains where I knew that water could be found.

I think that the most awful part of it was the knowledge that the hours would crawl away before us like a worm, and that always we would be looking at that picture of blue distance, and that always we would seem to be as far away as ever, and that, even when the picture turned from blue to brown, we would still have a ghastly march ahead of us, and that even when we could see individual rocks and trees, still there would remain terrible miles before us. The clear air would take care of that. Yes, the moment would come, when we would suck our own blood to ease the horrible pain in our cracking throats. We both knew all these things. We both knew that it was touch and go for us. That was the reason that we wasted no breath in talk.

The sheriff simply cut the cord that tied my hands. I felt no particular gratitude for the act. It might be I who would hang onto reason the longest and be able to slap him on the back at the right moment and clear his own wits, or curse him into a greater manhood. On the other hand, it might be he. So we left the rocks, and we started our voyage, and we walked all the rest of that day.

I don't want to dwell on it. I don't want to recall the horror of that sun, or the way it laid its red-hot hand against the backs of our heads and fried the brains. I don't want to think of that day, because it makes my throat dry and crack—the mere thought. Now I can go and fill a glass with ice and pour in enough water to fill the interstices, and drink that water, and fill up the ice again, and sip once more, and let the blessed cold of it trickle slowly down my throat. But still it seems that the thirst can never be taken out of me. The water famine has its claws in my vitals once more, and I burn with it in imagination, almost as badly as I burned on that day.

Before night came, I knew that we couldn't succeed. Already my tongue was badly swollen, and my lips were cracking till the blood ran down my chin. It was a painful thing to have to move my eyes, because the balls of them seemed to be lined and set in sharp crystals of quartz. But we marched on.

The sheriff must have known we were beaten, too. His case was worse than mine, because he was a larger and a grosser man, and I could tell by his staring look, long before sundown, that he was looking his death in the face. But, you see, he would not be the first to weaken, and neither would I.

There was the strange picture of two men walking straight on toward inevitable death and never speaking about it, because each of us wished to break down the pride of the other and force him to be the first to whine. Twenty times complaints came pouring up into my throat, and twenty times I ate those complaints and said no word of them. And once—once only—I heard the sheriff curse, and his curse was a groan.

It was about the sunset time, when the next part of that adventure started. I mean to say, the sun was lying on its side in the west as hot and terrible as ever, nearly, but its cheeks were swelling, and it was plain that before long we would have the dark. Even that thought was no comfort because sometime during the dark of that night the knees would fail under one of us, and that man would sink, and the other would turn and give him one look, and then drop in turn because of the bitter comfort of dying beside a friend. As this sunset began, and the sky was starting to redden in the west, I saw the sheriff pause sharply and stretch out his arm.

It's begun, I said to myself. *The madness is on him, and eating his brain like a mouse nibbling at cheese. It's started on him, and he'll be raving in another moment.*

Then I saw it. Animals of some sort were coming toward us, strung out in a long string, etched strongly against the background of the western light and dyed and blackened by the contrast. While I watched them and saw the nodding heads of the horses, I groaned aloud with joy.

They were not wild horses. No, now I could see a rider upon the first of the lot, and I thought that must be the luckiest man in the entire universe, because he was in this desert, but he had a horse beneath him. Suppose he were thirsty. Suppose he had run out of water. Suppose he had a drink. Then he would cut the throat of one of his led animals—mules or horses—and he could drink the blood. What a delicious drink that seemed to me at the time.

The sheriff dropped his arm. "Chip!" he said.

It rather staggered me, that idea. I stared again—one small rider, with several horses or mules behind—yes, and at the tail of it all the little outline of the burro pressed against the ground, as it were.

"It's Chip!" I yelled, as though I had made the discovery first.

The sheriff grinned, and, as he smiled, the blood ran down his face from his broken lips. But he nodded, and, side by side, we turned toward that procession. It was Chip, and, after all, he cared for us enough to want to give us a hand.

We marched toward him. The sun sank in the west. All was red fire behind, when we came within shouting distance of that youngster. We saw him wave an arm to make us halt. We walked straight on. The wave of an arm could not stop us. Suddenly something struck the sand at my feet, and a shower of that sand was scattered over my legs. Then the clang of a rifle dinged on my ears. He was shooting to make us halt! Bullets have a persuasive power of their own, and we stood still.

"You want water, fellows?"

Want water? The very sound of the word worked at my saliva glands and made my throat crack again and widen in hope. We merely stood still and waved at him, like fools. But we had no voice to carry across that distance.

"I've got plenty of water here for you," came the voice of Chip again, "but before you get it, you make a bargain with me."

He paused. We both waved. What was the use of words? Of course, he could make his bargain on his own terms. If he had water, he was the king of the world, so far as we were concerned.

Then came the thin crowing of his voice again: "I've picked

up the whole show that you left behind you. I've picked up the saddlebag, and all your packs. I've got the money. And I want to know if I keep it easy and safe, or do I ride on and let you sizzle and stew here?"

Do you see the idea? He would offer us rescue, but he would only do so under the condition that we should agree not to touch him and the possessions that he had taken.

I began to laugh, the laughter sounding like a whisper. Heaven, how my throat hurt. Then I looked at the sheriff and saw that he was shaking his head from side to side with a long, slow swing, the way a bullock does, if you've ever seen one under a yoke. I was amazed, and I stared at him again. Refusing? Saying no to this offer of water—of life? By heaven, that was what he was doing! He was saying no.

He put out his hand and gave my arm a grip. "You go on," said this amazing sheriff. "You go on and get the water. But me . . . you know the way it is."

"I know that you're crazy in the head," I said. "That's what I know. I don't know how else it is. What do you mean, when you ask me if I know how it is?"

I shook him. He kept on swaying his head from side to side— saying "No"—not to me, but to something in himself. Yes, saying no to the infernal heat and wretchedness of thirst that was in him.

"You know how it is," said the croaking voice of the sheriff. "I wouldn't mind giving in. But I took a dang oath, when I took my office. You know how it is, Joe. I swore that I'd serve the people to the best of my ability. That means what? That means with my life, if I got to. That's what it means now. You go on and get your drink. Get it good and deep. You go on, and forget about me. I've got my job to do."

No, it was not craziness. It was greatness. That big roughneck of a sheriff, he was great. It hit me between the eyes. While I stood there gaping, almost forgetting my thirst, by thunder, Tug Murphy turned around and marched away with a good, long, swinging step, putting distance between himself and his temptation.

Chapter Nine

"Chip Decides"

I was no sheriff, and I had taken no oath. But all at once I wanted to read one of those oaths that public men take before they get into office. I think, with most of them, that what they swear to do doesn't ride them very hard. No, I think that they take it pretty easy. They just have the words read off to them by a judge, or something, and they put their fat, pink hands on a book, and they say—"I do"—and that's all there is to it.

But Tug Murphy was different. I could somehow see him with his head canted over to one side, listening, and nodding, and frowning, as he listened to the reading. I could see him go and take the book out of the hand of the judge and then follow the words for himself, underlining them with one blunt forefinger with a cracked and black and broken fingernail. He wasn't a pretty man, Tug Murphy. But he was a great man. Just then it seemed to me that he made everything else shrink—even the desert, even the thirst of it.

However, what tied him did not tie me. I went straight on toward Chip, and I went at a run, stumbling a little, my knees pretty loose.

When I got there, Chip was off his horse and waiting for me. He had a canteen that was wrapped up in sacking, and he had so much water that he had been able to afford to use some of it to wet the sacking, and the evaporation had kept that water cool. He shoved the canteen at me, and I grabbed it. I didn't just swig it down. No, sir, I sat on the sand, and Chip, he kneeled behind me and made a brace for my back. He kept saying: "Joe, old partner, you'll never forgive me for what I've done to you. And Dug Waters, he'll give me what for. He'll give me a regular lambasting. But, somehow, I didn't know what else to do. And I been suffering for you, Joe. And I've kept this here water cool for you, as good as I could. D'you think that you could ever forgive me, Joe?"

I hardly heard him. The words he spoke sounded far off and dim as the sunset on the borders of my mind. What mattered to me was that canteen which was shaking in my hands and the tin lip of it rattling against my teeth. I didn't pour it down. No, no! A thirst like that was a treasure, and I intended to use up every penny of it. So first I let a thin trickle flow over my broken, dead lips. Some of that water ran down my chin and dropped onto my chest. I took the canteen away from my lips before I ever had swallowed a drop, and I just sat there, leaning back against the knees of Chip, and I let that water soak through to the skin, and then I laughed a little, in spite of the hurt of laughter, to think that my skin was drinking before my throat had tasted a drop.

Yes, I laughed a little, and Chip, he grabbed me hard and said: "Steady there, Joe. Steady, partner. Don't let yourself go. Don't you let yourself go. . . ." And he began to blubber a little.

Chip was about as hard as they make them. Rawhide and whalebone was what he was made of. But still, he began to cry a little, through his teeth, fighting it down—crying in a high whine, because he thought that my brain was gone, and that the long drought had about finished me. But my brain wasn't gone. No, no, I was only thinking the thing out—and laughing because the water had touched my body before it touched my throat.

Then I raised the canteen again, and Chip put around one brown dirty hand and steadied it for me, and this time I let a thin trickle go floating right straight down my throat. Down my throat? I tell you, it percolated all through me, and I could feel it work. The strongest red-eye in the world never worked as sure and steady and straight as that water did, soaking around through my veins and telling me what life was all about. I don't want to exaggerate, but, while I sat there and slowly sipped that canteen full of water, it seemed to me that the desert had changed, and that the green grass was pushing up all around us, and that trees were putting down roots and lifting their heads. It was pretty good to me, I tell you, to sit there and think of all that and feel that I was in the middle of a land drenched with water to the core, and ripe and rich and flowing with green.

Perhaps I was a little twisted in the mind, after all. I don't know. I only know that before that canteen was gone, my head seemed to clear, and I sat up and made myself a cigarette, and Chip lighted it for me, and I began to smoke. I laughed as I smoked, because I thought of what a torture smoke would have been to me ten minutes before this. No, I sat there and smoked, and put a hand on my knee and wondered why it was shaking so badly.

Then I felt a tapping on my shoulder, and a voice tapping at my ear. Pretty soon the voice got in to where I could understand what it was saying: "What's the matter with him? Is he dippy? Why didn't he come with you? Shall I go and get him now? Is it all right for me to leave you now and go and get him, Joe?"

Gradually I realized everything all over again. I shook my head. "It's not all right. It's not safe for you," I said. "He's sworn his oath that he'll serve the people. And he won't go back on the oath. He knows that you've got the money. He came back to get it. And now that he can't get it, he'll go and die. That's all there is to it. If you go near him, he'll grab you."

Chip groaned. It was like the groan of a man. His heart was all in it. "Now I know what Waters meant," he said.

"Waters meant what?" I said. "What did Waters say?"

"That Murphy was kind of stupid, but that he was a great man, all right."

"Aye," I agreed. "He's a great man. I never saw a greater. He makes me feel like a puling baby."

"What're we gonna do?" asked Chip.

"We're just gonna think," I said. "We're gonna think it over and see what to do. Where is the sheriff now?"

"You can see the head and shoulders of him, marching off there," Chip said, pointing.

"Aye," I said. "He's thinking of his death. Every step he's taking is deeper into the ground, Chip."

The kid began to blubber again. He wrung his hands. "I dunno what to do," he confessed. "I meant it right. It took me time to get up to Freshwater Springs after I'd blown it, and after you came. It took me a lot of time. And then one of the mustangs threw half a shoe, and I had to wrestle with the part that was left, to get it off. And that was why I didn't come up to you quicker, Joe. I never meant that you should have to march half a day, thinking of water all the way."

"It's done. It's over with."

But I was wrong. It wasn't over with. The ache and the misery and the burn of it still come back to me, and they always will, and they make a groaning in my throat that sometimes wakes me up at night. However, I could understand what had been the way with Chip. He was playing his game against two grown men, and part of the time those two grown men had a rifle. There was a little nick in Chip's left ear. It was a fresh cut. It had been clipped out by one of the sheriff's rifle bullets. After all, he had been able to shoot pretty well, even by moonlight, and that was how close Chip had come to paying for his trick with his life.

"The sheriff . . . ?" Chip kept saying. "What'll I do? If you take him water and a horse, he'll light out after me, and he'll likely catch me. Because I'm mighty tired, Joe. Jiminy, I never seem to've known what being tired was like before." He shook his head and sighed.

I nodded. It wasn't easy. "You could cache the saddlebag somewhere. Then it wouldn't matter if he caught you."

"I couldn't do that," Chip said. "The saddlebag ain't mine. It's Waters's. It belongs to him, and he left it in my safekeeping. I don't dare to let it go."

"Then what'll we do for the sheriff?" I asked. "He's got to have water, and food, and a horse, or he'll never pull through. Because he's on his last legs."

There was a little silence between us.

Then Chip said: "If he wasn't such a man, then I wouldn't care. But he is. He's a man. Even Dug Waters ain't a much bigger man than the sheriff is. He kind of beats me."

"Aye, and he beats me, too," I said. "But help he's gotta have, or you'll never forget this day, Chip. I can't force you to do it, because I gave you my word before I came in."

"You don't have to force me," Chip said. "I'm only thinking. That's all that I'm doing. I'm only thinking. I'm trying to work out the right way."

He sat quietly again. I could see the size of his problem. If the sheriff got the help he needed, he would use that help to turn around and chase Chip, and Chip, as he himself admitted, was a pretty tired boy. He was tired when he joined me at my mine, and he hadn't had a full night's sleep since that time. He was shaking with weariness, and, when fatigue gets into the nerves, it rots them.

"Well," said Chip at last, in a dead, solemn voice, "I've got it now."

"What have you got?"

"He's got to have back what he had when he started," Chip explained. "Because he's played the game straight, and I'm gonna play it straight with him. I'm not gonna have no cards up my sleeve when I play it with him, partner."

"That's right, Chip," I said. "What will you do?"

"I'll send him back his two horses, and his pack . . . and some water. Water!" Chip said, breaking out in a mournful way. "Look what I done to the springs, too. I've gotta go back and try to blast it out deeper than ever, and make the water flow again, and build the rocks up around it again to keep the water cool. Oh, what a lot I've got on my mind, Joe!"

"I'll help," I offered.

"Good old Joe," Chip said, and put his hand on my hand. It was like a woman's gesture. "You go, and take the stuff to the sheriff. Just ask him if he'll give me an hour's start, for the sport of the thing. And I'll tie myself into the saddle, and try to last it out."

Chapter Ten

"One After Another"

I found the sheriff spread-eagled on the sand, absolutely sense-less. That final effort he had made to get away from the sight of us had been too much for him. But the mere touch of the wet lip of the canteen upon his mouth was enough to rouse him again. There was a world of vitality in that man. It surged up now. I stood by and heard him gasping, and the sound of the water gurgling down his throat. Then he got to his feet, swaying a little, pressing his hands against his temples, and I suppose that the temples were bursting.

"Where is he?" he growled.

"Look here, Tug," I said, "that kid has played fair with you. He's sent you this water. He's giving you your chance. You're not going after him now, are you?"

"I'd pretty near rather cut off a leg," said Tug. "But I've got my duty before me, and I'm going to do it. I've taken my oath . . . I'm going to stick to it. I've swore on a Bible, son, that I'd keep the laws in force."

I saw that he was as fixed as iron.

"He didn't beg," I said. "He only asked for an hour's start.

You'll give him that, Tug. You're not the man to refuse him that!"

"I'll see him hanged," said the sheriff, "before I'll give him an hour's start."

"You'll be damned," I said, feeling pretty hot, as he swung into the saddle on one of his horses that I had brought up to him from Chip's captured string. "You'll be damned, Tug, when people find out how you've handled this. You've got water, and you've got a horse and saddle from the kid, and still you're going after him!"

I was about ready to fight, although I'm not much of a fighting man, but the sheriff tamed me down with his answer.

He said: "It ain't me that's after poor little Chip. It's the law. I'm only one finger in the grip of the law, Joe. But I've got to go where she sends me, and close where she tells me to close. I've got no kindness, no friendship, and nothing to give a partner until the law lets me. It don't let me now, and heaven help my unhappy soul."

It was a good deal of a speech, coming from a fellow like Tug Murphy, who did most of his thinking by fits and starts and dished up his ideas in little portions. I had no answer to it, and, as the sheriff rode off, I got onto the other mustang that belonged to him and followed.

Out there in front of us, a small, moving finger of shadow, we could see where Chip was riding. Well behind him was the burro. We passed that burro at a trot. It only shook its long ears at us as though to say that it comprehended what we were up to and was only glad to have man go on his way. I was sorry to see that burro drift behind me. He was the small ship that had brought my fortune out there into the desert. I had sighted my course for a good many days between his ears. Somehow, just then, he seemed to me like my tangible road to ordinary, law-abiding humanity.

I fairly hated Dug Waters. I had very little affection for Chip, even. I only heartily wished that I had been allowed to stay on at my daily grind, chewing out the hard quartzite and taking its gold away in morsels. I never would get very rich at that work. But I'd get on from day to day, with the taste of the calm, lonely life deepening all the while in my mind. For the best company a fellow can have is the stuff that comes up in his own mind during long silences.

Now I saw the burro soaked up by the night that followed us, and far away before me I could see the outline of the boy, swaying up and down a little among the horizon stars—so I knew that he had his mustang at a canter.

"He'll beat me tonight," said the sheriff. "But I'll get him tomorrow. I just wanta keep fairly close." He spoke with great surety, and he was not a man to be overconfident at that.

He certainly did not catch the boy that night. My brain was staggering with exhaustion. My thoughts would not run in a smooth flow. But the sheriff, like a bulldog, hung on. In front of us, the boy faded out of view. He was too light in the saddle for us to catch him, and that mustang kept on at a steady, good rate. I was mightily relieved when the outline of the kid melted away from our eyes, wavered back into view, and then was lost again. But the sheriff did not seem disturbed.

"I know where he's going," he said. "I'll catch him tomorrow."

I wondered that he could be so sure of himself, but he held to a steady course, pointing a little west of north all the while. I sighted this course on a star and saw that he kept to it. But after a time I let my head sag. I grabbed the pommel of the saddle with both hands, and so I sat the saddle, more than half asleep, surging to this side and to that, as the sleep overmastered me for a moment. The mustang followed along behind the sheriff, head down, almost as tired as its rider. Now and then my head cleared a little, and my eyes, and then I looked ahead and saw that the sheriff was pushing along with his head high and his shoulders squared. It made me sick at heart to think of the will power that man was using—and on a job that he hated. It was the strangest ride I ever had taken. It was the strangest ride that I ever will make.

In the dawn, we saw thunderheads around the mountains before us.

"The kid's in my hand," said the sheriff. He said it without enthusiasm.

Then we climbed through a dizzy pass and dropped into a narrow valley, and at last we saw the boy. He was going down the slope before us, very slowly. He was riding the mule now, and the mustang followed, and the body of the youngster was all slewed around to one side, so that I guessed he was sleeping in the saddle, held by the rope with which he had tied himself in place.

If you had seen the trail that he was riding, you would have caught your breath. A mule has extra brains in its feet, but even that mule was navigating the trail slowly, step by step. Now and again it stumbled, and rocks rolled before it and went bounding and beating down the sheer fall of the mountainside. But still the boy did not move. He was like a limp, dead thing.

The sheriff set his teeth, and pushed ahead. He dismounted, and, leading the mustang, he went on foot, because that way of going was both safer and faster for the moment. I never saw a man look worse than the sheriff did this morning. The black about his eyes seemed to be painted on the skin. The skin itself was wrinkled deep with chisel strokes about the corners of the eyes, and the muscles about the base of his jaw were always bulging. He reminded me of a violin, tuned too high, tuned so high that the strings are about to break.

I dismounted behind and went on down that horrible trail, and we gained rather fast on Chip. I began to think of shouting a warning to him, but there was no need of that, for in another moment one of the rocks we dislodged went leaping like a jack rabbit down the trail. It was a good fifty-pounder, and it went like a cannonball. It jumped to this side, and it jumped to that, and finally it went by the mule and missed it by inches.

The *whir* of it wakened the boy. Up in the saddle sat Chip, and he swayed violently from side to side. Then he looked back and saw the sheriff coming. It seemed that he could not make the thing out. I suppose he had been traveling so steadily all the night that he could not imagine we were anything less than miles behind him. I saw him rub his eyes and stare again. Then he went out of the mule's saddle and whipped onto the back of the mustang. He moved like a young cat. He pulled out a rifle from the saddle holster and turned and scanned us again, with the air of a man about to shoot. But shooting was not really in his mind. He shoved the rifle back again, and then he gave us an exhibition of horsemanship that to this day makes my heart stand still.

For he pushed that mustang into a trot, and, once that was accomplished, gravity did the rest. The little horse could not stop. It began to career and stagger, and slide from side to side. Sometimes it swiveled halfway around. It was fighting for its life. And Chip's life was in the saddle.

I stood still and watched, my eyes aching with the nerve strain, and there was a sort of disbelief in me, as though this thing could not be. There was something about the dazzling brightness of that morning, and the sheen of the rocks, and the voice of the river in the bottom of the valley that made my senses reel. It was a dream-like moment, with all of its horror and its vividness.

I say that the river was sounding in the bottom of the valley. It was running white and brown—not the brown of mud, but the brown of the multitude of rocks that were taken bounding along by the current. It was one of those rivers that flow perhaps two months in two years. Sometimes a year would go by without a favorable rain more than to moisten its bed, and then a torrent poured, and the little river became a giant, and a mad giant, at that, and ran all foam and thunder, and shouting, and leaping, and tearing its hair, so to speak.

That was the way it ran this morning. Not very far away, the current would widen out on the desert, and those swift waters would run slowly and more slowly, and finally they would stumble out in a frothing, muddy tide, and one would hear the sands drinking, and so all that dashing water would sink away into the desert and be lost. I knew that was what happened to the stream, but, looking at it now, I found it hard to think of that final picture, all my eye was crowded by the actual strength of the little river and the uproar it made, like an army fighting on the ground, and an answering army bellowing and threatening in the upper air.

Half hypnotically that confusion of noises worked on me; that was the greater part in the dream-like quality of the morning. But there before me, scurrying down the trail, went poor little Chip, and the sheriff was moving more slowly behind him.

I heard the sheriff cursing furiously, and I knew that it was in admiration of the boy's courage. Just then, as he was prepared to make every possible effort to catch Chip, I knew that the sheriff admired the boy more than he admired any other thing in the world. But that was the bulldog beauty of the sheriff's character. Now young Chip got to the bottom of the slope, and I saw him hesitate, looking first to one side and then to the other. At the same instant, I could see his dilemma.

Chapter Eleven

"A Perilous Crossing"

I could see, also, why the sheriff had been so sure of the capture of Chip, even long hours before. He had guessed what trail the boy would take, and he had known what the trap was at the farther end of the line. There was no getting upstream. A cliff came down there in a plumb line to the rim of the water. The way downstream was blocked by vast masses of rubble that had pitched down the mountainside in an avalanche. Half the breast of the height had been torn away to furnish this thundering confusion, and the boulders lay there as big as houses and piled on one another like stacks of chipped ice. I shall never forget the sheen of the raw edges of them, picked out with glints and wire-streaks of metal ores, here and there.

So there, between the two arms of the mountain, poor Chip was riding down to that singing and yelling river.

Now that we got lower into the valley, nearer to the face of the water, more and more there seemed to be one stream raging across the earth, and another roaring through the sky above us, the echoes flung down so loudly from the rimrock. I had a horrible sense of something great about to happen, something that would overwhelm ordinary human nerves.

The thing seemed impossible, too. Just when you've hunted the same grizzly for a fortnight, studying the sign, measuring the prints, learning the wits of the old campaigner—so after a thousand trail problems solved and as many thousand disappointments, at last you see the rascal before you, unaware of you, and in easy shooting distance, and the thing appears impossible, and you say that it must be another bear—in just that manner I looked down there toward little Chip and could not believe that the sheriff was drawing up on him and driving him into a corner. I had seen that youngster too often at his tricks. He had baffled grown men too many times. But there he was, against the wall, as it were.

All at once he looked pretty small, I can tell you, what with the cliff on one side and the great building blocks of the avalanche on the other. Behind him was the sheriff's rifle—and the mountain trail. In front of him was the mighty roar and the foam of the river. In a sense, of course, that was the smallest of his barriers, but it was a living one. It was beating and smashing to pieces boulders the size of a man almost. What would it do to a horse and rider?

In the middle of that arena, I saw Chip, like a wild animal, turn to this side and to that, and then he looked back toward the sheriff, who was coming on fast. He threw off the lead rope that tied the mule to the broncho, and, when he did that, I knew that Chip was about to attempt something. Only—what could it be? I knew that he was as cool as steel, but when he was surrounded by impossibilities, what out was there for him, in spite of his cleverness and his steady nerves, and all that?

He ran the broncho toward the ruins of the avalanche first of all, but, as he came under it, I saw him look up and measure the height and mass of it and shake his head. There was no scaling that wall in a hurry. He swung back toward the river itself, and stopped on the verge of it—yes, with the water curling around the forelegs of the mustang. I couldn't help admiring the control he had over that broncho. It might be a mean, kicking, biting wildcat of a horse, but it had courage. Otherwise, no rider could have forced it within ten feet of the verge of that river.

But Chip was staring constantly out across the water, seeing something on the other shore. Aye, what he saw there was freedom, or a ghost of a chance of freedom, I suppose. But how could he get across? Just then a chunk of the bank a little above Chip went down with a roar and dissolved in the thunder of the water, and turned the stream in front of him to a coffee-colored froth. The spume of it leaped as high as a man's head, and higher. But still the kid studied the face of the river like the face of a man when one waits for an answer.

That fall of the bank had changed things a little. For it had tumbled into the current some boulders so huge that even that ripping water could not budge them easily. I saw one of them tremble, roll slowly over, and then lie still again, shuddering, and seeming to grow light-footed, but still not swaying with the water again. Suddenly Chip gave the mustang the whip. The broncho shuddered and crouched.

The sheriff threw up one hand and knocked it against his forehead. He turned his face toward me, and I've never seen greater horror. What he shouted, I could not hear. There was no talking or hearing down there in the malstrom. Besides, I didn't care what the sheriff might say. I only cared what Chip might do. I've heard 'punchers tell of crowding wild horses too closely, and how they'll jump cliffs rather than be taken. Chip seemed like that—ready to die, but not to give up.

I screeched at him, I hardly know what. Something about not being a fool, I suppose. But I saw that whip flash twice again, and then the horse jumped. I blinked, as a man will when a fist flashes under his eyes, driving home on his chin. When I looked again, there was the mustang, perched like a goat on the big boulder that had just fallen from the bank. It was an amazing thing to see Chip there, crouched in the saddle like a jockey, and holding the reins hard with one hand while with the other he held the business end of a lariat. They were only poised for a second on that rock. The wavering of the thing made it a miracle that they could have kept their balance as long as they had.

Then the broncho jumped again to a smaller stone. And by

thunder, once more he landed and slipped, but did not fall off! It was only a thin strip of a river, but it was as dangerous as a cannon's mouth. Suddenly I told myself that they were going to get across.

The sheriff and I were both down to the foot of the trail by this time, but we did not ride on toward the river's edge. We did not even mount. We just stood still, frozen in place, and gaped and waited for fate to decide this thing one way or another.

The mustang jumped the third time. He had his head down. He seemed to be trying to use his chin as a fifth hoof when he landed, but the stone that they aimed for this time was almost lost in the spray and the boiling of the river, and, although the broncho hit the boulder fair and true, he went off it with a roll. He and Chip disappeared. No, not all of them. For, as the horse jumped, I saw the rope shoot out straight from the hand of Chip, and it landed the noose snugly about a head of rock on the farther bank. There were horse and rider underwater, and the lariat drawn tight like a dark ray, pointing. Then they came up. I saw the game mustang swimming hard, head upstream, and Chip striking out beside him. Something hit the broncho—some stone flung by the current. He went down. But up he came again, and now, as the lariat held and the force of the current beat down on them, they were forced rapidly in toward the other shore. They reached the shallows, and presently the broncho was scrambling up the farther side.

When he got to the top, with the kid beside him, they leaned together. I saw red running on the body of the horse. I saw red running on the face of Chip, and it was a sight that sickened me. He did not look back at us. He merely tried to mount, but his legs failed under him. He had to lead the pony to a rock, and from that he managed to half slide and half fall into the saddle.

The mustang, head down, badly beaten, started off at a hobbling walk, and I could see Chip tying himself to the stirrup leathers, his hands fumbling. He hardly could have finished the job, when he lurched forward along the neck of the horse and lay there like a sack.

The sheriff gripped my arm, and his fingertips sank to the

bone. I understood. I couldn't look at Tug, for my part. For what would happen, when that exhausted mustang fell with the kid on his back? What would happen to little Chip then?

We stood there with the danger of the river at our feet, and well we knew that neither the one nor the other of us had the courage to try what Chip had succeeded in accomplishing.

Chapter Twelve

"Dug Waters"

The sheriff was ashamed, but I was not. The crossing of that boiling creek was the most foolhardy thing I'd ever seen attempted. But still the sheriff seemed to feel that his duty to the law demanded that he make the attempt. That would have been suicide. With a grown man's weight in the saddle, no horse that was not a goat outright could have succeeded in jumping from one stone to another and keeping its balance. Even with Chip, the broncho had only managed to make two jumps. Still, it was half amusing and half pathetic to see the sheriff promenading on his horse up and down the bank, scowling and shaking his head at the water.

Finally he gave up, and we made camp there in the thunder and the silence of the cañon—the silence of our human voices, I mean to say, which kept us from speaking. But then, speech was not very necessary. Each of us knew pretty well what the other was thinking.

We cooked and ate a meal. We forced ourselves to it, although we were fairly shaking with fatigue. Then we lay down to sleep.

The Oath of Office

It was late afternoon when we were awakened by the absence of the thunder in the valley. Both of us sat up at almost the same moment and looked a question at the other fellow. Then we went over to the bank of the river and looked. Of course, there was nothing very surprising about it. The thunderheads that we saw from the far-off desert had poured their rain on the highlands and sent the rush of the currents down the cañon. That rain was used up. The bed of the river was now almost dry. So we had gone to bed in the midst of thunder, and we were waking in the midst of silence.

I cannot tell how to describe what a difference there was in the very look of the valley, now that the lion was no longer roaring. Still, the vibration of that uproar was in our memories so vividly that it seemed as though the tumult were only gradually fading away into the distance rather than completely gone. The valley itself seemed loftier and more grand in all its faces, now that it was not flooded by the noise.

We got the saddles on the mustangs and started forward again. We found it no trick to cross the dry riverbed, of course, and on the farther side the sheriff lined out on the trail of the boy. It was easily found and read for a little distance, but then it went out. The sheriff struck straight on in the direction of the boy's first line of flight. He said that Chip was so hurt and exhausted that, for once, he would not be able to attempt any trickery. But I decided that Chip might be more than half dead, but he would be always more than a fox. I had seen too much of him.

So I parted from Tug Murphy. He might have held me because he had found the saddlebag in my custody to begin with, but Tug seemed to have forgotten all about that. He was badly broken up by this job that he had before him. He even shook hands with me, when I parted from him, and he said: "Joe, I should have put a bullet into the kid, rather than let him get across the creek and safe away. The next time that we meet, maybe you won't want to look at me or be with me. Because the next time I meet with Chip, I'm gonna get him with a gun, if I can't get him with my hands."

I couldn't believe my ears. I said: "Why, Tug, you're talkin' like a madman. Shoot Chip? You don't mean that you'd draw a bead on old Chip, do you?"

His mouth twisted up to one side. "I've said it, and I mean it," he insisted. "You're gonna find that I mean it, old son, and a damn black day for me."

I said: "Man, you need a rest. You need a dog-gone good long rest. That's what you need. You look all battered, Tug. You can't do right or think right, when you're all jammed up like this. You know you can't. You turn in and make a camp for one turn of the clock, and I'll do the cooking for you. . . ."

He shook his head when I had gotten this far, and I stopped. He merely smiled at me. I saw what it was. It was the oath he had taken that was working like a red poison in the veins of poor Tug. By thunder, but I pitied that man. My heart ached for him. I gave his hand a good grip.

"I don't wish you any bad luck, Tug," I confessed to him.

"Luck?" Murphy said huskily. "I only wish to heaven that you'll find the kid first, and that you'll take him away where I'll never be able to see him again!" Tug meant it, too.

I have often thought about it, since that day, but I've never been able to understand the man quite. He was a little too simple, too close to the soil for me to have a complete understanding of him. He worked as a dog works, with its eyes and its heart fixed straight ahead on its duty.

We parted that day, and the sheriff went jogging off on one of his horses, and the other mustang he left to me. So I took it and asked myself, deep down, where the kid was likely to be and what would have passed through his mind. His own pain and weakness and his agony for the lack of sleep? I couldn't imagine Chip beaten down as far as that. He would always reserve the first place for the affairs of his friend and partner, Waters. Therefore, he would be concerned only with the safe disposal of that infernal saddlebag with the fortune inside it. Which way for that purpose? Why, right up into the nearest nest of the mountains perhaps. So that was the way I steered.

That last sleep had done me a great deal of good, but I was tired. I was soaked in weariness clear to the bone, because after you've been through a sleep famine and a water famine together, you need rest the way a horse does after its summer's hauling work. It don't rest up in a day. It stays groggy for two weeks on easy pasture before it begins to pick up its head and see that the old world is not so bad, after all. But I plugged away through the red-hot latter part of that day, steering for the first tangle of mountaintops that I saw. On the way I found mostly rocks that wouldn't take a print, but in one place there were six hoofprints made by an unshod horse that was going at a walk in the direction I had chosen. That decided me that I was absolutely right, and that Chip must surely have lighted out in the line I had guessed beforehand. So I felt a great deal set up, as you can imagine. This brightened me enough even to get part of a song out of my throat.

I pulled the mustang into a twisting gully that pointed for the high places, as it seemed to me, and, just as I was taking the first elbow turn, a voice sang out behind me: "Hey, Joe!"

I grabbed my Colt and turned around. My nerves were pretty jumpy that day, I guess, and there I saw Waters riding along behind me. He threw up his hands and laughed at me, and yelled: "Don't shoot!"

I took a good bead on him, which is not a polite thing to do. "I'd like to blow the lining out of you," I said.

"Sure you would," he replied. "You always did want to, sort of. What's the matter with you, old son? I thought you were up the line, somewheres, chewing on some quartzite for a stick of candy."

"Yeah. I been chewing quartzite," I agreed.

I put up the gun and scowled at him, but he didn't care. He shook hands. There was something a little aloof about Waters. He never seemed to mind very much what other people thought—except for Chip. Chip could get under his skin with a single glance, of course.

"Well," said Waters, "if it hadn't been for quartzite, I'd've been an honest man to this day."

"You?" I said. "You never could be any straighter than the hind leg of a dog."

"What's the matter with you, boy?" he asked. "You're riding me pretty hard, it seems to me."

"Yeah, I'm riding you hard," I admitted. "And I'm gonna ride you harder."

259

"Go on," he said. "I see that you're mysterious." He laughed a little, softly and sort of in the high hollow of his throat, and then he curled up the ends of his short mustaches and sparkled his blue eyes at me.

Damn him! I about hated Dug Waters, just then. I said: "Chip is right, it seems."

"Right about what?" said Waters. "Chip is always right, the little rat." And he laughed again.

I hated that affected laugh of his.

"He's right when he says that you're a danged dude," I said.

"Hold on! Did Chip say that?"

He looked alarmed. I suppose there was a covert insult in the fact that he cared not a rap what I might think of him, but he was pretty badly jarred by the boy's opinion.

"Yeah, that's what he said," I answered.

He looked away from me and then back again, like a man who has received a pretty hard blow. "He thinks that I'm a dude, does he?" he repeated. He said it in a low voice, thinking the idea over.

"You know," I explained cheerfully, "he thinks that you're too fussy about clothes and such things. You know how it is. Curling your whiskers too much, and all that."

Waters blinked. "I'm kind of surprised," he said. "I didn't think that he'd notice, somehow. You know how it is. I didn't think that he'd pay any attention, you know, old son."

I nodded. "He's got a pair of eyes," I said.

"He's got everything," said Waters. He meant it, too.

"Well," I said, "he's not blind, anyway."

"I'm on his trail," remarked Waters. "I thought that I might find him farther on, where you were working."

"I'm working now," I informed him.

"At what?" asked Waters.

"To try to find the kid before the sheriff does."

He flinched. "The sheriff?"

"Yeah. Murphy," I said.

His lips twitched, and his eyes narrowed. There was murder in the look of Waters just then. I never saw death and destruction more clearly promised in the face of any man.

"He's been after me long enough," Waters said softly and almost to himself. "Now I'm going after him."

"All right," I said. "You go after him. You catch him. You catch him before he catches the kid."

"He's lining out for Chip, is he?" Waters asked.

"Yeah. That's what he's doing."

Waters showed his teeth. "I'm going to kill that son-of-a- . . . ," he promised himself.

I looked him in the eye. "You hurry, then," I urged. "Before he kills the kid."

"Kills the kid?" He was blank enough now. All the sleekness and the smoothness were worn out of his manner.

"That's what I said," I told him.

"Look here," demanded Waters, "what's happened?"

I told him, and I made it strong. I told him how Chip had come, and how the sheriff had trailed him, and how Chip had nearly been the death of the pair of us, and how he had come up in time to save us, too, and how the sheriff had started again on his trail. I told about the riding of the river, too, and, when he heard that, Waters put up a hand as though he wanted to ward off a blow. But the blow went home, nevertheless. His mouth began to work for a moment before he could speak.

"I've been a dog to load the kid down with that sort of a responsibility," he stated.

"Yeah," I agreed. "You've been a dog!"

Chapter Thirteen

"Chip Changes"

Things were drawing to a close. I felt that as I went on, with
Waters riding beside me. I felt also that evil was working in the
air, and that this trouble might be one big enough to blast everything—Waters, Chip, the sheriff, and myself. For, somehow, I
sensed an inevitable crash, such as one feels when the thunderheads are piling over the mountains. The same picture had been
painted before. I mean to say, the sheriff and Chip and Waters
and I had all been involved. That time the air cleared. This time
I guessed at the worst. And this is what happened.

We went through a rocky gap into an upland valley, where
there was a dark cloud of pines—not big ones, but good to eyes
that were so used to glittering rock and white sand. Out of the
distance, we could hear the trickling of water, and the soft, easy
song of it, and, riding up that valley, we took off our hats, I
promise you, to the smell of clean pines and breathed it to the
bottom of our souls.

It was pretty cold. I had piled my slicker on top of all the
rest of my outfit to turn the edge of the wind, and, when I saw

a twist of smoke above the trees, I suggested to Waters that we go in there and warm our hands, at least.

Waters stared at me. "Why d'you think that we've been going in this direction for the last mile?" he asked me.

"You saw the thing from away back?"

"Yeah. I saw it. Maybe it's what we want."

"Chip?"

"Or the sheriff," said Waters.

"Come along, man," I said. "You're not hunting for trouble with the sheriff, I know. Let the sheriff go. He's only doing his duty."

"I'll only be doing mine," answered Waters, "if I blow his head off. I'll take a chance with him, anyway."

I argued no more. There's no use arguing with a bull terrier. You may beat him half to death, but in the finish he'll put his teeth as near the other dog's life as he can.

So it was with Waters. His face was gray when he thought of the sheriff, and his nostrils worked. I don't think it was because he laid such a great heap of blame on old Murphy; it was because he was ashamed on account of Chip. When a man is ashamed, of course, he's a ton more dangerous than when he's justly angered.

We went on through the woods, and we came at last close up to the smoke, and I was for riding straight in, but Waters slid off his horse, threw me the reins, and went sneaking ahead on foot.

After a moment I heard a shout, and I went crashing straight through to find Waters doing his war dance in front—not of the sheriff, but of young Chip. Chip was sitting up with his back to a tree, and on his wrists there were handcuffs, and from the handcuffs ran a rope that circled the tree. His blankets were under him, and it looked as though he had been sound asleep when Waters discovered him. I mean, his hair was all tousled and he was yawning and laughing at the same time.

They began abusing each other in a good-natured way.

"You pie-eyed little snake," Waters said, "what made you crawl away off up here? I never gave you any such marching orders as that. What brought you up here?"

"I'll tell you," said Chip. "I just got tired of riding alone, so I came up here and found the sheriff."

"He was pretty glad to see you, I guess," said Waters.

"Yeah, he was glad," the boy said.

"So glad he wanted to be sure you'd be here when he came back?"

"That's right. He put these things on me just to remind me to stay. There ain't hardly any attention that the sheriff don't seem ready to pay to me." He laughed a little as he said it. Then he nodded to me. "Hello, Joe," he said.

"Hello, Chip," I answered. "How does it go?"

"You know," Chip said, "it goes along all right. I ain't dead, and neither is the sheriff. So there you are."

"Where's the sheriff now?" asked Waters.

"He's gone off to have a look for some venison," Chip said. "He says that he could eat a whole saddle himself."

"I hope he has luck," said Waters, "because he might have some help in the eating of that venison. He might only be the host, in fact."

Chip looked him squarely in the face. "You mean to make trouble with him, do you?"

"Why shouldn't I?" Waters asked. "How much trouble has he made for you and me?"

"Leave me out of it," said the boy.

"Yeah? Leave you out, Chip?"

"Yeah. I've got nothing ag'in' the sheriff."

"Come along," Waters contradicted. "He's hunted you like a fox."

"That's what I've been," Chip said. "He had a right."

Waters merely blinked.

Chip went on: "You poke a man in the nose, ain't he got a right to poke back?"

"Why, I suppose he has," Waters answered.

"You bet he has," said Chip.

"When did I hit the sheriff?" Waters asked, scowling.

"Whenever you broke the law," said Chip.

Waters snapped his fingers. "You like that Irish stuff pretty well, don't you?"

"What's better blood than the Irish?" Chip questioned.

"Oh, bah!" Waters erupted.

Chip growled in his throat. "You'd rather have your dang English blood, I reckon," he said. "You'd rather be one of them sneakin' aristocrats, maybe, or my lord what-not, and of all the lyin', sneakin', worthless . . ."

"Shut up," said Waters, very hot.

"I won't shut up," Chip responded.

"You will," said Waters, "because I'll make you."

"Give me my hands free and it'll take two like you to make me," said the boy.

"I'll free your hands for you," Waters stated. "A thrashing is what you need. A good caning, and I'm the man to give it to you."

"The whole blankety-blank red-blooming island of England couldn't thrash an Irishman!" screamed Chip.

"Any one Englishman is as good as three Irishmen," Waters said.

I thought the boy would twist himself into a knot. "You lie!" he shouted. "You lie, and you lie ten times, and, if I had my hands free, I'd show you just how bad you lie!"

Waters was just as hot. "Policemen and boodle grabbers and crooks is all that Ireland turns out," Waters hissed.

"Real crooks is what they turn out," Chip responded instantly, "and not poor, dawdlin' excuses like Dug Waters!"

"You little puppy!" Waters said through his teeth.

"The sheriff will be back in a minute," Chip reminded Waters. "You'd better run for it as fast as you can, because he's Irish, too, and, when he catches hold of an English-American like you, he'll just start by bashin' in your face for you, and I wouldn't like to see your skin broke, Waters, because it would give everybody a chance to see the yaller that's in you!"

It was a foolish business to try to talk down that boy. When he got worked up to it, his punch in language was worse than the punch of any man.

Waters looked to both sides at once, but he couldn't find a proper answer. I came in and tapped his shoulder. "It's no good," I said. "You cannot keep that game chicken still. Don't try, old son. He'll always win out."

"Wait till I free his hands," said Waters. "I'm going to teach him manners. That's all I'm going to do. He's too long out of school. That's the trouble with him."

"I'll show you what I've learned out of school," said the kid.

Waters leaned over, and, with a little picklock, he barely touched those handcuffs, and they fell away.

"I wouldn't even get up to pay no attention to you, Waters," the kid goaded him.

"I'll warm you up enough to move you." Waters caught up a flexible switch from the ground.

I stepped in front of him and caught his hand. "Dug," I said, "you're making a wrong play. You can't touch the kid. You know that you can't."

"Back up," Waters said. "You want a hand in this, do you? If you do, fill your hand before you start."

I was badly scared. Of course, all he wanted was a chance to explode, and he would rather have had me than a mere kid to work on.

"Dug," I protested, "I'm begging you to take one turn up and down the clearing here. After that, I'll do whatever you say. I'll fill my hand, if I have to."

"You'll fill it now!" Waters shouted.

He was white. The evil spirit was in him. It was no sight for anyone to see, not even a grown man. It put me pretty far back. It lowered my temperature a good deal to face him, I can tell you. But, after all, there's a point when even a rat is cornered, and I was cornered then. Somehow, I think that I would have knuckled under, except that another person was watching, and of all people that witness had to be Chip, who himself had no fear. At any rate, I reached for the handle of my gun and found and gripped it.

"Start your play," Waters said, or, rather, the evil spirit that was in Waters then.

But just at that, with a split part of a second to go, Chip pushed in between us.

"Leave off this!" he ordered.

"Get out of my way!" Waters said, and, with a back-hand cuff, he knocked the boy sprawling.

Then he saw, in a flash, and I saw, too.

There wasn't enough force in that blow to have floored the

real Chip, made of rawhide and whalebone as he was. But the boy had gone down, and, staring in wonder at him as he lay on his back, I saw a red-stained bandage around his right leg, above the knee. Waters saw it, too, and groaned as though a bullet had torn through his own flesh.

Chapter Fourteen

"Waters Weakening"

In an instant Waters was down on his knees. Chip, clawing and fighting to get to his feet, whacked his small fist into Waters's face to knock him back.

He might as well have hammered on cast iron, on white iron.

"Hit me again, Chip," said Waters. "I want you to. Slam me good, Chip. It's coming to me. *I* hit you. *I* did it! What a cur I am!"

Chip sat back against the tree. He put his hand to his face and wiped away a drop of red that was rolling down from his mouth toward his chin. I don't think that Waters had hit him very hard, but just enough to break the thin mucous membrane of the lip.

"Suppose you fellows leave me be for a minute," he said.

"No, no, Chip," Waters argued. "I want to tell you that . . ."

I grabbed him by the shoulder—for I had seen—and whirled him away. He was pretty angry at being manhandled in this manner, but he endured it. I got him through the trees until we were just out of sight of the little fire by which the boy was lying.

"What the dickens do you mean by this?" asked Waters, turning on me again.

"You chump," I said, "Chip was beginning to cry! Didn't you see that? The tears were coming into his eyes."

Waters put his hand against a tree and braced himself, closed his eyes, and groaned. I wanted to make him suffer a little, but hardly as much as this.

"He'll pull out of it all right," I assured him.

Waters shook his head. "He'll never forgive me. He must have known that you saw it. He'd forgive me the other things, and even the blow. But never for shaming him. Never for that. There's too much proud Irish in him for that." Then he added: "Was there blood on his face?"

"Aye"

Waters groaned again. He began to walk up and down along a short course. "I've drawn blood from him," he said, "and you know what he's done for me?"

"I know something," I answered.

"He's shed his own blood for me. He's dared everything. Just to please a whim of mine, he's done it."

"He's a grand kid," I confirmed. "There's nobody like him."

Waters cursed softly and steadily for a moment. "I've been nothing but a curse and a drain on him," he declared. "But I wanted to make up, one day, when I had my pile. Then I would have put him in clover. You know. I would have fixed him in the greatest style in the world. I still will. Only . . . I know that he wouldn't take it. He'll never look at me again until he's old enough to go gunning for me."

I nodded. That seemed pretty clear. Everything about that lad was the clear strain, and he was not the likely one to forgive or forget insults.

Then I remembered. I said: "He loves you, old son."

"Aye, and that's why I've treated him like this."

"Well," I told him, "you know, Dug, that everyone worth knowing understands how to forgive a friend. Chip is worth knowing."

He whirled about on me. "You saw that bandage?"

"Yes," I said. I saw that bandage."

"That cur of a sheriff drilled the kid before he got him," said Waters.

"It looks that way," I said.

"Then I'm going to get Murphy," declared Waters. "And I'm going to get him good." He continued walking up and down. He controlled his voice, and it came out steadily. "I had my wad. A quarter of a million . . . that's enough for a start. It's enough for me to begin on, and try to make my way. If I can't do it with that, I'm no good at all. You know, Joe, that I've been no good all my life. I've taken the easiest way. You know why I want to take the hard way and be straight?"

"Because of Chip," I said, getting a flash.

He was amazed at me. "How did you guess that?"

"Well," I answered, "because Chip is straight himself, and because he means more to you than anyone else does."

He nodded slowly, like a man thinking a thing over from the start. "That's right," he said. "It's Chip. He's so damn straight. You know what used to happen?"

"What?" I asked.

"After I'd made a haul . . . sometimes Chip had helped me more than a little . . . I used to try to split the proceeds with him. I used to try to give him his whack. But he never would take it. He used to say . . . 'I work for the money that I get.' Mind you, he never used to tell me that I was a crook or anything like that."

"He loves you, old son," I repeated.

"I'm going to give him the best break in the world," he said.

"Of course, you will."

"Murphy drilled him!" he spit.

"Murphy had his duty to do," I responded.

"Duty? To shoot a kid?" said Waters, boiling.

"Yes. Duty means a lot to Murphy."

"Duty's going to bring him to his grave," Waters said.

"Well, he knows that," I answered.

He stared at me. "Knows what?"

"He knows that this job'll be the finish of him. It's no pleasure to him to go gunning after kids."

"You're a friend of his, it seems," Waters stated, cold and still.

"Yes," I answered. "I'm a friend of his. He's one of the best."

"I'm going to kill that friend of yours."

"You'll hang for it, then," I said.

"He's not the first man that's gone down, when I pulled the trigger," he said, sneering.

"It's the first honest man," I replied.

"What?" shouted Waters.

"Why, you poor loon," I went on, "you've never taken a fall out of an honest man. Not with slugs. Crooks and thugs, on one side of the law or the other, you've put them down. But you haven't put down the straight-shooters. You know it. You've used your guns where the using was pretty near a virtue. Am I wrong?"

He stared again. "You're trying to make me out nearly virtuous, aren't you?" he said.

"Aw, Dug," I answered, "you've never been a bad sort. You've taken the easiest way, almost always. But that's the end. Your heart's been straight."

He gaped. "All right," he said, "if that's the way you think about it." But he was badly dented by what I had said, and he showed it. "D'you think that I can go back to the kid now?" he asked.

"Of course, you can," I responded.

"I'm going back to ask his pardon, on my knees," said Waters.

"I'll walk the other way," I said. "I'll give you fifteen minutes to do what's right."

So I took a walk through the pines, and I waited until I thought that the fifteen minutes were about up, and then I added another quarter of an hour for luck. The pines were as still as a funeral, and even the squirrels scampered along the branches and had lost their voices, or so it seemed. As I walked there, I got to thinking about Waters, and Chip, and the sheriff, and wondering how the thing would turn out, but all that I could see was murder, in the end. Because Waters would never forgive the sheriff for the bullet that he, a grown man, had put through Chip's leg.

Finally, when the time was twice up, I strolled back and got the smell of the fire through the trees, and then I followed on and came to the place where Chip was lying. He was stretched out on his back, and Waters was beside him. Waters was talking, and this was what I heard: "You know, Chip, that dog-gone dog knew all about me. When I came down in the morning, he gave a sniff to my boots, and he knew by the sniff of them whether I was going out hunting or not. If I were not going, he went and curled up in a corner and went to sleep again. But if I was going, then he'd just follow me at the heels all around the house, and crawl under my chair at breakfast."

"Jiminy," said Chip, "that's the kind of a dog to have." He laughed a little. Then he said: "Wouldn't I give my socks for a dog like that?"

"I'm going to tell you something," Waters confided. "That dog is going to be yours. That very same dog."

"Go on!" said the kid.

"I mean it. He's yours."

"I wouldn't take your dog," Chip said with a quaver in his voice.

"Everything that's mine is yours," said Waters. "You know that. We've agreed on that."

"Jiminy," said the boy.

"And then," Waters continued, "you're going to pick out a school that you like, and you're going to go to it."

"On what?" Chip asked. "It costs money to go to school."

"Aw, I'll find the money. Don't you worry about that," Waters said, and he laughed a little.

"Have you got it?" Chip asked.

"Yes, I have it now."

"Then it's crooked money," said the other.

Waters jumped. "Hold on, Chip!"

"I mean it," answered the kid. "It's crooked money, and crooked money is not good enough to buy me a sardine sandwich, let alone sending me through school."

I listened, and my heart nearly stopped. I could guess that this was worse than a bullet through the heart of Waters. But he held on.

"Suppose I make honest money?" he asked.

"Save it, then," Chip said, "and make yourself into an honest man. I'm mighty tired of having a crook for my best friend."

There was a little silence after this. I began to walk softly away. It was a scene, I could understand, where there was no place for me, so I just backed out of it. The last that I could see of them was Waters, sitting rather humped over, thinking, and both of them not saying a word.

Chapter Fifteen

"A Dead Man"

The next thing that I said to myself was: *What about the sheriff? And what will happen to him when Waters gets on the trail?*

So I just dropped down the valley a little in the direction in which the kid had waved when he said that the sheriff was off looking for venison. Perhaps there was very little that I could do. On the other hand, if I saw old Tug Murphy, it might be that I could turn him. I doubted, but I was willing to try. It was worth any effort to stop the meeting, if it could be managed.

So I went on through the woods, feeling smaller and smaller, and all the while more ready to turn back on my traces. And, by and by, what do I see but the sheriff himself. Yes, there he came riding out of the woods, and a nice picture he made, with the deer meat packed around his saddle, and his rifle balanced across the pommel, and the wind furling up the brim of his hat above his eyes.

I had an idea. I backed away behind a rock, and from that shelter I drew a good bead on the sheriff with my revolver as he went by, and, when he was right opposite to me, I sang out—

"Hands up!" I added a couple of good long curses to make the thing sound more real to my own ears.

Tug Murphy's horse stopped of its own accord—which was enough to make me laugh later on—not just then.

Then Tug sang out: "Who's there?"

I yelled: "Never mind who. One that'll drill you clean, if you don't stick up those mitts of yours."

He was actually beginning to raise his hands, when suddenly he said: "Why, it's old Joe!" He laughed, and simply turned his horse around toward me, still laughing as it wheeled.

"Put them up!" I roared at him again. "Put them up, or I'll let the light through you!"

He sat in his saddle with one hand on his rifle and one hand on his hip, and he laughed at me, and the bull-like bellowing of his laughter still, in a sense, is ringing in my ears. I actually tried to pull that trigger, but I couldn't, and he knew I couldn't, and I knew that he knew that I couldn't.

"A rotten murderer is what you make, Joe," Murphy said.

"I'd like to plant you one between the eyes," I said.

"Come out from behind that rock, will you?"

I came out, with my gun still in my hand.

The sheriff just grinned as he looked me over. "You ain't the kind that could shoot an old partner."

I looked soberly into the face of the sheriff. He was quite a new man. He had lost thirty pounds, I think, in his hunt for Chip. His clothes sagged on him as if his body were a mere scarecrow frame.

"Old son," I said, "you came close to trouble, when you didn't shove up your hands."

He shook his head. "You ain't that way. So you come up here and found me, did you?"

"Yes," I said, "I found you. And I found the kid, too!"

The sheriff's brown face turned yellow. "I couldn't run my hoss no faster," he said. "I begged him and hollered to him to pull up. But he wouldn't. And his weight, it was a mighty lot less than mine, and pretty soon his pony begins to gain on me . . . and so I up and fired. I meant to fire lower. I aimed just to chip a nick in the calf of his leg for sort of a warning, but just

then his pony give a big jump. . . ." He paused. He raised his
hand to his face but could not screen the agony that was in it.
I was pretty deeply touched with pity.

"It's all right, old son," I said. "I understand."

"You understand, Joe," he said, "because you're my friend.
That's the reason that you understand. You understand because
you've got a heart in you, and you know what my duty means
to me. But other folks ain't going to understand. This here is
my last job as sheriff. They'll laugh me right out of office. I'll
have to resign. It's the finish of my career. And . . . maybe I'm
glad of it."

He was *not* glad, though. The pain was still staring at me out
of his eyes.

"Aw, go on, man," I said. "Don't you worry. Besides, I've
got something else to tell you about. Don't you go blundering
back to your campfire so dead careless and free as you were
riding along just now."

"Why not?" he asked.

"Because things there are not as they were when you left the
place," I told him.

"What's happened?" he asked me.

"Chip's free," I said.

"Free?" he exclaimed.

I wanted to let the news in on him gradually. "Yes, free."

"Man, man," he shouted at me, "if you've been tampering
with the irons that are legally . . ." He stopped himself. "How
did you manage it?" he asked curiously. "Did you smash 'em
with a rock?"

"I didn't do the trick myself," I explained.

"Not yourself? Was somebody with you?" the sheriff questioned in a suddenly grave and quiet voice.

"Aye," I said. "Somebody who simply seemed to touch the
lock and it flew open."

"You mean it's Waters," the sheriff said with a snarl in his
throat.

I nodded. I said: "Now's the time, old fellow, to play cautious
and to back up. You know that Waters is too handy with a gun
for you to have a chance with him. You know that."

"It's Waters," repeated the sheriff, his face turning grayer than ever. "Then I guess this here is the last day that I'll ever see the sun."

As he said this, he gave a wild sort of a look about him and then upward through the green gloom of the trees to where flecks of blue were shining.

I merely laughed at him. "You're wild, sheriff," I said. "You'd be a fool to take on a fight with the two of 'em armed to the teeth, and expecting you to come back. Nobody ever would ask you to do it. . . ."

"Nobody ever would," the sheriff agreed, "but the oath that I took to the people. That would make me. Joe, so long for a while." He wheeled his horse about and went plunging at full speed up the valley through the trees toward the site of the camp.

I followed as fast as I could leg it. I could have spotted an antelope fifty yards and beat it in a mile that day, and with every jump of me my heart was crashing and dashing right in my throat.

But I saw the sheriff, riding like a madman, swirl out of view through the trees, and then, a moment later, as I strained and struggled to sprint faster, I heard two voices shouting loudly, and then the rapid clanging of shots. Then there was silence. Not the same silence as before, but a thing that crawled and reeked in the very air around me.

Then, as I came closer and broke through into the ring of the trees, I saw a thing to make your blood run cold. I saw the sheriff down, shot clean out of his saddle, as I supposed. I saw the great Waters down, too. The sheriff was pulling himself together and starting for Waters, and Waters was already getting to his feet, very white in the face and with a shine in his eyes. Chip had hobbled to the place, and, as Waters tried to drive forward with his gun lifting, Chip threw his arms around him and begged him not to shoot.

"Or they'll hang you, Dug!" he screamed. "They'll hang you! They'll hang you!"

What a thrill and a screech was in the voice of that boy. It was like the horrible cry of a frightened woman, but deeper than that, and more in it than that. It was Chip himself, the old indomitable Chip, who was crying out like a girl.

"Chuck up your hands and tell me that you're beat," Waters

ordered, "or I'll surely kill you, Murphy . . . you boy murderer!"

"Guard yourself," said the sheriff and brought himself to his feet with a gun in his hand, too.

"Make your move!" Waters said, trembling like a tiger.

"Make you own move first, and I'll blow your head off," the sheriff declared. "I'm gonna take you in. I'm gonna take you in with a rope around your neck. . . ." But he wavered where he stood. I managed to get in between them.

"Stand away, Joe, or I'll go at him through you," Waters shouted.

"He's helpless!" I yipped over my shoulder, a chill shooting faster than a bullet through my spinal column. "He can't move his shooting arm."

"You lie!" Murphy yelled. "You lie . . . you've always lied, you yellow . . . !"

But then he reeled outright, and I caught the gun out of his hand. He staggered, and, as he sloped toward the ground, I caught him.

There we laid him out. There we cut away his clothes and saw what had happened. The bullet from the gun of Waters had gone straight through the body of the sheriff, and, in going through his body, it had gone through his right arm, too. How he had managed to keep a grip on his revolver, I can't tell, but he had done the thing.

Waters was over his fighting madness—there was no other word for it—by this time. He was helping with the care of the wounded man. When he saw the direction of the wound, he said to me slowly: "What made him stand up there like that? What made him ask for it a second time?"

I looked back into the eye of Waters. "Don't you know?" I asked.

"He was game. He was dead game," said Waters. "I never saw a gamer one than he. But what made him stand up there like that, when he was a dying man?"

"It was the oath that he took to his people," I said, "when he took office. That's what made him stand up. And who are his people? Why, you and I, and Chip, and everybody on this range. And now he's a dead man, and heaven forgive the lot of us . . . because the law never will."

Chapter Sixteen

"Reprieve"

No, he didn't die. I know a doctor who saw the scars afterward, and who said that he *must* have died, and I remember how we fought to save him. We had three wounded men in the camp, but the wound through Chip's leg was doing well. The graze of the bullet that had clipped along Waters's head amounted to nothing. So all three of us worked on the sheriff, night and day.

The weather turned colder, and we had to build a lean-to, and the food played out, but we kept at it until, one day, we looked down into the ghostly face of the sheriff and saw that his eye, at last, was clear and strong. He said nothing, but we knew that he would live. And live he did.

That day Chip dragged the saddlebag, containing the stolen money, to Waters and pointed to it. There was a great, dark stain covering half of the leather.

"What did that?" Waters asked.

"The sheriff. He bled all over it," Chip said, and he stood there, looking first at the bag and then at Waters.

"What do you want me to say?" Waters said.

But Chip said nothing, and merely fastened his look straight on the eye of Waters.

Waters moistened his lips. "What's in your mind, Chip?" he said.

"It's in my mind," said Chip huskily, "that there's still a chance for you, Dug. If you'll try to take it."

Waters said: "You mean for me to give up this? This is a fortune! This is yours and mine, kid . . . with a slice for Joe."

"Joe don't want it," the boy stated. "And I don't want it. There's blood on it. And there's blood on you, too, so long as you keep it. You're stained with blood already, but not this kind. The other things that you've done, they'll wash off, but not this."

Waters blanched. He looked from Chip to me. I nodded gravely back at him.

"What would you do if you were me?" Waters said to the kid.

What Chip answered stunned me like a club stroke.

"I'd go in with Murphy," said Chip. "When he can ride in, I'd go in with him, and give up the loot, and take your chance with the law, and try to get clean. Because you're stained, and that's the truth. You're worse than a pig. You been wallowin' and takin' it easy in worse than mud. That's what you've been doin'."

That was how miracles happened that caused so much talk.

It was Chip's idea, and Chip's persuasion that worked it. The result was that we all went down to town together, and in the dark of the night we all came to the jail.

The sheriff was completely puzzled. "I dunno what to think," he confided to me. "I've tried to do my duty. But it looks as though my duty's bein' finished for me by other folks. An oath is a terrible powerful thing, Joe. Look how it's working on all these others. Heaven knows what'll come of it. I hope not too much harm to Waters. The rest of us, we're puppies. But he's a growed-up bear."

I suppose there was truth in that. I never saw a nobler face than that of Waters, calm and resigned, as he gave himself up. One hand was behind his back, however, and that hand gripped hard the fingers of Chip. But this I was the only one to observe.

It was a strange act and a great act, in its way, and it had a great result, I'm thankful to say. For when the governor heard of the return of that quarter of a million and of Waters's resolution to lead a life with clean hands, he sent down a pardon that freed Dug from jail and left him with no trouble in the world, except worry about Chip and Chip's future. But, for that matter, there were already half a dozen strong men worrying about the very same thing.

Only Chip was at ease. He went off on a hunting trip with Tug Murphy and left his partner, Waters, behind him to sit down and do the thinking about the future.

About the Author

Max Brand is the best-known pen name of Frederick Faust, creator of Dr. Kildare, Destry, and many other fictional characters popular with readers and viewers worldwide. Faust wrote for a variety of audiences in many genres. His enormous output, totaling approximately thirty million words or the equivalent of 530 ordinary books, covered nearly every field: crime, fantasy, historical romance, espionage, Westerns, science fiction, adventure, animal stories, love, war, and fashionable society, big business and big medicine. Eighty motion pictures have been based on his work along with many radio and television programs. For good measure he also published four volumes of poetry. Perhaps no other author has reached more people in more different ways.

Born in Seattle in 1892, orphaned early, Faust grew up in the rural San Joaquin Valley of California. At Berkeley he became a student rebel and one-man literary movement, contributing prodigiously to all campus publications. Denied a degree because of unconventional conduct, he embarked on a series of adventures culminating in New York City where, after a period of near starvation, he received simultaneous recognition as a serious poet and successful author of fiction. Later, he traveled widely, making his home in New York, then in Florence, and finally in Los Angeles.

Once the United States entered the Second World War, Faust abandoned his lucrative writing career and his work as a screenwriter to serve as a war correspondent with the infantry in Italy, despite his fifty-one years and a bad heart. He was killed during a night attack on a hilltop village held by the German army. New books based on magazine serials or unpublished manuscripts or restored versions continue to appear so that, alive or dead, he has averaged a new book every four months for seventy-five years. Beyond this, some work by him is newly reprinted every week of every year in one or another format somewhere in the world. A great deal more about this author and his work can be found in *The Max Brand Companion* (Greenwood Press, 1997) edited by Jon Tuska and Vicki Piekarski.

THE ROCK OF KIEVER

"Brand practices his art to something like perfection."
—The New York Times

Here are three of Max Brand's classic short novels, all carefully restored from Brand's own manuscripts, and collected in paperback for the first time. In "Range Jester," Barry Home, once a free-spirited cowboy, now an ex-convict, returns to the small town of Loomis. "Slow Bill" is the story of young Jim Legrange, who leaves home for an abandoned gold rush town where he runs into an old prospector who has a photograph of Jim's father. But he calls the man in the picture Slow Bill and says he was once his partner. And in "The Rock of Kiever," Texas Ranger Charlie Stayn swears vengeance against his best friend's killers and defies the ranger code, heading into the Kiever Mountains to track them down.

___4719-5 $4.50 US/$5.50 CAN

Dorchester Publishing Co., Inc.
P.O. Box 6640
Wayne, PA 19087-8640

Please add $1.75 for shipping and handling for the first book and $.50 for each book thereafter. NY, NYC, and PA residents, please add appropriate sales tax. No cash, stamps, or C.O.D.s. All orders shipped within 6 weeks via postal service book rate. Canadian orders require $2.00 extra postage and must be paid in U.S. dollars through a U.S. banking facility.

Name_____
Address_____
City_____State_____Zip_____
I have enclosed $ _____ in payment for the checked book(s).
Payment <u>must</u> accompany all orders. ❑ Please send a free catalog.

DUST ACROSS THE RANGE/ THE CROSS BRAND

MAX BRAND

Here, together in one volume, are two thrilling novels by Max Brand, the master of Western fiction. "Dust Across the Range" presents the story of Harry Mortimer, a free-thinking, college educated man who knows the brutal devastation that a dust storm can bring. As part owner of a ranch, he has been trying desperately to put his new ideas of soil conservation into practice. But it's only the elemental forces of nature that can show the reluctant ranchers and townsfolk the error of their ways. Will they see it in time? In "The Cross Brand", Sheriff Harry Ganton and Jack Bristol have been friends since they were young. But when Harry accuses Jack of trying to steal his girl, guns blaze and the sheriff is shot. Jack, believing he has killed his friend, flees town, only to run into two mysterious hardcases, one of whom has a cross brand on his forehead . . . and a date with the hangman's noose in his future.

___4743-8 $4.50 US/$5.50 CAN

Dorchester Publishing Co., Inc.
P.O. Box 6640
Wayne, PA 19087-8640

Please add $1.75 for shipping and handling for the first book and $.50 for each book thereafter. NY, NYC, and PA residents, please add appropriate sales tax. No cash, stamps, or C.O.D.s. All orders shipped within 6 weeks via postal service book rate. Canadian orders require $2.00 extra postage and must be paid in U.S. dollars through a U.S. banking facility.

Name_____
Address_____
City_____ State_____ Zip_____
I have enclosed $ _____ in payment for the checked book(s).
Payment <u>must</u> accompany all orders. ❏ Please send a free catalog.
        CHECK OUT OUR WEBSITE! www.dorchesterpub.com

SOFT METAL
MAX BRAND

Collected here for the first time in paperback are three of Max Brand's greatest short novels, all restored to their original splendor, just as the author intended. In "The Red Bandanna," Clancy Morgan returns to town to warn his best friend, Danny Travis, that Bill Orping is heading there, looking for a confrontation. But when he gets there he finds that Orping has arrived before him and was shot in the back—and it looks like Danny was the killer. "His Name His Fortune" is the story of a young gambler who falls in love with the daughter of a wealthy rancher who despises him. And in the final short novel, "Soft Metal," Larry Givain, fleeing from a posse, meets a beautiful woman at a deserted cabin belonging to one of the men in the posse. Her brother is also holed up in the cabin, pursed by a notorious gunfighter. With death drawing ever nearer, Givain realizes his life will never be the same again.

___4698-9 $4.50 US/$5.50 CAN

Dorchester Publishing Co., Inc.
P.O. Box 6640
Wayne, PA 19087-8640

Please add $1.75 for shipping and handling for the first book and $.50 for each book thereafter. NY, NYC, and PA residents, please add appropriate sales tax. No cash, stamps, or C.O.D.s. All orders shipped within 6 weeks via postal service book rate.
Canadian orders require $2.00 extra postage and must be paid in U.S. dollars through a U.S. banking facility.

Name_____

Address_____

City_____State_____Zip_____

I have enclosed $_____ in payment for the checked book(s).
Payment <u>must</u> accompany all orders. ❏ Please send a free catalog.

THUNDER MOON AND THE SKY PEOPLE
MAX BRAND

Thunder Moon has often proven his bravery in daring raids and bold battles, but now he is setting out on his greatest quest. He is determined to return to the long-forgotten home from which he was abducted as a child by the chief of the Suhtai band of the Cheyennes. He sets out to return to the white people of his childhood, accompanied only by his faithful friend, Standing Antelope. What he finds among the unfamiliar whites is much more than he expects, but still less than the consternation the Cheyenne hero brings to those who have not seen him since he was an infant. Yet, during all his perils, Thunder Moon cannot escape the spell cast on him by the enigmatic Indian beauty Red Wind.

___4673-3 $5.50 US/$6.50 CAN

Dorchester Publishing Co., Inc.
P.O. Box 6640
Wayne, PA 19087-8640

Please add $1.75 for shipping and handling for the first book and $.50 for each book thereafter. NY, NYC, and PA residents, please add appropriate sales tax. No cash, stamps, or C.O.D.s. All orders shipped within 6 weeks via postal service book rate. Canadian orders require $2.00 extra postage and must be paid in U.S. dollars through a U.S. banking facility.

Name_____
Address_____
City_____ State_____ Zip_____
I have enclosed $_____ in payment for the checked book(s).
Payment <u>must</u> accompany all orders. ❑ Please send a free catalog.
     CHECK OUT OUR WEBSITE! www.dorchesterpub.com